MW00533647

The Conspiracy

JAAN KROSS was born in Tallinn in 1920. He studied Law at the University of Tartu and worked for two years as a teacher until his arrest and deportation, with countless other Estonians, to Siberia in 1946. In 1954 he was released and returned to Tallinn, where he devoted himself to poetry and to translating the classics, including Shakespeare, Balzac and Stefan Zweig – in the Gulag he had taught himself several languages. Later his interest in Estonia's chequered history, that has continued to be a live issue, made him turn his attention to the historical novel, and he established his reputation as one of the great practitioners of this genre. His books are now translated into every major language.

ERIC DICKENS lived in Finland, Sweden and Poland before settling in Holland. He has a remarkable range of languages at his command, including Estonian, Finnish, Swedish, Polish, German, Dutch and French. His translations include works of non-fiction from Swedish and poetry from Finnish.

Jaan Kross

THE CONSPIRACY
& OTHER STORIES

*Translated from the Estonian
& with Notes by Eric Dickens*

THE HARVILL PRESS

LONDON

With the exception of *Tubatoos* "The Ashtray"
these stories first published in book form in Estonian
with the title *Silmade avamise päev*
by Kupar, Tallin 1988
First published in Great Britain in 1995
by The Harvill Press
84 Thornhill Road, London N1 1RD

"The Ashtray" was first published in Estonian in
the literary monthly *Looming*, 1990.
First published in Great Britain in
Leopard II: Turning the Page, 1993.

Second impression

A CIP catalogue record for this book
is available from the British Library.

Jaan Kross asserts the moral right to be
identified as the author of this work.

ISBN 1 86046 005 4 (hardback)
1 86046 006 2 (paperback)

Photoset in Linotron Janson by
Rowland Phototypesetting Ltd,
Bury St Edmunds, Suffolk

Printed and bound in Great Britain by
Selwood Printing, Burgess Hill, Sussex

CONTENTS

Introduction

Jaan Kross is nowadays considered the most accomplished writer of Estonian prose and a lively illustrator of Estonian history. He was born in the Estonian capital, Tallinn, in 1920, some months after the truce with Germany which marked the *de facto* start of the interwar period of Estonian independence. His father was the son of a machine-tool craftsman and Kross was sent to the local equivalent of a grammar school. In the late 1930s, Kross began studying Law at the University of Tartu, situated in the second city in the southeastern part of the country. These studies were interrupted by the Soviet Occupation of Estonia (1940–41), which was a result of the Molotov-Ribbentrop Pact where Hitler and Stalin carved up Eastern Europe into two spheres of interest. Then came the German Occupation (1941–44) as the Germans, ignoring the terms of the Pact, pushed the Soviet forces out of the Baltic states.

After being imprisoned for a short while by the Germans, on suspicion of membership of an Estonian nationalist organisation, Jaan Kross continued his Law studies, now under Soviet rule (1944–91), only to be arrested in 1946 to spend the next eight years in prisons and labour camps in Russia, a fate shared by many thousands of his compatriots. Under the first and second Soviet Occupations of Estonia, in 1940–41 and again during 1949, a total of 80,000 Estonians from a population of around one million, were deported to the Komi Autonomous Republic, the Kola Peninsula and elsewhere. Furthermore, 70,000 or so managed to flee the country in 1944, either illegally in small boats and fishing vessels, or officially in large passenger vessels which ran the risk of being torpedoed, and ended up mostly in Finland, Sweden or Danzig and subsequently as far afield as Canada, Australia and the United States. A few thousand ended up in Great Britain.

On his return to his native country in 1954, Jaan Kross made his début as a Modernist poet and published a collection under the unpromising title of *The Coal Concentrator*. During the 1960s, he was a major influence on other poets, some twenty years his junior, such as Jaan Kaplinski and Paul-Eerik Rummo, who are now leading cultural figures and who began writing during that same decade.

But by 1970, Kross had changed horses to become a writer of historical fiction. The genre was not new to Estonian literature. Eduard Bornhöhe at the end of last century, and K.A. Hindrey during the 1930s, had both written epics in the style of Walter Scott. But between 1945 and 1965 only three historical novels were published in Estonia. In the 1960s, Karl Ristikivi (1912– 1977), exiled in Sweden, did start writing historical prose and completed a dozen or so novels before his untimely death. But while Ristikivi concentrated on events and figures from mediaeval Europe, Jaan Kross brought something new to the historical novel: the Estonian of equivocal loyalties, at times almost the anti-hero. And to this day, Kross has continued to examine historical figures who have in some way been significant for Estonia.

Kross' first major breakthrough came with the tetralogy *Kolme katku vahel* (*Between Three Plagues*) published between 1970 and 1980 and dealing with a sixteenth-century Tallinn urchin Pall (Balthasar) Russow, who rose to become a chronicler of Baltic events and finally the Mayor of Tallinn. From that time onwards, Kross has published novels and novellas nearly always dealing with the lives of protagonists of lowly birth who have risen up in Baltic German or Russian society, gaining status, power and wealth but being obliged to sacrifice their Estonian identity in the process.

One exception to the rule is the hero of Kross' most successful novel *Keisri hull* (1978; translated as *The Czar's Madman* by Anselm Hollo, Harvill and Pantheon, 1992). It concerns Timotheus von Bock, a Baltic German aristocrat who marries an Estonian peasant girl. He is foolhardy enough to trust his old friend Czar Alexander I so far as to begin sending him letters criticising serfdom. Bock is imprisoned in the fortress of Schlüsselburg (the present-day Petrokrepost, on Lake Ladoga) and is, on his release, declared to be insane and kept under house arrest, in order to prevent him from being taken seriously and thus becoming a danger to the Russian Empire. Readers in the late 1970s could not fail to see parallels between the fate of Timo von Bock and that of the more outspoken Soviet dissidents of the day . . .

Kross' other novels include the story of a luckless legal adviser to Czar Nicholas II who assists him in his negotiations with Kaiser Wilhelm of Germany just before World War I, and who almost wins the Nobel Peace Prize – *Professor Martensi ärasõit* (1984; translated as *Professor Martens' Departure* by Anselm Hollo, Harvill and The New Press, 1993); the life of Bernhard Schmidt, born on the island of Naissaar in the Bay of Tallinn, who loses a hand in a firework accident while still a teenager, but becomes a lens-polisher and a renowned designer and builder of astronomical telescopes in Germany during the rise of Hitler – *Vastut-uuleläev* (*Sailing into the Wind*, 1987); the fates of a number of ex-pupils of a famous Tallinn grammar school, growing up in a society which is a far cry from what they had been led to expect – *Wikmani poisid* (*The Wikman Boys*, 1988); the exploits of Peeter Mirk, a young man returning from the labour camps in the mid-1950s, unemployed but keen, who, while helping with an archaeological dig, finds a mediaeval book, written by a leper, whose contents do not square with the historical "facts" the Soviet authorities wish to highlight, and conceals it from the rest of his colleagues – *Väljakaevamised* (*Excavations*, 1990); and, most recently, the life of the ill-fated Jüri Vilms, member of the Provisional Estonian Government during the struggle for independence who was shot by the Germans while trying to escape to Helsinki – *Tabamatus* (*Inscrutability*, 1993).

Peeter Mirk, protagonist of the novel *Excavations*, is also the protagonist of this volume. Kross' historical prose is always based on the lives of historical figures, and these stories are no exception. All six are based on real-life experiences, this time those of Jaan Kross himself. Peeter Mirk is, to a large extent, Kross' *alter ego* and appears in a number of further stories not included here, such as *Eesti iseloom* ("Estonian Character"), *Halleluuja* ("Hallelujah") and *Onu* ("The Uncle") the first of which has appeared in English translation in *Index on Censorship* in a slightly abridged version.

The first story here, "The Wound", is set in the chaotic days of 1939 when the Baltic Germans are answering Hitler's call for *Umsiedlung* (repatriation to the Fatherland) while the last story, "The Day Eyes Were Opened", is set in the post-Stalinist mid-1950s at roughly the same time as the novel *Excavations*. While Kross often adopts a tongue-in-cheek attitude as regards many of the characters and their foibles, he nevertheless makes a serious examination of ethical issues such as loyalty and betrayal, guilt and innocence, in the context of a country too small to remove foreign domination by force of arms. One of these leitmotivs especially, guilt, features in four of the six stories, where the narrator Peeter Mirk feels himself to share the moral responsibility for the death of a friend, colleague or fellow-prisoner. But owing to his sense of humour, Jaan Kross, who seems at peace with the world despite his years of incarceration, is a moral author, rather than a moralist.

To a large extent, these stories speak for themselves and it would be foolish to minimise their impact by over-introduction. Nevertheless, as Estonia is still quite unknown in Western Europe, some aspects of Estonian geography, life and history, obvious to the average Estonian but obscure to others, should be clarified.

Firstly, a word on the Estonian language in which the stories were written. This is a Finno-Ugrian language, closely related to Finnish and more distantly to Hungarian. Pronunciation is very regular, containing few awkward conglomerations of vowels, and none of consonants. Although Estonian, quite in accordance with rumour, sports fourteen cases of the noun (as opposed to German's four, and six for Polish and Latin), many of these are derived from a basic set of four. There is no grammatical gender, there even being a common word, unmarked for gender, for "he" and "she" in the singular (cf. the genderless English plural, "they"). The system of verbs is similar to that of many other European languages and, owing to Tallinn once having been a Hanseatic port, Estonian has a great many loan words from Low German and Swedish, while most nautical terms stem from the Dutch. Estonian is thus perhaps culturally and historically closer to the more well-known European languages than the linguists would have us believe.

Secondly, the geography of the stories. These are all set, at least partially, in the capital, Tallinn, or the second city, the university town of Tartu. While Tartu is a small, fairly compact town, bisected by a river, Tallinn consists of a number of straggling suburbs sprawling around a large bay – the Bay of Tallinn – which opens out onto the Gulf of Finland to the north. Helsinki is four hours away by ferry under normal circumstances. But as can be seen from stories such as "The Stahl Grammar" and "Lead Piping", normal circumstances do not always prevail.

To the west, the Bay of Tallinn is bounded by the Paljassaare peninsula with its harbour facilities and the Kopli goods station. Next comes the residential suburb of Kalamaja (where Kross himself was born) followed by the Old Town and the city centre. The bay then sweeps up to the northeast of the centre via the suburbs of Kadriorg, where the Presidential Palace stands, and Lasnamäe on whose slopes the two Tallinn lighthouses (plus, nowadays, a depressing high-rise suburb) stand, up to Pirita with the ruins of the St Birgitta Convent (and the present-day Olympic Centre) and Merivälja in the north. Out to sea, west to east, lie the islands of Naissaar, Aegna, Prangli and Aksi and to the south of the city lies the garden suburb of Nõmme which consists to this day of large, privately-owned villas. Peeter Mirk's uncle, the doctor Aadam Veski, who is a frequent visitor to the Peeter Mirk stories, moves out to Pääsküla, on the edge of Nõmme, when his city-centre flat is burned to the ground during the firebombing of Tallinn by the Soviet Air Force on 9 March, 1944. This tragic bombing raid, referred to on a number of occasions, was one in which many people died and a number of buildings in central Tallinn were destroyed. It is commemorated every year in typically low-key Estonian fashion by placing lighted candles at one of the bombsites, on a wall near the Niguliste (St Nicholas) church. Tallinn street names are now more or less the same again as they were in the 1930s, after fifty years or so of being named after Soviet heroes and politicians.

Kuressaare and Kärdla are the main towns on the western islands of Saaremaa and Hiiumaa, respectively, and Paldiski is a harbour town to the west of Tallinn where the Soviet Navy have had a base until 1994. Viljandi is a medium-sized provincial town in the south of the country, while Otepää is smaller and lies to the southwest of Tartu, on the road to Valga, a town split in two by the Latvian border.

Finally, a number of historical events which are of importance for the understanding of these stories and of the Estonian nation as a whole (notes for each story specifically appear at the end of the book and are numbered in the text):

Apart from the firebombing of Tallinn in 1944 (Tartu and Narva were also badly damaged during the war), and the mass deportations of 1941 and 1949, the Estonian nation has suffered countless indignities and tragedies such as the battle at Velikiye Luki near the Russian town of Pskov (Estonian: *Pihkva*), to the southeast of the Estonian–Russian border, which took place at the end of 1942 when Estonian soldiers conscripted into the German Wehrmacht and the Soviet Red Army were obliged to battle against one another and where many thousands died on both sides. This event is remembered with great bitterness in Estonia and has become a symbol for the vicissitudes of a small nation.

And during the last years of Stalinism, from 1944 to 1950, Estonian libraries suffered the loss of approximately *four million* books. To quote Jaan Kross himself in a recent essay published in the German periodical *Estonia*: "*Anyone entering the University Library in Tartu around 1950 could not help but notice a man with an axe standing under the plaster statues in the foyer, a pile of books, still whole, to his left, to his right a pile of those books already hacked to pieces.*" Those who wonder whether or not the Estonian nation errs on the side of nationalism, that most fashionable of sins, might consider what cultural murder of this sort, performed in such an outrageously crude manner, must do to the psyche of the nation undergoing it.

I hope, therefore, that making these stories available to an English-speaking audience can, apart from being enjoyable in themselves, contribute towards a better understanding of the fate of the Estonian nation during the last half-century.

Eric Dickens
Blaricum, Netherlands, November 1994

The Wound

The Wound

I took a seat upstairs in Café Kultas[1] and threw a glance at a copy of *Päevaleht*[2] which someone had left lying on the table: the Uluots[3] government was in its second week of office. A Soviet naval unit had arrived in Tallinn harbour on an official visit. TASS was vehemently denying the rumour spread by the *New York Times* that the Baltic states were being Sovietised. *Es war eine rauschende Ballnacht* starring Zarah Leander was playing at the Gloria Palace and Dick and Doff's *Blockheads* was playing at the Ars. And the 14,000-ton *Der Deutsche* and other vessels lay at anchor waiting to welcome on board those who had heeded Hitler's call for repatriation to Germany. The bustle of departing Germans had been going on for several days.

"Hello, Peeter . . ."

I raised my eyes from my newspaper.

"Hello – Karl . . ."

Yes, it was him alright. And on that grey October afternoon in 1939, our encounter here amid the gentle buzz of the Café Kultas seemed perfectly normal and not in the least fraught; for all that, it was quite accidental.

We had not seen one another for fully a year – since the time we entered university together and I had stayed on in Tartu while Karl had soon moved back to Tallinn, only travelling down to take the odd exam.

"Well – take a seat."

He was his usual elegant self. A little supercilious. With an affectation of melancholy, as always. But in spite of any such difficulties, the general impression he made was an amiable one. Difficulties is perhaps too strong a word – for it need not be taken as referring to anything more than what someone had told me eighteen months previously during our last days at grammar school. We were contemporaries then, he at the Tallinn commercial college, I at Granberg's and we had long known one another by sight. Just before the matriculation exams, I suddenly found myself at their place. I do not remember how, but no doubt on Karl's invitation. And on that occasion someone had said to me: that Karl is only sucking up to you because you'll be useful to him, come the exams – as an unpaid tutor! Hadn't I noticed?

I didn't take the remark seriously. It even made me feel a little uncomfortable: for the person who made it was a girl who all too clearly wanted to keep me well away from Karl's home. And the reason for her endeavours was Karl's sister, Flora. Indeed yes, it was not Karl's interest in receiving free lessons, but my interest in his sister, Flora, that drew me more than anything else to that in some ways strange Ventsel household in the May of '38.

The first time I went there was certainly on Karl's invitation – to go through the physics exam questions together. Then, Karl's mother offered us dinner. And alongside kindly Mrs Ventsel with her hair the colour of rust, her page-boy style coiffure and her rolls of fat there appeared at table the daughter of the house – and even if I had originally intended to refuse dinner, I now stayed put.

Flora was one year younger than Karl but left school at the same time as ourselves and had just finished her matriculation exams the week before. And as I looked at her like this across the table, eyeing her from close to, I could not get over the fact that I had never noticed her in town or in the course of school activities. For Flora was a girl with beautiful grey-green eyes and flowing auburn hair and a face which could be described as slightly Grecian but without the inert quality of a sculpture. The

impression she gave was, somehow, one of excitement and fresh-
ness and her movements, one moment startlingly quick, the next
unexpectedly languid, were lithe and intriguing.

I ate dinner at the Ventsels', gazed at Flora and provoked her
deep laugh on one or two occasions (with the cheap wit of a
nineteen-year old lad, of which I had a good stock) and conversed
as best I could with stout Johanna, her mother, who, with all her
rings, earrings and bangles, but even more so with her ready
tongue, was altogether different to the women of her generation
whom I had had the opportunity to observe at close quarters.
Not that I knew that many of them: my own mother and my
aunts on her side of the family, solemn deaconesses; and my aunts
on my father's side with their rustic ways, also the mothers of a
couple of my classmates, dowdy little middle-class ladies whom I
had met at their houses; add our entirely institutionalised women
teachers and, finally, one or two women who had crossed the
threshold of my parents' home, the virtuous spouses of factory
foremen or middle-grade civil servants. Against this backdrop,
Flora's mother struck me as an almost alarming phenomenon.

Flora's father I first saw only for a moment – in slippers and
braces, wearing a white shirt and no tie, the tall, gaunt master of
the house darted into the room shaking his grey locks indignantly
and asking his wife where his patent leather shoes had got to.
But she did not put herself out to find them for him:

"Wherever could they be? But Felix – they'll be exactly where
you left them the day before yesterday!"

"Well, where did I leave them, that's what I'm asking!"

"Why ask me? I was asleep when you came home. It was
four o'clock in the morning, after all. So you'll just have to ask
yourself."

And she returned to chatting to her children and myself. And
it seemed to me that she even winked at us as if to say: "You see
how comic dad can be. And how neatly we keep him in his
place . . ."

It turned out that Mr Ventsel was on his way to play bridge
with some business colleagues at the Vigint Club (his firm were

representatives of some foreign chemical products company).
Later on, I obtained the impression that he was an assiduous
player of the game and that ladies played a key role among his
bridge partners. And when I had observed Mrs Ventsel every
evening for a week, with her peals of laughter, her protuberant
brown eyes with their meaningful glances, her puffing and sigh-
ing, her childish frocks which took no account whatsoever of her
abundant kilos and her ample figure, I began to a certain extent
to understand why Mr Ventsel escaped from home – in spite of
the fact that family habits here differed fundamentally from those
I was used to.

But this in no way (or hardly in any way) affected my relations
with Flora. As is usual with nineteen-year-olds. In whom the
novelty of the play of hormones carries more weight than observations of character or social standing. Since the former takes
place within our bodies themselves while the latter, however surprising these observations may be, fail (on account of our inex-
perience) to offer us sufficient grounds for conviction.

That summer the three of us, Flora, Karl and myself, had to
prepare for our university entrance exams. Karl and I had decided
to study Law, while Flora was going to enter the Department of
Philosophy. This meant that we would be swatting together for
the same Estonian Language and History exams. So from the
middle of July to mid-August the three of us, or sometimes two,
sat together at our books for several hours each day. More, in
fact, than was strictly necessary for study. And the nearer we got
to the exams, the more our sessions were conducted not as a
studious trio but as a twosome – me and Flora – up on the third
floor of the solid stone-built block of flats at the end of what was
then the beginning of the Tartu Road, in the Ventsels' expensive
but always surprisingly higgledy-piggledy apartment, on the sofa
in Flora's little room or, as I remember, in the glass recess resembling a conservatory adjacent to the lounge, under a huge palm,
whose green foliage offered you a moment's shelter from anyone
bursting in unexpectedly.

And we soon began to need a certain amount of shelter. To

conceal from Karl, and especially from Flora's mother, the fleeting advances, kisses and embraces which two young people of our age could permit themselves forty years ago, fettered, in her case, by the constant threat of her mother walking in through the door, in mine, by the unfamiliar surroundings. Karl never caught us unawares. But he must have suspected our intimacies. All the more, since he was interested in such matters in a slightly womanish kind of way, far more so than in the classification of Muuk's classification of the 1,166 Estonian word-models, or the latest discoveries of archaeologists at the Lehola dig. But Flora's mother did catch us *in flagrante*. She stalked silently (which was not at all her usual way of doing things) from the dining room into the lounge while we were kissing behind the palm and evidently stood looking at us for a minute or two. And then said so suddenly that it made us jerk apart:

"Well children, I wanted to offer you a nice cup of coffee. But now I feel I must offer you something stronger with it. Would you like a Martell or a rum?"

My embarrassment at being found out was mingled with the relief that Johanna, instead of throwing me out, had taken the situation in her stride. And I also felt the adolescent joy that my escapade had been inevitably condoned – since the daughter of the house had allowed it. But a moment later, when we were sitting at the table sipping our tiny glasses of Martell, I felt an incomprehensible confusion – as if by accepting that glass of cognac – God damn – I had been accepted as a member of the family ... Luckily just then, in walked Mr Ventsel and took a seat at our coffee table, and in his presence the subject was not aired. So that I never did get to find out how Johanna would have expanded on the subject.

Soon afterwards, we went off to Tartu and all managed to get into university within the space of one week. In Karl's case this did not particularly surprise me. With a reasonably easy essay topic and a bit of luck with his history questions, acceptance by the university seemed quite likely. But even allowing for Flora's "4" in her written paper – her subject was "Woman and Culture", which allowed the greatest scope for waffle – the results of her history oral bowled me over nonetheless.

I waited for her at the hotel on Vallikraavi Street where she and Karl had been staying for the time being. Karl had gone out, so I sat and waited in the hall. Flora arrived smirking and humming a tune, and holding a bunch of marigolds she had bought in the street. Before even reaching me she cried out:

"I've passed!"

I did, of course, congratulate her and asked, when we had reached her room, *how in the world* she had managed to do so.

"I'll show you. Sit down over there at the desk."

I took a seat at the hotel room table which was covered in faded green baize. Flora placed a chair in the middle of the room, one-and-a-half metres away, and sat herself down, the bunch of flowers still in her hand. And I suddenly noticed that she was wearing a poison-green dress which deepened the green of her eyes in a strange sort of way and highlighted the copper tint of her hair. Not only was the dress extremely tight, but also unexpectedly short. And when she crossed her right leg over her left with the languor of a princess, this once again affirmed for me that her legs were of a divine shapeliness. I saw that she had dressed for the exam in expensive black fish-net stockings and ballroom pumps with golden straps. And that movement of her legs, which had seemed entirely unstudied, opened up unprecedentedly promising vistas for the imagination to work on. Thus I had a quite physical sensation of being unable either to look away, or at her . . .

Flora noticed this and explained, a look of triumph on her face and cooing with delight:

"Well, you see, it was like this. There were only men on the exam board. And the girls had been saying to me only the day before yesterday: use your legs! Tartu girls. If you get my meaning. They know their old Piilmann. He was the chairman of the examining board. A bald daddy in his fifties. I didn't really believe what they told me. I had to pass somehow, though. And it turned out to be true. Sure enough, he got into a real pother. He didn't listen to a thing I said. Well anyway, I did manage to remember a few key facts about the time of National Enlightenment. And when he started asking me additional questions about Kreutzwald's *Vambola*[4] – or was it some other work, I don't quite remember – I simply started going like this . . ." Flora lifted her right leg with dignified ease up off her left knee, then recrossed her legs, "and I started telling them about the romance between old Kreutzwald and young Koidula. Mum had once told me the story. She'd once seen a play about it. And then Mr Piilmann's eyes narrowed slightly behind his glasses and he said:

"Good, good, good, good. Well, I think that we can give the young lady a 4."

At first, I found Flora's exam-passing technique rather uncouth. There was something a little alarming in possessing a skill such as this. It was in too great a contrast to the serious, clever and modest behaviour by which everyone in my circle of friends was judged, especially the young ladies. Even so, Flora's trick was, to my mind, most inspiring: the girl came, saw, *dared* and conquered . . .

I got up and went over to Flora. I took her in my arms and carried her to the ramshackle hotel bed. And she let it happen. When she was in my embrace she looked at me absently from behind her almost shut eyelids and brushed my eyes and lips with her bunch of marigolds. And I was ready to seize the whole world and lift it off its pedestal. In the pride of knowing that such a desirable girl had merely *teased* the old baldies but actually allowed me to . . .

I do not know how much Karl could have noticed when he came back to the hotel an hour later. He did not, at any rate, say anything. He only mentioned that he would be taking the afternoon train to Tallinn and we could now all go and have lunch. We ate lunch in the small restaurant of that same hotel and saw Karl off at the station at five. He was going to return a week later for the start of term. On climbing up into his carriage he said no more than:

"Well, don't do anything I wouldn't . . ."

*   *   *

Our fairy tale, children's story, or so it seemed at the time, our all-embracing novel, lasted until February. Just before Christmas, Flora's mother came to see her daughter in Tartu. We were by then living in digs, Flora in the home of a lawyer on Veski Street in an old patrician dwelling where nothing was permitted; me in the small house of a retired librarian on Meltsiveski Street where lodgers had the run of the place for weeks on end, since the landlord spent a good deal of his time out in the country. When, incidentally, my landlord was in town, he was busy giving Latin lessons to those students who needed them. And Flora really did need them – in preparation for the forthcoming Latin exams – and took lessons of a sort from my landlord. So that she had a superb excuse for coming over. As for Flora's mother, I met her in Café Ateena, Flora having asked me to come there to sit with them for a while. And it was at that point that I understood with mixed feelings, part triumph, part embarrassment, that our relationship which I thought our closest friends may have had an inkling of, but which was not supposed to exist as far as our families were concerned, was in fact perfectly obvious to Flora's mother. And not only did she know about it! She immediately began talking about it! With relish, interest and, while munching her way through her flaky *Napoleon* pastry and sipping her coffee, she eyed us with curiosity over her silver fox pelt which followed her generous contours:

"You know, children, *I* say: the main thing is that you are content with one another. I have always said: why must girls pine and do foolish things and young men visit places of dubious repute – when it can all be done in a way that is socially acceptable? *Denn das Leben will doch auch vor der Ehe gelebt werden, nicht wahr?*"[5]

She burst into peals of laughter at Flora, who was blushing a deep pink, drained her coffee cup with obvious relish, took the cigarette from between Flora's fingers, stubbed it out in the ashtray, pushed some 20-*kroon* notes into her hand instead, and billowed away to call on the Ladies So-and-So.

Auch vor der Ehe . . . At the age of nineteen, I had never of course thought seriously about marriage. Particularly, as child marriages were far from fashionable in those days. I had always warded off such thoughts with an inner blush, for even I realised that I was ridiculously young for such things – though at the same time, being married ... No, no – all that sort of thing – legality, domesticity, finality should crystallise and develop *later*. Not, at any rate, for shall we say, a couple, or three, or four years from now ... And yet – or for that very reason – Flora's mother's *auch-vor-der-Ehe* formula smacked unpalatably of foregone conclusions, a fact which disturbed me ...

I travelled up to Tallinn for Christmas, told my parents of my life in Tartu, about what an edifying and by no means time-wasting place the Students' Guild "Amicus studiorum" was and about how irreproachably hard I had been working. I even had a couple of respectable marks to show for this, my first term. I also mentioned in passing, how independent I had already managed to become – thanks to the few dozen *krooni* I had earned contributing articles to some periodicals. About Flora I did not breathe a word. But then I went off to visit Aunt Sandra on Girgenson Street.

This older sister of my mother's was then in her sixties, a little bony, a little stiff, but irritatingly observant, with her amazingly large, inquisitive and stern eyes, grey as the sea. People said she had been quite a beauty in her day. Judging by what she looked like now, it must have been a chilly and somewhat perilous beauty. When already past thirty, she had been married for a few years to some photographer who died young. But marriage seemed not to have changed her character one jot. It must have been moulded much earlier and given a final polish during those fifteen years that she had spent in Saint Petersburg as governess to a count who was Chief Prosecutor. The Prosecutor had, incidentally, been a Liberal. But Aunt Sandra had remained a devilishly logical woman all her life. I had once heard how Aunt Sandra had driven past a prison in a coach with her Prosecutor and uttered some remark that included the word "criminal". The Prosecutor had sighed and raised his eyes to the heavens:

"Oh, Alexandra Ginrikovna, please refrain from calling them criminals! You should think of them as unfortunate souls!"

Upon which Aunt Sandra had given her employer a withering look (I can just imagine how she would have looked at him as if through a lorgnette which she would not at that time have possessed) and said:

"By all means, Lev Ivanovich. But if *they* are not criminals, then *you* must be."

Aunt Sandra chatted with me in her usual slightly aloof but not unfriendly manner and, as always, she offered me a cup of coffee and a couple of cubes of dark green candied jelly which she had bought at Stude's confectioner's. She then said:

"I've heard you've been courting Flora Ventsel."

This was no question. This was a statement. But demanded some kind of answer, nonetheless. I said:

"One of your friends could quite well have seen us once or twice at the Vanemuine Theatre."

Aunt Sandra asked: "Only in the bar? Or in the auditorium, too?"

"Well – we were in the auditorium as well."

"I see." She looked at me through her lorgnette which was now very much part of her, and asked with a somewhat strange emphasis: "Do you happen, by any chance, to know the young lady's *mother*?"

"Well, erm . . . yes I do, actually. What of it?"

Aunt Sandra raised her right eyebrow and smiled with the left corner of her mouth. Almost imperceptibly. Satanically:

"Then, I need say no more. Then, you will know."

"What will I know?"

"What is awaiting you in twenty years' time. If you take a serious interest in her daughter."

I could not say what most affected the course of events in the relationship between Flora and myself. To a certain extent private factors made their presence felt as well as public ones and, forming a backdrop to the latter, the world events of those strange months. As for the private factors, I should in the first instance mention that we had taken our relationship too much for granted and that, as far as I was concerned, it had come prematurely. As for public ones, I am thinking of the fact that the family took everything for granted in the same fashion: Flora's mother sanctioned our conduct with her motherly goodwill, which caused a kind of *metamorphosis* in our relationship. But also Flora's mother's attitude in general: her ardent condescension as if she were matchmaking (I did not dare admit it to myself but I felt at times that her behaviour smacked of pimping) – and in addition, her somewhat unseemly understanding, not expressed in so many words but hinted at nevertheless, that Flora's marriage, Flora's future, Flora's future social status, even Flora's *happiness* need not have anything to do with this relationship ... When I mentioned "world events" as factors affecting our romance, I was thinking primarily of the tense situation of the pre-war world in general. It seemed, in that tense atmosphere, as if advances which were destined to succeed were likely by their very nature to flare up in true unity, while those which were flawed were likely to fissure sooner than they would have done under normal circumstances ... Perhaps Aunt Sandra's poisonous prognostications gnawed at the roots of our burgeoning love and I began to imagine, perhaps unconsciously, that there was indeed a dangerous likeness between the Flora of future days and her mother, and began to detect in the present-day Flora the seeds of her mother's painful obesity and ridiculous fussiness. However, all these factors, taken one by one at least, were no doubt secondary – compared to the appearance of Inga.

This was a stage in life when you were sometimes susceptible to tragedy but fully open to fantasy, where you never took anything particularly seriously apart from yourself, a time when you could find ample leisure for the most varied activities, and I took to attending lectures on all kinds of subjects other than those which my own Faculty of Law had on offer. Towards the end of January, during a lecture by old Gustav Suits[6] on French Classicism which

was being held in Lecture Theatre 4 of the main building, I
found myself sitting next to a girl with hair the colour of wheat
and a peach complexion, and I had to ask her why I had never
seen her there before. She looked at me for an instant with her
surprisingly serious, sparkling dark-brown eyes. Just as she began
answering me, Suits entered the auditorium and I heard her reply
through the scraping of heels. So she turned towards me and
pressed her full and well-formed mouth against my ear, so that
I both heard her words and felt her breath:

"I'm here for the first time. I'm actually a first-year economics
student. But I feel it's not really my thing. I'm getting to know
the university."

And I decided to get to know her.

The discoveries of this friendship are another story. Except
for the discovery that Inga's charms as such were that much
closer to my in-built demands for propriety and the like and
which, for some, go under the name of petit-bourgeois prejudices,
than were those of Flora, or at least those of her mother . . .
And I felt that this was precisely how a young girl ought to
behave . . .

At the beginning of February and before, I am sure, she was
even aware of a rival, Flora travelled up to Tallinn. She had to
stay there for a few days. She stayed a week, two, three. So I
discovered to my surprise and joy, as well as with slight pangs of
guilt, that her absence, which three weeks previously would have
had me at least worried or morose – suddenly suited me admirably
. . . A week later, someone told me (and this is the blessing and
the bane of such a tiny country and pocket-sized community such
as ours): Flora had been seen in some restaurant or theatre, or
both, with her mother and a certain Mr Kimmel, a successful
divorced wine-merchant in his forties and the Consul for Luxem-
bourg . . .

I can still clearly recall how the news *struck* me – like a blow
with an iron bar in the solar plexus. And how the feeling of pain
sank for one very long moment through my body and down to
my groin, making my knees shake for an instant, then flowing

out through the soles of my feet. And how around my heart (yes, literally around my heart!), my temples and the root of my nose, a feeling of freedom grew. My fuzzy-chinned ego had been dealt a blow, but my mind told me jubilantly that such liberating synchronicity rarely occurs in such separations ... True, the wave of anguish knocked my youthful self-esteem on a couple more occasions when Inga was not present to ward off such feelings. Such as when I received a postcard from Flora at the beginning of March:

> Peeter!
> Mother wants me to live at home, after all. It won't make much difference to my studies anyway – and you won't miss me that much from what I can gather. Do give me a ring when you are in Tallinn.

I never did give her a ring. Since I never went up to Tallinn. Which no doubt showed that I had not quite got over the whole business. I stayed in Tartu until the spring exams were over. In mid-June, when Inga had gone off home to Otepää, I took the train and went to visit my cousin in Kaunas, then the capital of Lithuania. And now in October 1939, after the fall of Poland, the outbreak of the war, the establishment of the bases and the autumn exams which demanded full concentration (Theoretical Statistics and Forensic Medicine – so that I wouldn't have them hanging over me until Christmas) I was here again. I had travelled up to Tallinn to visit my parents during these troubled times. I was too happily in love with Inga for the journey to arouse in me any desire to meet Flora and cause myself, or her, the pain involved.

And now I was sitting here looking at Karl, and over his shoulder, to where the young Jossif Schagal was putting his violin under his chin, preparing to play a lunchtime concert with the ensemble, and smiling back in the direction of anyone who happened to smile at him. Most people smiled because this boy's violin playing was one of those heartening threads of normality in the ripping canvas of the epoch. And one or two smiled at

him because he was reputed to be the nephew of the great Marc
Chagall. I watched him play, and his capriccio helped me back
to present time and place – and was all the more surprised when
Karl, who had already taken a seat, said cheerily:

"What a good job we bumped into one another. Flora and I
were saying only this morning how nice it would be to see you
again. What are you doing this evening?"

No, no, I couldn't bring myself to refuse this invitation as if I
were afraid of something. When I had in any case heard that
Flora must perhaps by now be engaged to Kimmel, into the
bargain . . .

"Nothing really. Why do you ask?"

Karl picked up the copy of *Päevaleht* and pointed to the picture
of the 14,000-ton *Der Deutsche* in the sea roads:

"We're leaving too. It would be nice for us to get together
this evening – Flora, you and me. And I could bring Bella along
as well."

"So you're also leaving?" I was genuinely surprised. Taken
aback. No, not for Flora's sake. Or if for her sake, then really
only *in part*. Chiefly because the Ventsels' departure was yet one
more incursion of abnormality into normal life . . . And I could
not stop myself from asking pointedly:

"What kind of Germans are you, then? Your mother went to
German Grammar School – and now the whole family has sud-
denly become German – Papa Ventsel on the strength of Mama
Ventsel's choice of school . . . !"

Karl suffered my comment and said, drawing (with visible suffering) on his "Elba" cigarette:

"Peeter – you know how things stand . . ."

I knew all too well how things stood. A week before, the papers
had announced that Hitler was inviting all Germans living in
Estonia and Latvia to return to the Fatherland. The following
day, a German government delegation had arrived to discuss the
arrangements. The commissions had worked frenetically day and
night for two days running. Germans began selling their possessions and packing. By the third day the ships lay at anchor in

the sea roads. The furniture of those leaving had already been collected up and placed in bonded warehouses. At the doors of the banks there were queues of those wishing to exchange money. By the fifth day, the first voyagers had climbed aboard. The area outside the Customs Office was clogged with taxis. The newspapers were full of such announcements as "I bid my friends farewell on account of my departure abroad . . ." Or "I wish to declare I do not intend travelling anywhere and that all rumours as to my imminent departure are quite without foundation . . ." It was a disciplined, if contagious, panic. I, of course, knew as well as everyone else that among those departing were quite a large number of pure-blooded Estonians. Many of those whose cultural affinities were German, were gripped – some by an urge to make a decision for complex biographical motives, others out of sheer naked fear. The urge to make a decision affected those who had, perhaps for generations, vacillated between being German and being Estonian, adopting whichever identity was the more pragmatic at the time – and who were now obliged to answer the question: which of the two am I? And the fear – well, fear had seized those who considered that they would have something to answer for, against the background of our new orientation towards Moscow. But to obtain an exit permit, a citizen need not be on the list drawn up by the German Administration for Cultural Autonomy. It was quite enough to be in possession of papers from the Estonian Ministry of the Interior stating that you were a German. And since the whole of this half-dreamlike drive towards repatriation took place with feverish and sinister haste, people with the right connections found it quite easy to obtain a certificate declaring them to be German.

Karl continued: "You know how things stand. I didn't make the decision. Father did. He says the Russians would make short shrift of the likes of him. He says he has experience of this from the events of 1918. I don't know. Nowadays you can't be sure of anything any more. And I'm not sure either whether he's doing the right thing or not . . ."

I enquired when they were leaving. It turned out that the older

Ventsels were already on board and would be departing the next morning. Port of destination: Stettin. But Karl and Flora would be leaving on the evening of the day after next. When I asked why they were travelling separately, Karl replied vaguely: "Well, it just turned out that way . . ." I asked:

"Is it true that you will be resettled in the Posen area?"

Karl replied: "Yes. For the time being."

Hitler had, of course, announced that repatriated Germans would be given comfortable living quarters in the areas which the Reich had reconquered. I wanted to say: OK, why not? You can make yourselves at home there – once you've washed the blood of the departing Poles off the floor . . . But I held my peace. For I could see Karl's weary and nervous face – the bluish stubble on his narrow jaw was more visible than he would normally have permitted – and it was obvious that he was not in the least happy. That observation alone may not have made me keep my mouth shut. But at that point the thought crossed my mind: what if my father had decided to leave . . . ? This was, thank God, unimaginable – on account of his love of his home district, his naïve nationalism, his attitude to Germans in general and Hitler in particular – and his attitude to "his" factory into which he had invested fifteen hundred *krooni* of his money and forty years of his life. But you do not choose your own father! If he had been different – and if he had decided to leave – for some reason I was not aware of and whose roots could be traced back to a time before I was born – what could I have done about it? And what would I have actually done? Would I have acted any differently from Karl? Hardly . . . The ensemble were now playing Fibich's musical poem, then gliding smoothly over into Schubert's somewhat supplicatory songs. I asked:

"And what were your plans for this evening?"

"Well – we thought – you could come round to our place. The house is all topsy-turvy, our things are all packed and three-quarters of them are already gone. So it's no longer much of a home. But we could go, the four of us, to a restaurant and eat a farewell dinner there. Who can tell when, how, even *whether* we shall ever meet again. There's war in the West. And God only knows what's going to happen here . . . Flora thought you could come by around eight –"

"How could she think that – when only yesterday I . . . ?"

"She phoned your mother this morning and heard."

"Oh, I see . . ." She had never before phoned my mother.

I have to admit that at that moment I had entirely forgotten the fact that it was I who should, or at least could, have been asking for forgiveness. So I thought to myself: Very well. I'll accept their invitation. I'll forgive Flora. Since we'll be saying goodbye for goodness knows how long. Let her go. I can forgive her and her Kimmel. Perhaps I was also thinking: since the Lord has obliged her to depart, and has punished her enough with her flight abroad.

I asked (despite my decision to forgive Flora): "Flora's – new admirer – Mr Kimmel – he's not coming – this evening, is he?"

"Oh no, no –" said Karl hurriedly, "He won't be going to Germany. He *should have been*. But he decided to stay here."

I thought: all the more reason for him to come! But then again, all the more reason for him not to. How do I know? I don't care one way or the other.

In the end, we agreed that I would not go to their place, after all. That seemed necessary for me to save face. So we would meet at eight at Brenner's Restaurant by the seashore out at Pirita. Karl phoned straightaway from a phone booth and booked a table for four for eight o'clock.

When we parted company, it was five. I remember ringing home to say that I would be returning late that evening. Then I went on Inga's request to Keisermann's bookshop and bought her a copy of Cronin's *The Stars Look Down*. She wanted to read it herself and then give it to her sister for her birthday. And as the bookshop was right next to the florist's, I also entered the florist's after a slight hesitation. From the meagre October selection I bought Flora three pale roses, since life lay before us, did it not, and yet this would be our last meeting. Pale roses – since anything brighter would have been a lie. And I bought those three roses out of devilment too: the official Estonian name of these roses "*Staatspräsident Päts*"[7] seemed to offer the opportunity of making a double-pronged pun which I wanted to think out in detail on the way to the restaurant – one thorn for the recent "Germanophilia" of President Päts, and the other for the back-sides of the Estonian *Umsiedler*[8] ... I remember that, as I still had one-and-a-half hours to kill, I went to the City Library and flipped through their card-index. By the time I got on the bus it was already dark. Out of the bus windows I could see that the darkness was intermittently dampened by drizzle. The bus turned into Narva Road, then into Pirita Road and I thought to myself, shrugging my shoulders: why would Karl have chosen a restaurant so off the beaten track ... ?

Brenner's Restaurant was almost empty at eight in the evening and I was the first of our foursome to arrive. The waiter showed me to our table which had been reserved quite unnecessarily. I asked for a vase to be brought for the roses and a cup of coffee for myself, took a seat and had a look around.

Five or six pink night-table lamps on the few occupied tables were the only lighting in the room with its dark timbered walls. A monotonous foxtrot was being pumped out on the violin, piano and saxophone and a few couples were shuffling across the badly waxed dance-floor. In the rosy half-light and over the heads of the dancers sailed a four-masted model schooner under whose keel the taller dancers instinctively ducked. We had been given a comfortable corner table by a red curtain, behind which was the window. I looked out at the view and saw the bay and the city lights beyond in the misty darkness. I remember lighting a cigarette, screwing up my eyes and trying to compose my salu-tation, in spite of noise from the saxophone, and knocking together something like this:

> To lighten the burden of my sins,
> O Flora dear, I take these verses as support
> And, while I bargain with my poet's wings,
> To kiss your hand, so newly German, I do sport;

And, as is the current fashion now,
Salute you with the *Staatspräsident* –
Under the sailing prow ...

Well, my not quite twenty-year-old ego was rather satisfied with
my spot of versifying and I imagined, smiling wryly, how I would
rise as they arrived and hand Flora the roses from the vase while
declaiming ... And at the same time I planned – or perhaps even
promised myself – to be a gentleman after that, keeping silent
about all those dubious events, Flora's flight from Tallinn,
Kimmel, rumours of betrothal and the Germanification of the
day before yesterday ... And at that very moment Karl entered
the restaurant with his sister and his Bella. Karl stepped inside,
in advance of the girls, then let them pass by, exactly in accordance with the etiquette of the day – and as they crossed the floor
towards me I saw with a start: Flora was wearing that selfsame
tight, poison-green dress and the same shoes with golden straps
– the dress and shoes of her history exam – and I wondered, with
a mixture of joy and anxiety: Why? Why? To remind me ... ?
And as she approached in that green dress with her copper hair
agleam between the tables and past the little islands of pink light
cast by the lamps, many things were going through my mind:
can weariness so embellish a girl's face? So those legs are German
now? Kreutzwald's *Vambola* – ha-ha-haa ... Shameful to recall,
but such things are *also* important – for the sake of the quality
of future generations ... God knows ... But what was the name
of that Watteau painting now? *The Departure* – to where? Which
island was it now ... ?
      Then they had come right up to me and I shook Flora's hand.
But before I had time to present her with the roses and open my
mouth to recite my lines, Karl steered Bella in my direction, saying:
      "Do say hello to my wife too!"
      "Wh-a-a-at?! Your wife!"
      "Yes. We've got married. This morning. I could have told you
when I saw you just after lunch. But I decided to keep it as a
little surprise for this evening."

"Well ... you really have surprised me ... I wish you all the best, of course ..."

I shook hands with them both. As is the custom. We took our seats. I was thinking: one surprise after another. Bella, that pale, silent, dark-eyebrowed girl, who was nicknamed "Banana" and who played the piano so nicely, and whose fleeting presence I had seen in Karl's company from time to time, so that I was on first-name terms with her – Bella Luide. You could read in the papers about such lightning weddings among those heading for Germany: those leaving had been given that privilege. The fact that those two had suddenly taken such a step was yet another one of those tremors, those earthquakes beneath your feet which could be felt all the way up to your heart ...

"So you'll be leaving together the day after tomorrow ...?"

"That's right," said Karl, "we're leaving."

And I wanted to cry out: How can you? It's simply impossible! Quite absurd ... But I said nothing. For they knew better, no doubt. Nevertheless, I looked them both in the face as if to assure myself that they were still fully sane. Bella's father was an Estonian, to be sure, a bank official and a house-owner and with his Baltic German wife he fitted nicely into the motley mass of emigrants. But his first wife, Bella's mother, the young Mrs Luide, now some ten years dead (I heard this from the family of my uncle the doctor) was the daughter of a well-known Jewish aurist! Although Bella with her would-be German father and her German stepmother and a husband who was, since the previous day, also a German would seem to have been well-covered, her emigration to Germany was in my opinion, one of those leaps into the abyss which others in her position were desperately trying to avoid. For even if not obvious before, it had during the last year become plain since Hitler's *Kristallnacht* pogrom that Jews of all people ought to understand that in present-day Germany they had nothing else to look forward to save interminable horrific and unexpected violence ... By what yardstick were you supposed to measure the recent announcement in the Estonian press where you could read that Berlin had announced officially that Jews in

Germany would be issued with food rationing cards on the same
basis as Germans but would not, for the time being, receive ones
for buying textiles – since they had, up to now, been employed
primarily in that particular sector . . . ? When even announcements intended to mollify foreign opinion were intrinsically
taunts, what did the *reality* of the situation look like? But there
was really no point in bringing that up here -- when they had
made up their minds and had to leave the day after next . . . I
took the three roses out of the vase and presented them to Bella
– without any versifying, just some awkward words and a strange
feeling that I had seen those broad-based upright thorns in connection with some entirely different and ominous event . . .

I decided to devote my attention to the Flora beside me while
she was still here. I looked at her. Her greenish eyes seemed to
me to be particularly dark, almost black, and against her classical,
lightly freckled but nonetheless clear profile, her smile seemed
doubly hesitant. She had sat down, not next to her brother, but
next to me, as if this were quite the expected thing to do. On
the chair arm she rested her right hand, five centimetres from
my left. I looked at her hand with its small girlish gold ring and
grasped the situation: whether I took hold of this hand, or
desisted, would set the tone of the evening. If I did nothing, the
whole dinner would become a pretty formal affair. If I did take
hold of her hand and she pushed it away, likewise. But if I took
hold of it and she let it happen and went partly, or wholly, along
with my little game, then bitterness and sweetness would be the
inevitable result . . . I remember considering for a long moment
what it was I actually wanted – a cool, more or less amicable
farewell, or something more. I remember: reason told me that
the first alternative would be the only sensible and right one. But
all the other forces in me, from irony and patriotism to sympathy
and lust, gainsaid reason in an avid whisper. I do not know how
this struggle would have ended (or I can at least say that I do
not know), had the waiter not appeared at that very moment
to take our orders. So that I could not do otherwise but take
Flora's hand in mine and ask her what she would like to have . . .

Whereupon I said (noting at the same time the fact that she did *not* withdraw her hand):

"I think we should take something light. And then some coffee with a Napoleon brandy – don't you agree?" (I took it as read that I would be paying for Flora and myself and anything more expensive was quite beyond my pocket.) But Karl started to protest immediately:

"*Today* – there'll be no penny-pinching! Understood? I don't suppose you know but we can only take along fifty *krooni* per head! Anything over and above that sum will have to be deposited with Scheel's Bank. They'll transfer it for us God knows when, at God knows what rate and God knows where to. But there's no way *we* are going to stand there queuing at the bank! On principle! And we've got over three hundred *krooni* left over. To be spent by the day after tomorrow – you understand! So we can let the bill run up to at least one hundred *krooni*! And I'm paying! No two ways about it!"

From my visits to the Ventsel household I had received the vague impression that the well-to-do middle-class life they had led used to place certain strains on them from time to time. Clearly their financial situation was not all that rosy and that brilliant uniform which had to be kept in trim in order to maintain appearances sometimes betrayed rather tight stitching. For instance, when Mr Ventsel would borrow twenty crowns from his wife, or when Mrs V. would go through the pockets of her husband's trousers hanging in the cupboard to find money to send the maid off to the cake shop to buy some pastries. Against this background of heightened observation on my part, Karl always made a business-like, frugal impression, and I had never observed any spendthrift tendencies on his part. Then there sprang to mind a conversation I had held with Doctor Seidel in Café Werner in Tartu, only the week before. That young doctor, who came from an old Baltic German family and whose name was in actual fact *von* Seidel, had recently graduated from the Tartu Faculty of Medicine and was a passing acquaintance of mine from goodness knows where. He confessed to vacillating

between leaving and staying. And foreshadowed days of tough
ethical decisions ahead, both private and public. According to
Seidel, emigration would lead to a tragic disintegration of society.
He explained how such a conservative ethnic group as his would
suffer doubly in the process of emigration. On the one hand,
the more moth-eaten (as he put it) elements tend to become
even more neurotically withdrawn, while the other, more
vigorous elements would suffer from unimaginable moral
decline: marriages breaking up, complexes emerging, shifts in
character occurring. He went on to give examples: eminently
respectable older women beginning to play the whore, honest
businessmen no longer honouring their debts, old rams of
virtue beginning to tup. The main reason: the crumbling of the
old system of moral checks. Which was just one aspect of a
phenomenon which had no equivalent in the Estonian language:
Entwurzelung[9] . . .

It seemed to me that there was a good deal of truth in what
the keen and brisk Dr Seidel was telling. It just seemed that the
conclusions he was drawing were a little too categorical and dras-
tic. But Karl's way of throwing money around did make me
think: when it came to the crunch, wasn't this a symptom of that
selfsame *Entwurzelung* . . . ? Anyhow, I didn't argue with Karl
and said:

"Do as you think best . . ."

And I do not remember what we finally ordered. We were
brought some kind of aperitif and some cold cuts. A nickel-plated
ice bucket containing a bottle of schnapps covered grandly in
condensation and wrapped in a white serviette tied in a bow was
placed beside Karl's chair. Next, we were served some kind of
cutlet and red wine. And as we were wined and dined and Karl
and Bella opposite us whispered, planned, cooed and teased one
another (as theirs was more than purely a marriage of convenience) and as we, now and again, found ourselves back in a
different time and space and needed to stop things from slipping
into oblivion, Karl and I would shout by turns: "Karl, don't you
remember . . . ?" or "Peeter, wasn't that what happened . . . ?"

And now and again I would give Flora's cold but responsive hand a squeeze, and finally asked:

"Flora – was this evening your idea?"

I expected her to look at me with her dark green eyes, but she returned my question, her eyes fixed on the tablecloth:

"Does it bother you?"

I answered: "Flora – not in the least ... Quite the contrary, in fact. I'm positively glad. That we have forgiven one another." I took a sip of the red wine with its flavour of oak bark and felt an unexpected flash of anger at the thought that Flora's gorgeous knees, which were right next to me, were nevertheless treacherously and irrevocably beyond my grasp – for the whole of our affair was still too much part of me despite all the forgiving and forgetting. And I heard myself say:

"By the way – just that I know *what* exactly I'm forgiving you for, were you, or are you, engaged to that Kimmel fellow?"

Flora now looked me straight in the face and asked with an unexpected glint in her eye, but in a strangely muffled voice:

"Listen – are you engaged to Inga, or not?" She paused and as I said nothing, continued: "You see, how such questions don't get us anywhere." (But she made no attempt to remove her hand from my grasp.) "If you really want to know, Kimmel was Mum's idea. And our departure is going to save me from him."

I asked: "If you had stayed, would he have got his hands on you?"

Flora looked down and said: "Oh God, I really don't know ... Not if it was up to me, at least ..."

I freed my hand from hers in order to pick up my wine glass and said (though I felt: I shouldn't be doing this. But it had all been seething inside me, clearly more violently than I myself realised):

"Either way, he's been a swine twice over in the way he has been treating you ..." I expected Flora to ask me in what way, but she remained silent so that I was forced to add, making me feel more wretched than ever – though I continued nevertheless:

"Firstly, by letting you go. And secondly, by staying behind himself."

Flora did not reply. And I felt: now I must stop this. It was compensation enough that she wasn't defending her Kimmel. I felt: God help me! Don't humiliate yourself or her any further. And yet I still said:

"There again, it's a good job you finally got rid of the boor. Now you can have a hundred German lads kissing your knees."

I have to admit that I shocked even myself by the crudeness of that remark and I waited to see what she would do now. I had the feeling that it might result in floods of tears, or in her jumping up, running away or boxing my ears, all of which were in the air, anything could happen . . . I waited. Then Flora took my hand:

"Peeter – I would like to think that I've got – when I'm over *there* – that here there'll be some period of my life, some place and *somebody* – I can think back to. And I thought that if we could forgive each other today, as you have already said, then I will have."

She said this quite softly, in a manner far removed from all theatricality, in a way I had never heard her speak before. And I could feel my inner turmoil and how intolerance, which was really hurt pride, was struggling vainly against emotion. I, in turn, took Flora's hand, stroked it and said:

"Flora – we've been rubbing salt into old wounds. And you have proved the wiser of us two. Forgive me for what I said. Let us accept one another's apologies. Then I too will have, over there in Germany, more than just unpleasant things [I tempered the phrase by using "unpleasant" so as not to offend her] or distant and alien people, or goodness knows who – or even some whom I wish well, such as Karl and Bella – but well, you know, somebody whom I can think back to with fondness . . ." And then I added – (Oh, even in old age it is not always easy to know where the limit lies for words before they start to hurt. At twenty it is incalculably more difficult, when we are so full of the power of our words and constantly want to test *if* and *how* seriously they are being taken . . .) I said:

". . . In a different world – if we had been given the opportunity to think things over." (God, I certainly now felt that my words were impermissible in relation to Flora – at the very time when we were trying to separate without hurting one another – and that they were something of a sin vis-à-vis Inga, who was absent – and a sin as regards the book I had bought Inga and which lay in my briefcase in the cloakroom, forty paces away – but I finished, nevertheless) –

". . . maybe we would have come back to one another."

Flora remained silent. Then suddenly she said: "Come on, let's dance!"

We stepped out onto the dance floor. It was quite crowded by now. One middle-aged gentleman with a small moustache greeted Flora, and several of the men dancing eyed her over the shoulders of their dancing partners, or turned their heads to look at her. The ladies did not pay her any attention or if they did, then only by swivelling their eyeballs. Flora spoke into my ear – in a more lively tone somehow, than I had been led to expect:

"Would you believe it – even out here there are familiar faces! I especially asked Karl to find an out-of-the-way place, since there would no doubt be people we knew at the Gloria or the Pariis and other such places. You always have to *explain* everything to people you know. You know what I mean. It's such a bind. Those who are staying behind commiserate, those who are going support you. Some express sympathy, others wish you luck. By now, I've heard it all. Even the jibes. Traitor to our nation. I shrug my shoulders – what else can I do? – and say: Do you know, my grandfather was an Estonian, that I admit, but a Germanised one, nonetheless. Who made boots for the people of Paide. He didn't write the Estonian epic. So why not go and find out why the granddaughter of Kreutzwald, the man who did, became a German and emigrated! Just leave *me* alone!" She remained silent for a moment, then continued: "But you, I'll write to you. Not often, of course. Let's say two letters a year. Plus a card at Christmas. That won't endanger your relationship with Inga. Listen – are you going to marry her? I don't know her, but I don't think

you will. But do as you think best, of course. I'll write anyhow.
And I'll send you books. What's the name of that publisher's
again, the one which was supposed to publish such good books
– Behr's?"

"No. Wolff's. But they've closed it down now."

"Then I'll look for them in second-hand bookshops. Are you
listening to what I'm saying?"

"Yes. Thanks for the offer."

"Peeter – let's go and get my wrap from the table – no, I don't
need my coat – and let's get a breath of fresh air."

"You'll catch cold."

"No, I won't."

We went to our table. Karl and Bella had gone to dance. We
took Flora's spangled black and green plaid from her chair and
went outside.

The October night was chilly, as could be expected. But we
had been drinking wine and spirits and the cold did not reach
us. Beyond the circles of light thrown by the lamps at the entrance
to the restaurant, everything was in pitch darkness. But the fog
had dispersed and the sky had partly cleared. One or two stars
twinkled through the clouds. I hummed snatches from the theme
tune from *The Stars Look Down* . . . – and this gave me the courage
to put my arm round Flora. We strolled the fifty yards down to
the shore. The asphalt was wet and black. The sea was invisible
in the darkness. So that it was only from the lapping of the waves
that you could imagine its presence down there below the railings.
I remember thinking: kissing her would be just as noble as not
kissing her . . . The swathe of city lights glowed in the distance
through the thin mist, serving as a backdrop for the liners – what
were their names now – *Der Deutsche*, the *Weissensee*, the *Köln*
and the *Oldenburg* . . .

We watched the vessels. I wanted to kiss Flora. For why should
I not do so when I was sure it would be neither less nor more
noble than refraining! Suddenly she turned her back on the sea.
I could feel her shudder. She cried:

"I don't want to look at those ships! Don't you understand!

It's terrible . . . Here, they're all bathed in light. But once they
put to sea – I know what they do, they extinguish all the lights.
Out at sea they are as blind and dark as coffins! You understand
– the ship, the sea, Germany – all of this from tomorrow evening
on – blind and dark – like a coffin!" She grabbed my hand –
"Come on, let's get away from here."

She pulled me along and began running back in the direction
of the restaurant. I ran, my hand in hers, close behind her, alongside her – in front of her, then pulling her along in turn. I did
not ask her where she wanted to run. For I feared, consciously
or otherwise, that she would answer: back inside . . . Though she
had said: Let's run away from here! And I felt – swathed in the
lights, the darkness, the chill of the night and the glow of the
wine – that this darkness could, indeed must, mean something
more: an escape not only from the shore and the panorama of
those fateful ships, but escape as such – an escape beyond space
and time . . . I acted on that belief, that fancy, that hope, that
impulse. I doubled back to the right, off the asphalt road, into
the shadow of a line of spruce hedges dragging Flora along with
me.

My right hand still retains the memory of that pull: the sudden
weight of Flora at the first jerk, and the unexpected lightness at
the second. I have spent much time since, analysing what lay
in that pull. Jealousy of goodness-knows-who. Jealousy of that
wretched, rich, vile and idiotic man-of-the-world, that enviable
wine merchant whose appearance I could but vaguely remember.
Anger directed towards him as the bastard who had dared to take
Flora and then, the shit that he was, had gone and dropped her
– anger which had, to a certain extent, turned into a mixture of
hostility and sympathy towards Flora . . . And, of course, jealous
rage at that apocalyptically lethal and – as Flora had just described
it – *blind, dark* beast, against Germany, that had in actuality
already swallowed Flora up . . . And anger towards Flora for
being so willing to let herself be swallowed up. And a helpless
sorrow at the violence being inflicted on us. Till the presentiment
of an intention entered deep into the loam of my consciousness:

take her again, there among the spruce trees and prevent, for some short while at least, forty million Germans giving her German children ... And in that jerk of her wrist there was also undoubtedly a reawakening of our recent intimacy. Love, if you like. A blinding surge of tenderness. And wrapped within it, always that feeling of naked lust. Which left me, as I fled the light of the street lamps, and shielding my face from the claws of the spruce trees, with the fleeting image of myself fleeing through a translucent but infinitely thick wall: Inga – I hope you will understand – it can't be helped if you don't ...

And then Flora fell. On account of her damnably tight dress which had not allowed her to follow me – and which she was wearing on my behalf ... I tried to prevent her from falling completely by jerking her back up onto her feet. So that a combination of her own momentum and my pull meant that she slid a metre or two, scraping her left knee, shin, thigh along the asphalt. No, she did not break any bones. With my assistance she was up on her feet in an instant. When we stepped out of the shadow of the hedge into the light of the street lamps, which we had just tried to flee, we could see: Flora's stocking was bloody and torn and a stretch of her leg above and below the knee was grazed and covered in dirt.

We sobered up instantly and grew serious. We went back to the restaurant. The head waiter showed us to the manager's office where the First Aid cabinet was located. I went into the restaurant itself and told Karl that Flora had grazed her knee and asked Bella to come and help us. The girls did not make a fuss. Bella brought a bowl of boiled water from the kitchen and washed Flora's leg carefully and pedantically, disinfected it with cotton wool soaked in spirit and then applied iodine to the wound. And Flora pursed her lips at the sting of the disinfectant but did not begin to whimper. When Karl came in and said in a dismayed and slightly reproachful voice: "Oh dear, oh dear – what have you two gone and done, now?" Flora, now that Bella had finished applying the iodine, pulled my face down to hers and gave me a kiss in front of them both.

No, Flora was no spoilsport. She threw away her stocking covered in blood and dirt, rolled up the clean one and put it in her handbag, wrapped her plaid around her in the form of a skirt and swept back into the restaurant in her dark green, Mexican-style, fringed, ankle-length evening dress. But the party spirit had gone out of our farewell party and all that remained were the farewells. We drank a quick cup of coffee and got into a taxi. When I left the taxi at Vene Square in order to walk the rest of the way home, I promised to ring them next morning at nine.

In the morning, instead of calling, I went over to their place at half past eight.

Their apartment was a battlefield of packing cases. The furniture had disappeared from five of the six rooms. The floor was strewn with pieces of wood, nails, rope and wrapping paper. A couple of old sofas had been pushed together in the living room. The paintings had been removed from the walls, revealing the bright patches on the wallpaper where they had once hung. Flora was lying on the faded sofa under the palm – our palm – whose leaves had become so shrivelled from the lack of water that they could no longer shield anyone from view.

Flora said that her knee hurt a little. She had apparently twisted it while falling. When I took her hand, it felt as if she were running a slight temperature. I suggested she took it, but the thermometer could no longer be found. My involvement in the whole affair goaded me on. I said:

"I think a doctor ought to take a look at you and say whether you need an injection."

"What kind of injection?"

"Against tetanus."

Flora did not think it was necessary. There would be a doctor on board ship the following day and he could do the necessary. But then Karl, who was always rather fussy about matters of health, said:

"Listen, why put things off. The best thing would be to call Dr Kukk, now wouldn't it?"

Flora did not argue. She had in fact inherited her mother's somewhat agitated concern for health care. And Dr Kukk was their family doctor of long standing. He had once even treated my pneumonia when I was still at junior school. A pleasant enough old codger. During Czarist times, he had consistently written his surname with a "ck", but had been writing it with a double-k, Estonian style, for some twenty years now ... So Karl phoned him right away. The doctor's wife answered and I could overhear the conversation:

"*Doktor Kuck ist leider nicht da.*"[10] The doctor's wife replied in German to Karl's Estonian request, and I thought with a wry smile that the time of the " – ck"s had returned ... She explained: The doctor has gone to the German Embassy. Yes. Oh, Herr Ventsel Junior. With Fräulein Flora? Oh dearie me – poor child ... No, no. Not any longer, I'm sorry to say. We're leaving *too*. Everything has been sent off, packed in, or sealed up. Tomorrow. Pardon? Ah, I see, you'll be sailing on *Der Deutsche*. No, we're taking the *Oldenburg*. So we won't meet on board. But listen – A young friend of my husband's is here right now. A very good doctor. A German doctor. But he's not leaving as yet. I'll send him over. He'll be only too glad to come. Right away. A Doctor Seidel."

Karl looked at us to obtain our approval. I immediately said: "Let him come. I know Seidel. Quite a philosopher in his own way."

"I can ask him to come immediately, if you want." Mrs Kukk's voice repeated over the phone.

"Then tell him to come. You know the address. *Und wir sind Ihnen sehr dankbar.*"[11] And Karl replaced the receiver.

Half-an-hour later, I opened the door to let in Dr Seidel.

"Well – they told me the patient was bound for Germany. Surely *you're* not leaving, as well?"

"God no – not me, at least."

Dr Seidel put his doctor's bag on a chair, hung up his coat, stood for a moment in the middle of the hall, shut his eyes and wrinkled his nostrils – "That's the bathroom door – from the smell of plumbing." He hurried into the bathroom (it was indeed the right door) and explained through the open door as he washed his hands: "But *I* will be leaving as likely as not. You know – your circle of friends, your community – whatever – you still belong to it. And if you have to do without, then things can also get very tough, I fear."

I said: "So you're not afraid of moral decline setting in?"

"Well, you know, I've weighed up the pros and cons. Seeing the other side of the coin is an interesting experience." He guffawed, flashing his white teeth. And he only gave a cursory glance at Flora's leg:

"I'm afraid you'll have to have an anti-tetanus injection. 'Fraid so. I've got one with me. Frau Kukk told me what the trouble was. I went by the chemist's on the way here and got the serum."

It was all over in five minutes. Dr Seidel showed how to disinfect the wound again later that evening and said farewell with a cheery briskness. Bella made some coffee but the conversation seemed to fizzle out after a couple of spirited volleys. The departure – or perhaps some kind of premonition – filled the silence of our conversation. Flora was feeling poorly and I left at around ten, promising to phone and come by in the evening to find out what time I would have to see them off the next day. It was my idea to go and see the ship sail, which I am sure I would not have done had Flora not fallen.

The rest of the morning I wandered about, dropped in at a couple of editorial offices, the Tallinn branch of the "Amicus" Student Guild, the City Library, lunching at my parents' and sat in on the meeting of the "Golden Fleece" Literary Society in the afternoon. I had barely arrived home that evening and had just sat down by the radio (where a calm voice announced that Soviet troops would continue to travel along the roads in the direction of the bases, as agreed in the treaty), when I suddenly remembered that I had promised to give them a call. But before I had managed to do so, the phone rang. It was Bella. She spoke in a half-whisper and with agitation:

"Peeter, come quickly. Karl's gone to the Commission to get

our final papers. But Flora's very feverish and now she's having convulsions."

I remember how I ran through the city streets in the direction of where Tartu Road begins and the Ventsels lived – or had lived. People bumped into me and got under my feet. Theatre-goers dressed for an evening out were quietly entering the *Estonia*. The shop windows along the Kalev shopping arcade was all lit up. People were flowing into the Workers' Theatre. A stiff policeman in blue stood on the street corner. The windows of the synagogue glowed. People were pouring out of the Modern cinema onto the pavement after the performance. Elated, laughing, grim, opaque, indifferent faces ... I could feel the entire mood and the real problem of the time – where does the *truth* lie if you consider those who half-secretly hope for deliverance and those who feel they are on board a sinking ship? – crumpling up inside me like a sheet of newspaper – in which is wrapped the millstone which was my responsibility for what had happened to Flora ...

Karl had not yet returned. Flora was lying on that selfsame sofa in the living room of the empty apartment. She had a raging fever. Bella had borrowed a thermometer from the neighbours. It showed 39.7° Celsius. I took Bella into the hall and asked her to describe Flora's convulsions.

"Horrible ... Twice ..."

We phoned Dr Kukk. The maid answered. The doctor and his wife had gone to have their crates of furniture put on board ship. I phoned Dr Seidel, but the line was dead. We phoned the Greiffenhagen Clinic. Dr Kukk had worked there. The clinic told us he had already left. And that their patients had all been sent to other hospitals on account of the fact that their staff were leaving, and that they could no longer accept any new patients. Terribly sorry. And that they had no doctors on duty. And then she had her third convulsion. Flora brought her balled fists up to her throat and thrust her head as far back as it would go. Her terror-struck face underwent a metamorphosis, becoming uncomprehending and ghastly. I had never seen an epileptic fit but I imagined that this was something similar. And our total helplessness made the situation doubly horrific. Bella gave her smelling salts to inhale (I have no idea where she got them from) and after five horribly long minutes the cramps subsided. Flora wept from pain and fatigue and we sensed the hollowness of our words of comfort. I said:

"Bella, I'm going to phone my uncle, Dr Veski."

I had not thought it necessary to mention to my uncle anything about my acquaintance with the Ventsels. I do not quite know why. As likely as not, because of the fear of hearing sarcastic remarks made by Uncle Aadam's sharp-tongued wife, similar to those I had heard Aunt Sandra utter. I dialled his number –

"So long as Uncle Aadam isn't at his chess club . . ."

He wasn't. He was round at the Ventsels' within twenty minutes. Thank God Karl had arrived home (or what was left of a home in this resettlers' bivouac) by then too. Bella described the convulsions to Uncle Aadam, and he examined the patient, pursed his sensitive lips and stood thinking.

"She hasn't, by any chance, received any other injections recently? Before the tetanus one yesterday?"

"Yes. A month ago. And without any complications."

"What sort of injection?"

"Against diphtheria." Karl now turned to me for some reason. "Kimmel's little daughter had diphtheria. Flora had been in contact with her, and mother insisted she be inoculated."

"Hmm," said Uncle Aadam, "have you still got a phone?"

I showed him into Ventsel's bare and echoing study. The phone was on the window sill.

"She shouldn't have been given such an injection! Not under any circumstances! Do you hear me?" bawled Uncle Aadam, so that his voice reverberated through the empty room. As if what had happened was in effect my fault. I tried to explain: The departure. A mix-up. How it had no longer been possible to get in contact with Dr Kukk, the family doctor, who had administered the first injection. Dr Seidel hadn't asked. No one else remembered . . . I asked:

"Is it – dangerous . . . ?"

"Can't you see for yourself?" He picked up the receiver. "This idiotic panic – O God ... And what's urging them on – an invitation from *Hitler*, of all people!"

I murmured: "How are we supposed to know?"

"No, no!" yelled Uncle Aadam, his voice reaching a crescendo – "who would choose times like these to leave for Germany?" I could see how he was wrestling with himself to try and stay in control – so that he said in a voice, hoarse with strain, but quite quietly now: "Well –, I will of course – *treat* her ..." and I understood that what he had just added seemed a little too conciliatory to him, so that he ended in a mezzoforte: "... but no more than that!"

I had long noticed that Uncle Aadam could be very subtle and sensitive one moment, disproportionately brusque the next. At any rate, he rang the Central Infirmary for a Red Cross ambulance and Flora was taken there half-an-hour later. I am convinced he was doing all he could.

I never saw Flora again.

Or actually, I did. Four days later. In the bleak chapel, darkened by the falling snow, of the Rahumäe Cemetery,[12] surrounded by a few mourners, she seemed very peaceful, very serious, very small. Before they shut the coffin lid.

The Central Infirmary had, of course, done everything possible. The clash of the serums was considered dangerous but rarely, if ever, fatal. Fatal only if the patient was ill, run down, especially over-sensitive, or perhaps in a particularly susceptible state of mind.

We took the local train from Rahumäe back into town. A few of us, friends and acquaintances who had attended the funeral, a few of Flora's schoolmates, scattered throughout the other carriages, alighting at other halts. The three of us got off at the Baltic Station, Karl, Bella and myself, into the dusk, the driving snow and the biting wind. Karl and I both noticed how Bella was trembling. So we each took an arm and walked briskly into the city centre. They would now be departing in three days' time on the *Ozean*. In the empty basin of the fountain surrounding Raudsepp's statue of Eve swirled black leaves mixed with a mush of icy snow. I stopped, shook hands with them both and gulped a breath of air into my lungs – I wanted to say: Listen – don't leave *just now*! Bella has said that her father will try to get you to Holland. *Will try*? What good is *trying* in these times . . . ? You're leaving for a country racked by war and other horrors. Sooner or later, Karl will be sent to the front. And how will it *feel* to be living in the former homes of murdered or deported Poles? And at any moment, Bella could be – God Almighty – don't you understand?

But no, no, no! I remained silent. I swallowed my words. I had already been responsible for *one* death. I pulled my hands back out of theirs and hurried away around the edge of the fountain. I remember the gravel of Tornide Square crunching under my feet and their cries of farewell after me. I did not turn around.

I never did hear what happened to them. They did, of course, leave Estonia. Perhaps they managed to get to Holland. But soon Holland was no longer a guarantee for safety either. If you could talk of guarantees in those times. Or at all, for that matter. Karl and Bella – perhaps they are now living somewhere in the West, very well-off, a little less happy, and recall, very occasionally, that grey city where people were so young, so full of hope, so naïve . . . Perhaps they perished in the bombing of Dresden or Berlin. Perhaps Karl's bones lie buried somewhere in Russian soil and Bella's in the ash heaps of Ravensbrück . . . Maybe I should have tried to change their fate with pitiful, desperate, futile words. Should have tried to substitute one fate for another. Which fate for which? That, I do not know.

1979

Translator's notes for "The Wound"

1. *Café Kultas* a central Tallinn café now operating again under this name, after fifty years of being Café Moskva under the Soviet Occupation.
2. *Päevaleht* the main Estonian daily during the interwar years, revived in the early 1990s.
3. *Jüri Uluots* (1890–1945) a Professor of Law who became puppet Prime Minister under the influence of President Päts during the last months of the Estonian Republic; died in exile in Sweden.
4. *Friedrich Kreutzwald* [pronounced: kröytzvalt] (1803–1882) was the compiler of the Estonian national epic, the *Kalevipoeg*. *Vambola* was a superficial historical novel by Andres Saal (1861–1931). Flora's mistake is the rough equivalent of speaking of Shakespeare's "Robin Hood". Lydia Koidula (1843–1886) was Estonia's first major woman poet.
5. One has to live it up before one marries, don't you think?
6. *Gustav Suits* [pronounced: sooyts] (1883–1956): Professor of Literature at Tartu and Helsinki Universities and major Estonian poet. Fled to Sweden in 1944.
7. *Staatspräsident Päts* (German). The roses are named after Konstantin Päts (1874–1956) – President of Estonia during Independence. His autocratic government from 1934–1940 was unpopular, but he did manage to prevent the growth of Fascism as such in Estonia. Died in detention in Kalinin (Tver), Russia, reburied in Estonia, 1991.
8. *Umsiedler* (German) The people being rehoused in Germany after Hitler invited them to "return" to the Reich.
9. *Entwurzelung* (German) Deracination, i.e. becoming homeless both physically and mentally.
10. I'm afraid Doctor Kuck is out.
11. Thank you so much.
12. *Rahumäe*. Cemetery on the edge of Nõmme, south west of central Tallinn. Earlier this century the sculptor Juhan Raudsepp designed a monument there as well as the fountain which features towards the end of the story.

(The translator acknowledges a debt to a previous translation of this story by the late Tõnu Onu and has also consulted the Finnish translation by Juhani Salokannel.)

Lead Piping

Lead Piping

The autumn of 1943 in Estonia was exactly the same as any other autumn, before or since. And also contained more or less every kind of opportunity. Except, the likelihood of these opportunities being realised had changed significantly. The likelihood that people would succeed in doing a normal job of work had been reduced to a minimum. And what used to be normal work had taken on an almost criminal aspect. While certain activities, regarded as criminal up to then, had become normal work for many.

Tartu University too was still drawing breath during the autumn of 1943. Only that student intake had been reduced to one quarter of former levels. And a separate entrance had been constructed through the windows of the left wing of the façade with steps made of unplaned planks, since the main pillared entrance was being used by Herr Feldkommandant and his staff.

The students, insofar as there still were any, passed some exams more easily, others with more difficulty than they had hoped. For like so many other matters in this world, the criteria of the teaching staff had shifted ground: Anglophiles had become restive and liberal, Germanophiles careworn and tetchy. The Red professors, who would, in those months, have been able to recover their self-esteem, were either in concentration camps or under the sod, so the students did not get to know how they would have judged the results of the 1943 exams.

But the likelihood of a chance coffee-house encounter – over brick-hard biscuit fingers, made with a piping nozzle, with black chicory water to drink – leading straight to a one-night stand if the next air-raid warnings allowed it, were greater than ever before. And the likelihood of finding yourself caught up, at some fateful and yet quite ordinary moment, in a system of machinery which was quite beyond the normalities of life (in as much as life in Estonia and the rest of Eastern Europe in 1943 could be regarded as normal) – machinery whose *public* manifestations were barred windows in the metre-thick city walls, windows which were just as before and had always been there, but which had suddenly been brought to everyone's attention, and watch-towers and barbed-wire around barracks in pine groves and peat bogs, plus covered or, worse still, open prisoner transport lorries, but whose *secret* manifestations were whispered confessions through knocked-in teeth, kicks with jackboots and bursts of automatic fire – the likelihood of ending up in the cogs of this machinery had grown overnight, let us say four- or five-fold.

And all at once, even greater had grown – at least for boys born between 1919 and 1924 – the likelihood of falling into the grey funnel, into the grey lead piping. According to notices and wall newspapers published during March '43, such pipes were of two kinds. Notices and wall newspapers were, like death sentences and news of executions, printed in Gothic, in other words the script of the legendary Bible of our childhood, but which in the 1940s gave many the sensation of chewing sandpaper. Or sand. And the lead pipes, as already mentioned above, were, according to these notices, two in number. One of them spewed forth its load on to the front via the notorious Bad-Tölz training camp, that is to say, via southern Bavaria after a period of three to four months. The other pipe did the same, after a couple of weeks of basic drill at the Kohila or Elva training camps. Those spewed out of the first pipe wore SS uniforms and were told that they constituted the élite of *Neues Europa* and of the Estonian people. The second pipe spat forth so-called "Volunteer Assistants", who were in fact required to stay in the frontier zone in the same section as the prisoners of war stationed there. Both groups were constantly assured that they were there voluntarily. In the passes issued to boys sent to SS units, the so-called *Eesti Leegion*, or Estonian Legion, the words *SS Freiwilliger So-and-So* were printed there, in black-and-white. And the German name for the Volunteer Assistants was *Hilfswilliger*, a term which could be interpreted as including an element of free will – though their willingness to assist was more than questionable.

The idea of free will was based on the Jesuitical claim that those invited to come before the Recruitment Commissions were indeed presented with a choice: *either* the *Eesti Leegion or* the *Hilfswilligerdienst*. The Commissions had to work efficiently and resolutely. There was a moral pressure on those mobilised to choose the "*Leegion*". And in some cases this was more effective than pistol-pressure. The Recruitment Commissions, which were made up to a large extent of Germans, were often led by high-ranking war invalids. The citizens of Tallinn will still remember the albino *Obersturmführer* of a super-Aryan appearance and thoroughly arrogant, who had gained the Knights Cross but had lost his right hand: before such an exhibit, anyone among the conscripts who had retained any sense of proportion was obliged to keep silent about his trivial personal health problems in civilian life . . . Nevertheless, the old Czarist draft-dodging practices of our grandfathers' day such as smoking silk roll-ups or eating salt – at a new level of medical knowledge, it is true – were just as current again as was the fear. But as regards the new conscripts' state of health, the Commissions were more exacting for the *Leegion* than for the *Hilfswilliger*. In the case of the latter, it was said that the presence of both arms and legs was quite adequate, the presence of a head no real handicap, its absence indeed being a positive advantage. The *Leegion* Commission however tendentiously perfunctory they might have been as regards matters of one's health, nonetheless took health defects much more seriously. In the case of a fortuitous health defect (or one served up convincingly), the Recruitment Commission would give the conscript one, two or even three months' deferment. For this reason, there were conscripts who had put their names down for

the *Leegion* with the firm intention, sometimes fulfilled, of never
being required to serve at all.

But in general, the Recruitment Commissions were, as already
noted, resolute and swift in their judgments. And I remember,
from my own succession of appearances before the Commission,
the painful and anxious feeling when I suddenly realised (in
Tallinn, on Rataskaevu Street, in buildings always used by military committees in every age, on the top floor in a room with
bare green walls, outside the window a cobbled courtyard with
a couple of catkined trees, at a long table with a few monoglot
Sturmführer, plus a couple of *Scharführer* who had a smattering
of Estonian) just *how* hopeless it would be to try to get them to
share the sick joke made by my friends, who were about to be
fed into the thresher: if our alternative of *either* the *Leegion or*
the *Hilfswilliger* was indeed a voluntary choice, how was it then
with the people who, in accordance with Paragraph 407 of the
Criminal Code, belonged to the ranks of those destined to die?
That paragraph gave them the right to choose poison or the
noose. By the military logic of Groß-Deutschland, they had not
been sentenced to death, but were suicides.

Dangling between these two modes of suicide, in my pocket a
certificate from doctor acquaintances stating that I was suffering
from severe thyreo-oxycosis (shortage of oxygen 148), and having
obtained on that account a deferment to my call-up to the *Leegion*,
I had taken a seat one September evening in 1943 in a train
standing at Elva station and bound for Tartu. The platform was,
of course, blacked out, the carriage which at least had passenger
compartments and was not a goods truck as at the beginning of
the Occupation, was not lit up and was relatively crowded, as the
infrequent trains of the Occupation generally were. Into the
crowd of people who could only be sensed and which murmured
quietly in that way typical for these parts (for no heroic tipplers
of moonshine happened to be travelling), we were joined at the
last moment before departure by one more passenger. The
elderly village women on the opposite seat made room for him
in a motherly way. His short, stocky silhouette seemed somehow

familiar even in the darkness. But it was not until he struck a match to light his *Karavan* just before Peedu halt that I actually recognised him.

"Ilmar? Is that you?"

"Yes, it's me . . . Who am I talking to? *Peeter*! Well, well, what a coincidence . . ."

We fumbled a handshake.

"What have you been doing with yourself?" I hadn't seen him since the beginning of the war.

"I'm studying."

"What? Doric architecture?"

"No. How to use a spade in hand-to-hand combat. In Elva. In the *Hilfswilliger* camp."

It turned out that he had been here for almost a fortnight and would be sent to the front the following week. And all at once a thousand thoughts crowded into my brain.

This short boy, with his classical blue eyes of a village lad and his long blond hair, was the son of a parish clerk in a one-horse town out in the Western province of Läänemaa. We had entered university together four years previously, though he had in fact gone there to study Art History, but it was in the badly heated rooms of the "Amicus Studiorum" student club, the buffet and the library, that we had become what you could call friends. I do not know what he saw in me (friends must surely appreciate something in one another). He intrigued and yet irritated me with his country boy's clumsy, provincial vulgarity, redolent of the parish clerk, but which was somehow enviable for all that, with its hint of a moral upbringing. Beside these qualities, he had surprisingly wide interests and was an impressive conversation partner. He was nineteen when we first become friends. But you could talk to him, or learn something, about other things apart from the Ancient Etruscans and Knossos, which was, in some respects, his specialist subject. You would hear him expounding on the current debate around Wegener's theory of continental drift, he could give you a survey of the schools of thought relating to the transmigration of souls, and he would bring you up-to-date on Father Carrelli's most recent experiments on frogs' hearts. To our general amazement, he was able to read Estonian, Finnish, German, French and Swedish, which maybe does not stand comparison with the skills of Kristjan Jaak Peterson[1] at the same age, but was nonetheless far beyond the capabilities and exertions of average students like us.

I do not believe he was religious. But he was at any rate no cynical atheist. Though these are the two tendencies most likely to develop in a child brought up in a strictly Lutheran parish clerk's family. He seemed to be quite at harmony with the ideological inheritance of his home background. But he was less at ease with the customs instilled in him by his family – he often came to the buffet at the "Amicus" club with such bloodshot eyes, that his father with his little bushy blond moustache (I had seen him only in photos) would have grown positively livid at the sight. Or he would almost screech out satirical songs of the day in our library (this must have been in our third year at university). Such as:

> Oh Uncle Joe, why did you take,
> The whole of poor Estonia?
> Did you not promise that you'd make
> Do with a mud bath on Saaremaa . . . ?

But you could not help forgiving him with a laugh for his screeching, on account of his very adaptable and musical voice.

And then, in that dark train compartment between Peedu and Vapramäe it all came flooding back:

It had happened only two years before in the late winter of 1941. One evening, I bumped into *amicus* Harrak on the snowy pavement of Aia Street in Tartu, in the light of the street lamps and right outside the Vanemuine Theatre. Harrak was studying Art History like Ilmar. We stood there talking about the exams. Harrak was complaining: the syllabus was being radically restructured and the Devil only knew whether he would have any use for a pass in Gothic Church Architecture. I consoled him with the fact that I had just passed an exam in Roman Private Law, which was now quite useless, if the new syllabus was anything to go by. But this was of little comfort to him. I said:

"Go and find out about your Gothic Architecture from Ilmar. He seems to be pretty boned up on the subject."

We decided to obtain a couple of bottles at the theatre bar and then go over to Ilmar's place. We had heard that the head waiter at the Vanemuine, a kindly man by the name of Paakspuu, still kept a private stock of Kressmann's Barsac, but reserves were not unlimited. So, the sooner we got hold of some, the better. With good grace, Paakspuu took my grandfather's gold watch as security until the next day, and we loaded six bottles of the golden bubbly into Harrak's empty briefcase and continued on our way.

Ilmar lived on Lepiku Street in a room above the attic of a large block of rented flats, on what was, in effect, the fourth floor of a two-storey building. I had once paid a brief visit to his place and found out that to get to his room from the attic you had to climb a ladder, and that for the privilege of this inconvenience, plus the use of the bad and unreliable stove, his monthly rent was fifteen *krooni*, that is to say eighteen roubles, seventy-five kopecks in modern currency, for what amounted to virtually two rooms. Though the first of these doubled as lobby, and was in fact a windowless space with clothes pegs and a small table with an electric hotplate where Ilmar boiled his potatoes when he had run out of money to eat at the student refectory. But the living room itself was, as far as I can remember, unexpectedly respectable with its weatherboard walls and a sloping ceiling, angled down the middle, as this draughty student room was located directly under the full length of the eaves. And there were pictures on the walls which you would not have expected to see in a student room. One original Triik, a Norwegian landscape, a number of original Vabbe watercolours from the 1920s, and a small pastel drawing by Oskar Kallis.[2] Though everything in the room below the level of these works of art was, those couple of times I had been there, and permanently as far as I could tell, a hopeless Bohemian jumble.

We marched gaily up good old Lepiku Street, a cul-de-sac as it still is today, though somewhat quieter in those days, and climbed the stairs, and ultimately the ladder, filled with the anticipated joy of surprising and teasing him. We knocked at Ilmar's door, heard an indistinct cry and entered triumphantly – both doors being open. And grew abashed at the unexpected and strange sight which confronted us: Ilmar was in bed with a girl.

I had not known much about his relationships with girls. I had heard by way of the chance chatterings of a girl student about Ilmar's great love, a tall, red-haired, bluestocking daughter of a lawyer, a love with was not reciprocated by the young lady in question who – and this was even stranger – seemed now and again to become responsive, nonetheless – "So that your poor old Ilmar swings between bliss and despair."

It is hard to say what proportion of bliss and despair was in this bedroom scene we had so foolishly chanced upon. They had managed to roll over on to their backs and were still panting. The girl turned out to be not the lawyer's red-headed daughter but a swarthy lass with dark slanting eyes whom I had caught sight of on one or two occasions. She had in fact made a brief appearance at a few of the lectures held at the Faculty of Philosophy and had worked as a waitress for a short while at the Toome and the Central. But as for shame, she betrayed very little of it, considering the fact that she was stark naked. She made no attempt to pull the bedclothes up to her throat as did Ilmar, but simply crossed her arms across her breasts and smiled disarmingly at us with her slanting eyes in what was a bewilderment more feigned than genuine. Ilmar, on the other hand, hovered between blushing and blanching in his embarrassment and introduced us to the girl from his bed – and we impudently exercised our rights as boon companions and did not leave the room.

"My friends Mirk and Harrak . . ." stated Ilmar in a childish confused tone of voice, "and this is my girlfriend Piia." Whether he failed to mention her surname to spare her to that extent at least, or whether he simply did not know it was to remain a moot point. On account of their shared lectures, Harrak was closer to

Ilmar than I was and was clearly more *au fait*, as the expression goes. He said in his deep announcer's voice with surprising self-assurance:

"My dear friends, I can see that we have come at a slightly inopportune moment. No matter. Peeter," he turned to me "if you have no objections: we will give them a bottle to compensate for our behaviour . . ." He was already taking one of the Kressmanns from his briefcase, ". . . and we will retreat to the lobby until such time as they are ready. Judging by their faces, it should not take them long."

He was about to put the wine on the bedside table, but then took out his penknife and opened the bottle:

"Take a sip – my children . . ."

While this scene was unfolding, I was standing at Ilmar's writing desk and saw: three quarters of the table was covered in notebooks, photos, books, blotting paper, ashtrays, fag-ends, sharpened pencils and stubs, pencil-shavings, coffee cups and still-knotted ties along with an opened plan of the Parthenon in Athens complete with caption. I looked at all this, too embarrassed to look in the direction of the occupants of the bed – I had not seen such a detailed plan of the Parthenon before – and was informed (and remembered again in a dark carriage between Tõravere and Nõo, two years after): the fluting which runs the length of a Doric pillar is 299mm wide at the bottom and 233mm wide at the top, in the case of the Parthenon, but that its depth is constant (I do not remember how deep), which gives the pillars a certain optical relief. And that the grooves on each pillar are twenty in number. Twenty *cannelures*.

I do not know how Harrak was getting on, but I was liberated from my embarrassment by this curious word with its associations to the Estonian for harp plus lyre (*kannel* plus *lüüra*) and cinnamon (*kaneel*). I went out with Harrak into the lobby as agreed, my mind now at ease. Comedy, strangeness, shame, joy – *life* itself has its space, heartland and sense, incomprehensible as a whole but quite perceptible on account of their peaks . . . We closed the dividing door behind us. We found ourselves two stools and Harrak uncorked another bottle. I discovered two extra wine glasses for ourselves in the kitchen cupboard. Harrak filled them to the brim. God, then, if ever, was an occasion for a little smut. We were holding our glasses. I wanted to say: if we are Ilmar's friends then we have now become his Piia's too. At least for now and why not indeed for ever? So let them do it from behind and from in front, though not for too long, of course, and may they both be blessed. And as talking about a parish clerk's son, I wanted to finish with: "now and for evermore. Amen". But I merely said:

"To the Parthenon!"

I said "Parthenon" – ignorant of the fact that it means "The House of Virgins", but that knowledge would not have prevented me from uttering those words in the slightest. We drained our glasses, did so once more, and a third time, and that broad-faced, mustachioed Harrak did not descend to smut and so went up even more in my estimation. And then they called us back in. And only *then* did the fact strike me that we should have taken our coats from the peg, or need not have taken them off in the first place. We could have left them the remains of our bottle with, say, the message: *"Parthenon! 20 cannelures! T. & P."* and left. At least a quarter of an hour ago. But for some reason we had fought shy of the thought, and were still here and so we trooped back into Ilmar's room carrying the remaining four bottles with a mixture of mock-shyness and cunning on our faces.

They had dressed. They had made a noticeable, though futile, effort to tidy up the room. Four coffee cups had been set out on the small, low table. We added two of the bottles. The table had been carried over to the bedside. The four of us sat in a row along the bed Ilmar, Piia, Harrak and me. We filled two wine glasses and two egg cups and drank. Piia put on the coffee water on the hotplate in the lobby. When she returned and had taken a seat between us, Ilmar gave her a kiss, put his arm around her neck and said to her, and to us two:

"Piia's such a dear girl. She understands everything. Everything she should. And nothing she shouldn't. And does everything

I want her to. If it's a reasonable request. Don't you? And nothing a nice girl considers unreasonable. But these boys, Piia, are my very best friends . . ." (So that I started lightly and wondered with a slightly hollow feeling in the pit of the stomach *what* exactly I would have to do to prove that he was not erring in his judgment, at least in my case.)

He climbed over the bed from behind Piia's back, and sat between us with Piia on his right, Harrak and myself to his left, put his arms around all our necks and said with ardour:

"Piia, look at Harrak, at Tiit. A nondescript fat face. Hasn't he? A moustache, such a miserable one, grown with such patience – as if unsure of his own manhood. But what tentacles of thought he has! Or look at Peeter. Oh dear! If you want to shave your chin – sorry, you don't have a beard – if you want to shave your armpits – and you need something quite sharp – then borrow Peeter's logic! No need for a razor! As for me. Well, give me time. Piia, if we survive – then yon fat-chopped Harrak will become the Curator of the National Art Museum within ten years. He's got the necessary qualities under his belt already – he knows painting from Köler to Haamer. He's brilliant at enthusing people. And he'll get the new museum building finished. An unbelievable lad! And Peeter – in ten years' time he'll be a member of the academies in Tallinn, Moscow and Berlin. Without a doubt. Though I'm not quite sure in which field. The Berlin Academy? Of course they'll have built it up again in ten years' time. And as for me – Piia – my head's not full of shit either! In ten years' time my book will be ready for sure: *The Concept of Sacrifice from Ancient Times to the Present Day*. With the subtitle: *Holocaustomatica*. Piia – you'll never read it. But in ten years' time – when you, my poor dear lady, are walking along Ülikooli Street past the bookshop pushing a pram – then you'll all of a sudden stop in front of the shop window and read on the cover of a book: "Ilmar Timmas, *The Concept of Sacrifice*". Oh yes. And you'll push your fingertips into your mouth, think a little and then cry out: Eureka! – Ha-ha-ha-haa – no, not 'eureka', but: Oh my little nipper – that *Timmas* used to live on Lepiku Street

. . . If we survive. But, friends, survival is open to question. For the war in the East won't be long in coming. Though do you know what my brother told me? He's a student at the Tallinn Technical High School. And now and again does the odd job here and there. Me too, for that matter. For the money. Father can't support us both . . . And right now, in February, he's been out on weekdays at Tallinn harbour loading Ukrainian wheat on to German ships. What a paradox! But I'm telling you – survival is after all something dubious . . ."

He hugged us more tightly. He kissed Piia anew, then suddenly pressed our three faces up against one another and said – so that I turned my head to look at him as he had pulled his head back out of our circle:

"Piia – these lads really are my very best friends – give them a kiss! Help us all survive and kiss them!"

He was quite drunk by now, more drunk than we three others. His face was flushed and his dark blue eyes sparkled under his white angular brow. Piia looked at him and at us and back at him hesitantly, but then instantly turned her omnipotent smile on us and offered us her pursed lips. Harrak kissed her voraciously and I watched him jealously but with anticipation. And then I myself kissed her. I have to admit that I hadn't been able to wrench my eyes away from her for quite some time. That is to say I did manage to, but had to tell myself on each occasion: *now* I'm going to look at somebody else and had every time waited for myself to take the decision, *now* I'll look at her again: her slightly oriental sloping forehead, her small straight nose, her breasts of which I had seen more before than the light yellow pullover would now permit, and her knees – she had drawn up her legs under her on the bed and her short black skirt had ridden up above the knee revealing half her thighs, and she pulled it back down to her knees. I took hold of her freshly shampooed head and gave her a long kiss. So long that I had enough time to follow Ilmar over her shoulder, to look at him in two ways: with a certain grateful incomprehension but also with a little amused interest, observe *what* Ilmar was going to do after this so serious kiss, for Piia's response also suggested an element of unexpected ardour. This ardour so went to my head on the wings of the wine we had been sipping that my threshold of astonishment was raised almost to infinity. So that although what Ilmar now did certainly appeared strange at the more sober level of my mind, I had the feeling as if it was quite usual, as if I had known it would happen all along. Ilmar stood up, picked up a box of matches but did not reach out for his cigarettes. He fiddled with the box, sat down next to us and waited for me to let go of Piia. He then pushed his red-blotched though pale face, between us and said, with a slight slur, but with the utmost sincerity:

". . . Piia – please – be sure to rescue us *properly* –" Incidentally, his speech was in any case so unclear by now that I did not quite understand what he said, and am still unsure to this day, since I did not ask him about it then (nor did I do so there in Tõravere) and now I am unable to ask him: did he say "rescue *me*' or "rescue *us*"? But what he said next left no room for doubt:

". . . Piia – please – let these lads come to you – first one and then the other – yes, I mean it – now, immediately! You can see that's what they want. And you've got nothing against it, either. Be a friend to my friends! You don't realise it yourself but it has a profound significance. Here are two matches. A whole one and a broken one. Let them draw lots. The one who gets the broken one goes first, the other one after. The rest of us will wait outside in the lobby. Well, do you all agree? You want to do it, so what are you waiting for – friends?"

He pressed our four faces together, our cheeks, our eyes. I do not know what it was, or what it meant, for each of us – depravity, the aphrodisiac effects of the wine, an attempt to get closer to one another, an echo of the abnormal state of the world, a strange ritual, an attempt at placating the gods – but we were all prepared to go through with it, and Piia let us draw lots. I got the half-match and Ilmar and Tiit went with a half-bottle out into the lobby and afterwards I sat with Tiit and drank the other half-bottle while he talked loquaciously and repetitively about the temptations of his childhood and his stubborn attempts to get near to the church bells, while they were being rung, by way of a ladder and climb as near to them as his ears would stand. Towards morning, now enfeebled in pudency, but also with the wistfulness of conspiracy, we all drank the last bottle of Kressmann together and Piia kissed us all by turns in a motherly sort of way.

"So what are you travelling to Tartu for?" I asked, returning to the here and now of railway carriage, two-and-a-half years later.

"Toothache. One day's leave to go to the dentist's. Back the morning of the day after tomorrow."

"And what's it like where you are?"

"Real shit."

"And next week – departure?"

"Even deeper in the shit."

And in a split second I had made my decision. A complete plan, almost down to the finest detail, had presented itself in the twinkling of an eye. The plan seemed to embrace all the demands and considerations of the moment. And something more. Something which could be traced back in some way to that remarkable night in that weatherboarded room on Lepiku Street. As if I had to do something to release me from the feeling of debt for having possessed Piia. Or maybe something more – to, as it were, round something off which Piia had quite failed in doing . . . I said in a murmur:

"You're *crazy*! Only an *idiot* would go back now!"

I asked the old woman sitting next to Ilmar to swap places, and sat down beside him and said, speaking close to his ear in a voice inaudible to anyone else in the carriage: No intelligent person would join the German Army! You have to use every legitimate opportunity to keep out of it. Any method which doesn't bring harm to other people, or which would harm only the Germans, is legitimate. You should use your papers as far as you possibly can. If you can't get hold of papers, you simply have to go into hiding. And if hiding without papers proves too dangerous then you have to flee to Finland. They're fleeing there in their hundreds. Thousands. I've got one or two useful contacts. If the worst comes to the worst, even the Finnish Army is better than joining the Germans. But there are ways and means to move on from Finland. Harrak, for instance, has already been in Sweden for some months now. Rumour has it that he's got into the second-term course at Stockholm University. Yes, really! – I said right into his ear: *You* could manage to enter the fourth! You already know Swedish. And our very own Björkdal is now professor there, you realise, and would give you no less support than he has Tiit.

I explained to him how the problems of hiding and absconding had been with me every day for six months now. I told him how I had had my name on the list of international outlaws because my medical note certifying my illness had been issued late, but I was still moving about legally for the time being and was going to leave myself as soon as there was no other way out. And it was as if the Lord himself were giving him the opportunity to leave the camp legally to enable him to go on French leave.

I sensed him shaking his head in the darkness at my words and heard his peculiarly muffled mutterings:

"Oh hell, leave off, will you? I've given up. I've fiddled things too. Up to now. But I simply haven't got the energy any more."

That sounded very strange to me. The training camp for the *Hilfswilliger* must really grind the will out of people. At any rate, Ilmar's apathy redoubled my eagerness and I started all over again:

"Ilmar! Old chap! What's wrong with you? Are you really – forgive me for saying so – such a wet rag? You believe in Hitler's *Neues Europa* about as much as . . . I don't know what! Even less than in nutty Colonel Utuste's[3] folkloric Uku and Taara! Why the hell are you letting yourself be browbeaten into dying for such bullshit?! If you at least believed a scrap of what they said! But you don't! You simply don't believe a word of it!"

He muttered: "I've already told you: I've simply given up. Not that I've become a complete idiot . . ."

I cried out, so that I almost forgot to muffle my words:

"What do you mean *given up*? You can't give up, just like that! Or your friends will have to revise their opinion of you."

"What opinion?" he asked with some irritation as if such a revision involved his honour or lack of it.

"The opinion that you are a genius."

"Oh, that..."

I sensed how protest had welled up inside him. We travelled the rest of the way to Tartu in silence. We alighted on to the barely lit platform, walked through the throng past two field security officers with their machine guns who were surveying those arriving – their black-and-silver flashes glittering in the emergency lighting like the iron plates on graveyard crosses – and were again swallowed up by the darkness. Ilmar then asked:

"Do you have any concrete suggestions?"

"But of course!"

I revealed my plan for him. And in so doing, as is always the case, it sharpened significantly in detail in the process.

"Have you got lodgings? Are you going to Lepiku Street?"

"No. I gave the flat up. I've only got a suitcase full of belongings there."

I said:

"I've got the key to a flat near there on Tähtvere Street which used to belong to a student, a girl, who went off home. No one will ever look for you there. You can get some sleep there. Take a bath. I'll arrange a few things tomorrow. Better not to show your face out on the street. Oh yes of course – the dentist –" I deliberated for a moment and then said: "OK, let's go *now* to old Prof. Toome's. He'll do the necessary. And won't blab either. So let's go to Tähtvere Street and you can read Lawrence or Dostoevsky or whatever you want behind locked doors there until tomorrow. And then we'll take the night train to Tallinn. Tomorrow at five in the morning, when you're supposed to be returning to your Spade Wars in Elva, we'll be getting off the train in Tallinn – and the smell of the sea will hit your nostrils."

"But what if we're checked on the train?"

"It would be confounded bad luck if those field security mastiffs get you. First of all, they don't check you on the train. If they don't find any reason to. And even if they do, there's a way out. You tell them that you've changed your mind. That you've decided to join the *Leegion* after all. As you were not satisfied with being a *Hilfswilliger*. That you have understood that the *Leegion* is the proper place for an educated Estonian lad like yourself. So you are travelling to the *Meldestelle* in Tallinn. To sign up for the *"Leegion"* there. You have, of course, understood that you're not doing everything strictly by the book, but there again – and so on, and so forth. They won't believe you. The mastiffs never do. But if you spin them this yarn in good German, you'll be handed over to Hauptsturmführer Grote on Toompea Hill. So that they can wriggle out of any responsibility they might have had for you. As they always do. And Grote will believe you. He is the biggest pap-brain in the whole of the *Ostland*. You see: he was involved in Hitler's putsch in Nuremberg. He should, by all rights, be a Field Marshal by now. And he's got the ambition for three. But it didn't turn out that way. So he's now a Haupt-sturmführer. That just shows *how* thick he is. So he'll believe you alright."

Ilmar said: "But then I'll be even deeper in the shit than I am now."

I said: "Not in the least. Perhaps only if the next evening meat train to Bad-Tölz happens to leave in two days' time. But at present they're leaving once every ten days at the most. And even if they don't let you go home – there are no cells at the *Meldestelle*. It's not a prison, only a building belonging to the Ministry of Foreign Affairs. And they'll always let you out to buy a paper. So you simply nip round the corner, cool as a cucumber."

Although it was half-past nine at night, Professor Toome, a jovial old gentleman with the face of Cuvier, received us with the old-fashioned civility of a veteran alumnus. By way of my uncle, I knew him a little better than did Ilmar, who only knew him by sight, but this was quite sufficient for him. He showed us into his surgery, asked Ilmar to sit down in the dentist's chair and threw a cushion from the sofa over the phone. He noticed our quizzical glances and said while washing his hands at the sink:

"Well, you know, back in 1940 they suddenly started saying that world technology must have advanced this far. And the inquisitiveness of the world has always been so far advanced. But I want at least to be free to chinwag in my own home."

The old gent was certainly no great chinwagger outside of his home. Though he was known to have made a number of rounded statements in private circles. Via my uncle the doctor I had heard at least one of Old Toome's sententious utterances: "How the hell d'you expect a dentist of all people to make a living, if the whole world keeps its mouth shut!"

And so he ordered Ilmar to open his mouth and immediately cried out:

"My God – there's such a cavity in here as even Mussolini would fit in! And all that would be left of Hitler would be his quiff. Well, we'll pop a little arsenic in the hole – today's Tuesday – and at four o'clock on Friday we'll extract the nerve and do the filling next Monday. No matter which of the two roots it is, we'll stop 'em up, either way."

I said: "I'm afraid that's not going to be possible. We can't spare the time. Better pull it out right away."

"Can't spare the time? To have your teeth seen to? Wherever are you hurrying off to like that?" the old dentist asked Ilmar. (I have, incidentally, noticed that dentists have the habit of asking their patients questions when their mouths are so full of dental equipment that answering is rendered impossible. And I have thought: in this matter, dentists are just as inconsiderate as life itself. Neither doctor nor patient is really interested in the answer. And yet both the necessity and the trouble to answer are occasioned.) I said:

"He's got to go off – either from Elva training camp to the front – or – away."

"Hmm –" mumbled the Professor and pursed his lips – "well – if it's one of those departures – whether to one place or the other – then we'd better pull it out after all. That way you don't get a pain in the wrong place."

"But how are things going to work out in Tallinn?" asked Ilmar. "I haven't got anywhere to go there. Since my brother left the Technical University out at Kopli to join the Red Army."

We were walking in the dark in the direction of Tähtvere Street and Ilmar was beginning to feel the after-effects of the extraction, now the injection was wearing off. I said:

"We'll go to my uncle's. He's a nice old chap. A respected doctor. No one would ever think of looking for you there. All these years now he's been playing the absent-minded professor. If somebody should ask him – I can just imagine what he'd say: 'Ah yes, a friend of Peeter's . . . ? What was the name, again? Haven't the foggiest . . . What's he look like? Listen, I have a seven-room apartment – I can't *see* through walls . . . Young people wandering in and out all the time – but who and why, I've never really asked . . .' And his wife is quite a Bohemian. An actress. More or less lives at the theatre. Or God knows where else. You'll have all your creature comforts there, while I look into the question of transport to Finland. I imagine it'll all be arranged in a week."

In the darkness we turned, groping our way over the ruins of the Liberty Bridge destroyed the summer before but restored nonetheless, stumbling our way through recent bomb craters down to a street running along the river. Ilmar was shouting so loudly that I had in any case to hush him:

"But such a trip costs fifteen hundred marks! And I haven't got a penny."

"Shh!" I hissed. But the blackout was total and the darkness impenetrable and the riverside street quite deserted – so that I myself understood: I was in fact hushing him because suddenly, and quite unexpectedly, there was now talk of *money* and I felt I should have thought of this, and that my thoughtlessness was painfully childish. But the customs of recent years had been such

that this did not perturb me all that much. I said quite brightly
and with a clean conscience:

"Uncle will lend us the money."

Ilmar asked: "Will he now? Such a Croesus, is he?"

I explained: "He can agonise about five *penni*. I often stay at
his place, so I should know. A month back I went to the Vanemuine to see *The Golem*. He went to see the same play a week
later and asked me where I had left the programme. I said I had
no doubt thrown it away. So he cries out: What a waste! He had,
after all, told me he was going to go and see it a week later! For
God's sake. But at the same time he has helped chaps like yourself.
More doubtful cases than yours. Take it from me."

Ilmar was silent a while. Then he asked:

"How do you know that Harrak is in his second term at
Stockholm University?"

I said that I'd seen a letter.

Then we reached Tähtvere Street and stayed the night there.
The next day I went around Tartu attending to my university
business. After lunch I found somebody I knew who worked as
waiter at the refectory. I asked him to have a look around the
kitchen and find a one-litre jar and fill it with cabbage stalks –
there was no other food you could get hold of without ration
coupons, as the mushrooms which were much more popular were
finished. Then I went to the baker's with my coupons and put a
double four-hundred gramme ration in my briefcase alongside
the jars of cabbage. In the evening we stepped on the train at
Tartu station. Luckily, Ilmar was in civvies and this, in lieu of a
permit to travel to Tallinn (which he did not have), was a great
deal better than a uniform of any description. At five in the
morning we stepped out on to the platform at Tallinn and caught
the smell of the sea in our nostrils. I mean, I assume he also smelt
it though I didn't ask him. For I thought it rather inappropriate of
me to do so.

My uncle lived on the upper floor of an old two-storey wooden
house, now demolished, on Õuna Street. There were only the
two apartments in the building and behind the house lay an

ancient apple orchard which was surprisingly extensive for this central city district. I had keys to Uncle's apartment. We climbed the stairs with their faint smell of polish and stepped into the hall of the apartment. For some reason (or perhaps because we entered without switching on the light) it was the *smells* of the apartment which impinged on my consciousness on that occasion: the faint smell of ether emanating from Uncle's surgery into the hall and its extension which served as a waiting room; the faint smell of naphthalene which arose from the Biedermeier furniture in the living room, the faint smell of cooking oil from the dining room through which we groped our way and where rye flour pancakes fried in a drop of sunflower oil, obtained goodness knows where, had been eaten; the fragrance of *Soir de Paris* which seeped through his wife's door which stood ajar; the smell of the liquor store from the chink in the bathroom door, though this could have been mere imagination, since Uncle stored his several-litre stock of spirits in large flagons which stood in the bath which was half-filled with water as a precaution against fire and air raids; and then the comically coarse yet subtle whiff of tobacco from Uncle's own room (for he had, for donkeys' years, been smoking a weed grown by some patient or other and prepared with rose oil in his straight-stemmed pipe).

We slept a few hours in a small back room opposite the kitchen which I always used when visiting my uncle. When we emerged for coffee at around nine, Uncle was already God knows where but his wife, in her maroon silk dressing gown, joined us for coffee, or the black slops which went for coffee.

Aunt Ella was fifty years old, but well preserved and had the allure of an actress of the old school with her fake brunette hair and her genuine Grecian profile. She would flirt with boys half her age such as Ilmar as with coevals, and mother them like children. Her flirting could, of course, be the desire of a childless woman to play the role of the mother, could be some strange way of irritating her spouse, or, quite foolishly, simple flirting. With Ilmar, at any rate, she immediately chose the role of the mother:

"You are a friend of Peeter's, I take it? A fellow-student? Oh,
I thought you were even younger than he is. Aha, an art historian.
Oh, how charming. That, at least, is some something so much
more human than Peeter's law studies, don't you think? No one
has ever known what *justice* really is. But *art* is something pure
and eternal."

When their maid Anna, a moon-faced giant of a girl from the
island of Hiiumaa, had brought in the chicory slops under an
embroidered Japanese tea cosy, the saccharin bowl on a silver
salver and the barley-flour griddle scones spread with margarine
on a blue-patterned Meißen-ware dish, and had left the room,
Aunt Ella asked as she poured her black slops into the Meißen
cups:

"And what – Mr Timmas – happens to be wrong with *your*
health?" Adding, when Ilmar did not know how to react: "Or
do you work at such a fine place that you are not affected? In
which case – if you will forgive me for saying so – I will drink
my cup of coffee and hold my peace. For what good would it do
you if an old lady says things in your presence which she could
get hauled in for? And if you do work at such a place, then it is
impossible that a simple-minded actress like me should *not* talk
her way into getting arrested in five minutes flat . . ."

"Goodness gracious – no –" cried Ilmar, blushing, and I
added:

"Aunt Ella, his problem is that there is nothing wrong with
his health and he doesn't work at such an establishment. The day
before yesterday he went AWOL from his *Hilfswilliger* camp. To
avoid being sent to the front next week."

"Oh, how fascinating . . . !" cried Aunt Ella, arching her eyebrows – and I understood that the interest was more than polite
– "you mean to say that you've now gone – *underground*?"

"Quite so," I said.

"And what plans do you have for the future?" asked Aunt Ella
maintaining her interest.

"Peeter suggests I travel to Finland . . ."

"Oh, quite the wisest thing to do in the circumstances,"

conceded Aunt Ella, "but since you've left your training camp the way you have – do you have the equipment to make such a trip?"

". . . No. What equipment do you . . ."

"Oh dearie me! You haven't got anything at all, have you? All you've got is the clothes you're standing in. My dear young man – we are, after all, talking here about a sea voyage! A four-hour voyage, you will have heard. But that is by ferry under normal circumstances. Nowadays, people sail across in small boats. At night. The worse the weather is, the better. Sometimes with a stop-over somewhere out among the islets, so I've heard. Ten hours at least, hardly any quicker. Sometimes it takes twenty. And I don't know what contacts you have, but it can take weeks before you can find yourself a boat. You'll have to live somewhere by the shore. And it's September already. And as you may remember – in 1941, snow fell on the twelfth of October and didn't just melt away either! And *over there* – do you expect you'll end up working straightaway in the bespoke tailor's department in pre-war style Stockmann's?"[4] She held us all with her theatrical gaze: "Dear, oh dear, what children people can be, while imagining themselves to be adults . . . ! – Well, make yourself at home here. Peeter'll look after you. I don't have the time, I'm afraid. We'll meet at dinner this evening – no – not today we won't. I have a performance."

Straight after breakfast I set to work. For when Aunt Ella had gone out, and Ilmar and I had stayed behind in the dining room, I suddenly realised that this kindly flaxen-haired pal of mine with his relatively well-kept blue-grey suit, his white polo-neck sweater and his town shoes, slightly worn down at the heels, was now in fact my burden and responsibility. Resting *solely* on my shoulders . . . This adventure was beginning to take on an obligatory aspect.

I left Ilmar in the small back room. It had a huge verandah overlooking the garden. The door had not yet been sealed up for the winter. I showed Ilmar the verandah:

"Look, you can jump down from here in an emergency. Three or four metres down on to soft soil. The apple orchard is as good as impenetrable to the eye. There are four gates into the neighbouring yards. On to Imanta, Vambola, Lembitu and Sakala streets. So it doesn't matter a bugger which way you leave. Ideal, if you ask me. But I'm only joking, really. There's no danger of your being discovered here."

Then I took my ancient *Brennabor* bicycle up out of the cellar. In spite of its vintage it was in pretty good condition but had not been used lately. Since, three years ago, Uncle had made an unexpected purchase, on account of the value of the currency evaporating at the time, and had gone and bought himself a brand-new *Husqvarna*. He now went off to visit his patients on that. So I pedalled his old *Brennabor* out to the suburb of Kalarand. There, in a tiny house built against a rise and standing in a courtyard in the tiny Võrgu Street lived the Lööb brothers, Rudolf and Voldemar, former boatbuilder's locksmiths, whose markedly younger brother Aleksander had been taught by an aunt of mine at teacher training college. During Finnish prohibition, ten years previously, the brothers used to repair the boats of the Viinistu liquor smugglers, first their engines and later their fishing tackle, after they had been down-graded for use as humble fishing boats. They had now gone into the lucrative, shady, dangerous and mysterious business of conveying refugees to Finland. As I had been given to understand, this was run in such a way that they found a couple of hundred would-be travellers through friends, collected in the money, around fifteen hundred marks per head as far as I knew, and transported the whole group, in some wagon requisitioned from some Virumaa Province oil shale mine, with papers obtained God knows where, to the smugglers in Viinistu. The Lööbs got their share of the money, the smugglers the lion's share no doubt, but the local coastguard also got theirs – for turning a blind eye and for informing them of what they knew about the movements of the German patrol boats. The voyages were arranged on dark and if not exactly stormy, then at least windy nights. But the profits often made the smugglers take risks. So that at times they would set off with the sea like a mirror and under a full moon. This led to their coming a cropper on a number of occasions. As the former liquor boats, or ordinary fishing boats, with their old engines were, of course, no match in speed for the German coastal patrol boats. Those still on board would end up being interrogated for a month or two by the SD or Patarei bruisers, being roughed up nastily but without suffering any permanent injury, and then bundled off to join the army and to serve as a warning to the regular troops, making a public confession of their flight, and ending up (and this would surely have been so in the case of Ilmar) in the punishment battalion. Later, when general mobilisation was declared and the number of desertions had risen steeply, escapees could, at worst, end up with a court-martial and ten years. In which case, men with such sentences would of course console themselves with the fact that those meting out punishment were already in a particularly shaky position, though they did worry nonetheless whether they would survive the great collapse ahead. For the Germans were very likely to react in moments of crisis by lining up those prisoners with the heaviest sentences against a wall.

As far as I was aware, the Lööbs worked alternate shifts, one at night and one during the day. So that around ten in the morning the one coming from the night shift should have been at home asleep. But he could not have been so damned fast asleep that my knocking would not wake him.

I had in fact stopped knocking but was still standing on the couple of steps leading up to the door in the middle of the yard on Võrgu Street when I saw (reflected in a pane of glass at eye-level, the room inside being dark) that behind my back, in the house on the street side of the yard, a woman was looking out of the window. I took my bicycle which had been leaning against the handrail and made to leave the yard, with the intention of returning later that evening. Clearly something had changed in the Lööbs' working routine. When I passed the corner of the house facing the street, a woman, whom I could not actually see, but presumably the same one who had looked out moments before, pushed open the small ventilation window a fraction, and said in the direction of my ear:

"The Lööbs were taken away on Tuesday night. The yard's been under surveillance these last three days. Perhaps they're watching right now."

The window shut. I was on the street and looked both right and left. Nobody in sight. I felt my shirt sticking to my back and one or two per cent of this sensation was of wearing the Cloak of Nessus ... I thought rapidly: if I have to explain what I'm doing here, I'll say I've come to look up my old friend Leks Lööb who lived in that very same house. (Leks had in fact been six months in the Finnish Army, but I didn't have a clue about this at the time.) All the same, my heart was pounding perceptibly as I pedalled up the hill at Kalarand. When starting riding the cycle in town the thought hadn't struck me that someone might have been following me. Of course they would have written down the number of the bike – if anyone had been watching, that is. But on Pikk Street near Roheline Square back in the centre I jumped down from my bike and looked around – and breathed a sigh of relief. For I thought: *if* the Lööbs' house had been under surveillance, the duty officer would have rung the police station immediately and they would have replied: "A-11873 – just a moment – the bicycle belongs to a Dr Aadam Veski, Õuna Street 16, Flat 2." And a watch would be kept on Uncle Aadam and everyone immediately connected with him, Ilmar and I included. But I now realised that what I had failed to observe earlier, and which I had no doubt heard in one of Aunt Ella's ironic comments, was indeed true: Uncle Aadam had screwed the licence plate off the old *Brennabor* to affix it to his new "Husqvarna". Out of thrift. And as a small gesture of defiance against Groß-Deutschland. So that I had been riding an unlicensed and illegal bicycle, and had got away with it thanks to Uncle's niggardliness. But despite this little thrill of relief at my escape, my basic feeling was one of dissatisfaction as I made my way home. And instead of going straight to Õuna Street to announce our first fiasco to Ilmar, I dropped in at a couple of places *en route* where some old classmates and university pals worked, and for whom flight to Finland should have been a topical issue. I only managed to find one: the Secretary of the Merchant Bank, Endel Haak.

In the vortex of these torpid times of financial anaemia, the Secretary of the Merchant Bank (like the whole of the banking and business world) had little to do. But the Director of the Merchant Bank was a Students' Guild friend of Endel's father. Thanks to which fact the bank had also arranged a *Zurückstellung*[5] for Endel. The Merchant Bank had once had three or four Directors, each with his own office. As the volume of banking had been scaled down, there was only one Director left, and Endel made use of the one Director's Office, namely the one where the bank kept its very decent library which was by no means limited to financial volumes.

I found Endel behind his ex-Director's bureau. In front of the thin man with his narrow reddish face, slits of eyes grey as the sea and hair like toothbrush bristles, lay an open volume of the *Encyclopaedia Britannica* with a piece of tracing paper on top: he was copying a map of Anticosti Island.

"What for?"

"For fun."

He had always been a little secretive, a little ironic, something of a poseur, but quite shrewd in his own way.

"How long will you still manage to keep your head down?"

"Soon the mobilisation will widen the net. We'll have to see."

"What'll you do if things get tighter?"

He grandiloquently offered me a "Maret".

"Then – Sweden."

"But – how?"

"Hmm . . ." he looked out of the window over at the pigeons perched on the edge of the roof of the adjoining building, "I have my route."

"Would anyone be able to use it after you?"

"You yourself?"

"No. A friend of mine."

He blew a large, somewhat wobbly but perfectly joined smoke

ring and sent a second small and compact one elegantly through
it. I had never managed to learn such tricks. He said:

"I will look into the matter."

I said: "Look into it, by all means. It's urgent. I'll drop by.
When can you tell me?"

"Come back in a week's time."

I was already getting up when Endel added:

". . . But this route – *costs money*."

"How much?"

"I'll tell you when you return."

"Roughly?"

"Four, shall we say, five thousand."

As I rose, I merely uttered an "Ahaa". And resisted the temptation to tell him that in that case he might as well not bother.

In front of the Kalev shopping arcade I picked up my bike and,
without leaving the saddle, pedalled all the way to classmate
Jaak's. Jaak, with his angular head and his surprisingly thin neck
and his bitter little mouth looked straight at me with his brown
button eyes. I asked:

"Well, are you still under the protection of your "*Ostland Öl*"?

"Yes. Up to now."

The oil industry *GmbH* was indeed only a holding company
whose employees were as good as totally *zurückgestellt*.

"But if the mobilisation fans out, as it's rumoured it will?"

"Then I'll cross the Gulf of Finland."

"Got a boat?"

He shook his head.

"Well, how will you manage it then . . . ?"

Jaak smiled with relish: "I've got my dodge . . ."

"It wouldn't happen to be something for others, too . . . ?"

He turned his angular head obliquely over his right shoulder
and thought:

"Could be."

"Come on! Out with it then!"

"It's a long story."

"Anything to do with your oil business?"

"To a certain extent . . ."

"I don't think you need spell it all out right now. Come round to Õuna Street this evening. You've been there before. Uncle Aadam's got a drop of the hard stuff. Aunt Ella has some dried Hiiumaa whitefish. (I wasn't quite sure if there was anything left of the whitefish which the Hiiumaa giantess Anna had got hold of, but there *could well* have been. And in any case, that was a *délicatesse* which would appeal to the Jaak, who was rather fond of his dram.)

"I can't make it today or tomorrow. I'm working. But I'll come in the evening, in two day's time."

Jaak had been a bit of a fantasy merchant right from when he was a nipper. I remember how, one Monday, he had told the teacher in the Estonian class of Standard IV at junior school about his Sunday ski jaunt to Pirita. How he had whizzed down non-existent hills there. And how he had trapped a hare between the tips of his skis. But by the time he matriculated he had, despite a tendency towards laziness, become the best mathematician in class. A brilliant mathematician, at least by the standards of our grammar school with its focus on the humanities. And now, owing to the inevitability of the call-up (foresight, if ever there was!) he had left the second class of the Technical University to work in his own oil company. As a technician or whatever.

I cycled back to Uncle's flat in a slightly more relieved mood. Our chief hope had been crushed, that was a fact, and there was unfortunately nothing at all I could do for the Lööb brothers. But there was still a certain chance that something could be arranged two evenings from now. And finally, I could always have said that if we could scrape together four or five thousand . . . But when I turned into Õuna Street, cramp seized my intestines. For near number 18 of all houses, a couple of men in grey uniform drove past me on my bike in an Opel Kapitän and stopped right outside Uncle's front gate. I just had time to turn into the back gate of the neighbours' and from there peer out through the blackcurrant bushes to see what was going on. One uniformed soldier stayed at the wheel, while an NCO in *Wehrmacht* uniform jumped out on to the pavement and opened the rear door of the car. An officer, a major as far as I could make out, got out followed by – Aunt Ella. My first thought was that Aunt Ella had been arrested at the theatre and now they were bringing her back home to search the house ... Then I noticed that the sergeant was carrying some kind of boxes and the major had a suitcase in his hand. And Aunt Ella's grand gestures with her light-coloured gloves, as the Germans walked through the garden up to the steps, seemed too carefree for someone under arrest ... I waited a minute or two. Nothing happened. So I went through the neighbours' garden, and through the back gate into Uncle's, and up to the back door of the house. I put the bicycle in the cellar and stepped into Uncle's kitchen:

"What's happening here?"

Anna said from by the stove: "Oh nothing. I'm trying to stew this cow gristle which the Master has been given so that it might become soft enough to eat ..."

"But what are the Germans doing here?"

"Don't ask me. A couple of them helped the Mistress carry some packages or other – those over there. But they've gone now." Anna looked out of the window on to the street and I could see over her shoulder that the major and the sergeant had got into their Opel and were driving away.

I went into the back room behind the kitchen. Ilmar was lying on his stomach on the couch reading Meyer-Graefe's *El Greco*. He had not even heard the Germans come and go. As I left the room, Aunt Ella called: "Peeter, come and give me a hand to put these things in Ilmar's room!" I picked up the bundles and the suitcase which had been left on the floor of the lounge:

"Into Ilmar's room? You gave me the fright of my life, what with your Germans. What's going on?"

"Let's go in here. You'll soon see."

We went into Ilmar's room. He jumped up from his book. I put the bundles and the suitcase in the middle of the room. Aunt Ella said:

"Well, young man, now you've got at least the bare essentials for your journey."

I asked: "But what kind of Germans were those?"

"Oh, that was the arts editor of the *Revaler Zeitung*,"[6] said Aunt Ella, "he's always hanging about the theatre. I asked him to get a car for me and my packages. But he came in person. And ordered some NCO or other to assist him."

Out of two more or less new khaki rucksacks Aunt Ella took a number of thick homespun woollen jumpers, trousers, tunics, shirts, underwear, black and grey woollen socks and two pairs of ski-boots.

"Try them on. I imagined your feet wouldn't be larger than size 41, so I took 43s. Then you can wear a couple of pairs of woollen socks inside them."

And from the suitcase Aunt Ella produced, and placed next to the El Greco book on the couch, a shaving mirror, razor blades, a razor, scissors, two pocket knives, a corkscrew, a pocket compass, several mugs and tubes, two soap-holders with bars of soap, a raincoat, fishermen's leggings, a large torch with reserve batteries, a water flask, a dry fuel stove and thirty packets of "Karavan" cigarettes.

"Would you believe it, but I couldn't find an unused toothbrush. I'll go to the chemist's tomorrow and have a look if they've got any for civilian use. If we still can't get hold of one, then we can get Aadam to write out a prescription for one."

Ilmar was struck dumb with amazement. I asked:

"Aunt Ella – wherever did you manage to spirit up all this stuff from? Raid a second-hand shop, or something?"

"Don't be cheeky! From the theatre, of course. I told the props man roughly what I needed and he found it all for me."

"The cigarettes as well?"

"No. We don't have cigarettes there. I've taken them and some ointments plus the eau de Cologne from my own private stock."

"But my dear Mrs Veski . . ." uttered Ilmar, ". . . I can't accept all this . . ."

"Why can't you?" said Aunt Ella, coquettishly, "everything

will easily fit into the suitcase and the two rucksacks. And there'll be room for your food rations too. I'll see to them, just before you leave."

"...Mrs Veski, I..."

"Yes? What are you trying to say?"

And as Ilmar couldn't manage to continue, Aunt Ella laughed gaily, gave Ilmar's blond forelock a tug and said: "Oh, what a darling you are!" and breezed out of the room.

"Well, great," I said, "*why* can't you accept the stuff? Course you can! You make a judicious choice of what'll fit in one rucksack, and Bob's your uncle."

We had just managed to stack away Ilmar's travelling kit, which was four times what he would actually have use for, in the cupboard, when in came Uncle Aadam. Quick of step as always, always at a bit of a trot, a little absent-mindedly and awkwardly:

"Hello." He shook Ilmar's hand and eyed him through his thick spectacles.

I had long thought that Uncle Aadam must have been quite a colourless boy judging by photos taken in his youth, but with the years he had taken on, living alongside his pretty and theatrical other half, the quite professional, somewhat wearied, slightly worn, spiritually lean face of a popular actor playing the part of a humanist intellectual, in whom could be detected the makings of a dangerous fortune-hunter. Uncle said to Ilmar:

"Ella told me she stole a pair of boots for your journey. Jolly good. I gave her my old ones – to take back to the theatre as replacements."

"Not only the boots – Good Lord no..." Ilmar began enthusiastically but fell silent when I gestured to him, without really understanding why. Uncle Aadam, however, had not noticed anything and simply added:

"I know. A pocket compass too. A traveller needs one." He tried to light his pipe, but it wouldn't take. This action implied he needed time to think but refused to take too much time over it. I spoke to him briefly about my adventure with the Lööbs and his bicycle number. He puffed at his pipe, emitting smoke which crawled daintily and stank awfully, but his face did not betray anything of what he was thinking.

"And what do you intend doing now?"

I said: "We will have to find a new solution. And it'll no doubt be a more expensive one. The Lööbs took fifteen hundred. We'll now have to reckon on two thousand."

"Have you got such a sum?"

Ilmar shook his head, reddening. I said in what I felt was a rather abrupt voice – so as to make sure it was said unequivocally and that there was no room for misunderstandings:

"We'll have to borrow it from you."

Uncle Aadam turned to me out of sheer amazement and his voice was on the threshold of his falsetto register: "And where did you get it into your head that I've got so much money? I just simply *don't* have that much!"

I said, though I felt I didn't have a leg to stand on:

"Well, if you haven't got it right now, you'll devise some way of getting hold of some. Ilmar isn't just any old Estonian lad. He's an *amicus*, as you know. And everyone regards him as a genius."

Ilmar cried, his face blotched red as before: "Forget it! I'm not going to accept that kind of money!"

I said: "It's a *loan*, isn't it? Understand? Why shouldn't you accept it?"

He shouted: "Because *you* haven't got it to lend me!"

I still wanted to say: My dear chap, *that* you knew right from the start, but I grabbed that phrase by the tail and thank God I did. For I understood that in Ilmar's situation, which was to a certain extent of my making, uttering such a reminder would, despite the fact it may have been the truth, be rather below the belt.

"You mean to say you would accept the loan from *him*?" asked Uncle Aadam indicating me and looking Ilmar in the eye – "But not from me?"

"No," said Ilmar firmly – "because you (he did not say 'from you sir' but was obliged to *tutoyer* other *amici*) would have to go and borrow the sum yourself. And that would be quite alien to my way of thinking."

"*Ah soo –*" murmured Uncle Aadam and puffed an even thicker cloud of smoke into the air around him – "I think, young gentlemen, that you shouldn't get over-excited. No trouble for Ilmar to live here at our place for a week or two. And in the meantime, we'll come up with something."

He left the room with his usual quick step and Ilmar and myself bickered for a while about the limits of the permissible or impermissible as regards borrowing the money. And I tried (not with one hundred per cent conviction, but with a certain amount of faith based on experience) to make it clear to him that in critical situations Uncle Aadam was quite an open-handed man. Ilmar maintained that if someone has said in so many words that he has not got the money, then the question of open- or closed-handedness was quite irrelevant.

I don't remember the next two-and-a-half days in any detail. Maybe Ilmar was paler than usual. Perhaps his mouth was more set and his conversation sparser. I more or less left him alone during those days and tried to pursue the matter with other crossing agents, but beyond vague information which would require further investigation, I did not at first have any success. And at eight the following evening, Jaak turned up.

He walked into our place, as he had many times before, with his rather boyishly carefree gait, his hands in his jacket pockets. At that hour of the day, Uncle Aadam happened to be at home for a short while between visits to the hospital, the theatre, the concert hall, the doctors' association, the chess club and his private patients. So that before he left, he had time to tell Jaak a joke about Göring and the magnetic crane in a machine workshop he was visiting (the crane pulled his medals up to the ceiling and the Field Marshal along with them). And when the joke was over, although we were standing, I asked Uncle whether he didn't have a suitable amount (I said literally "suitable amount") of spirits for our little party. And I added: "Just enough *Mäe pisarad* to get him a bit more businesslike, if you see what I mean." After I had

said that, and after he had :
brought us from the bathr
he considered a suitable am
bedside table saying:

"From this you can make
40° proof. Just the right amc
And hurried off.

But Anna did have dried w
generous Hiiumaa portions th
sour cowberry cordial to rins
into the bathroom to fetch ano ....ed grammes.
I took it evenly from five flagons, so that it would take a very
observant eye to notice the difference. I said:

"Jaak – can you now tell us about the dodge for crossing the
Gulf of Finland you mentioned to me? Ilmar here is desperate."

Jaak looked at us, smiled and started to leaf once again through
a French edition of *The Arabian Nights* whose illustrations he had
been looking at. After a time he said:

"Well – it's all incredibly simple."

"Then spit it out," I insisted, "and tell us roughly what it's
going to cost."

". . . *Cost?*" He buried his nose in the illustration which
showed Ali Baba in the thieves' den counting out the pieces of
gold . . . "It won't cost you anything at all."

"Oh-ho! And *what* kind of *dodge* is it then?"

"Has it been tried before?" asked Ilmar.

Jaak turned the pages. "It has indeed. Last month, two of my
friends used it."

"Come on – I simply can't believe you. For free – in times
like these, when everything connected with such things costs
money."

Jaak looked at us with his dark stubborn eyes. The corners of
his mouth quivered with a smile of secret knowledge which he
did not want to, or could not, share. I cried:

"Tell us then! Like you usually do."

He put the book aside.

78

"What is there f
harbour?"
We had no
certainly h
in Ta
kne

...r me to tell? Have you been down to the

...t. Ilmar had last been there five years ago. And I ...adn't during the Occupation. I had spent more time ...u than in Tallinn. I had not had any business there. I ...w that the harbour had been badly damaged in '41, but had somehow managed to keep operating. But any curiosity on my part to see what was going on out there was inhibited by the existence of watchtowers and barbed-wire entanglements which were quite humiliating – in view of my frequent trottings down to the harbour as a child.

"Well anyway, can you imagine the road to the harbour?" said Jaak. "If you turn right along Mere Avenue into Sadama Street, you have on your left a number of two-storey stone buildings. Shops selling shipping tackle and so on. The windows are all boarded up now. Before you get to this line of buildings, there emerges from behind them a stretch of railway line leading to the quays. Can you picture it?"

I said that I could. I even knew quite precisely where they were situated. Jaak continued:

"That stretch of track is surrounded by a barbed-wire fence, about one hundred and fifty metres long. A dirty great fence, two and a half metres high. A gate at either end. Locked, of course. From the road end of that stretch of ground you can see the backs of the buildings. The harbour end is hidden by the buildings. In the enclosure stand the tanker wagons. But not all the time. The locomotive shunts them there on Monday mornings. Eighteen of them. They remain there right through Monday evening. At midnight the loco shunts them another three hundred metres further up. On board ship, in other words. A German barge. On deck there are two lines of nine wagons. The ship sails at one o'clock in the morning. Every Monday night. And on Tuesday morning at five, they arrive at the merchant shipping harbour in Helsinki. A locomotive pulls them on land a little after five. While it is still completely dark."

"And how exactly do you travel, then?" I asked.

"Well, the tanks are up to the usual German standard. There are no cabins for escort guards. A steel ladder up the side. An opening with a lid on the top. Forty-five centimetres in diameter. The lid's to stop the rain getting in. They are left unbolted. Unbolted for the whole voyage out. You take along a pair of wire-cutters and get into the harbour. By cover of darkness. You throw yourself into the nettles and wriggle under the fence. There are already two gaps but a newcomer wouldn't manage to find them. So you make a new hole and crawl in. It's quite safe. No guards, no dogs, let alone a searchlight. You stroll along the row of tanks and pick one out, right? One that appeals to you. Count odds or evens from the loco; or what's left when the train is split in two, either towards the head or back of the train. Or the second or third from the end. Well, there are all sorts of possibilities. In a word, you pick out your tank, silently, of course, at any event. You grope around till you find the footboard, climb up, ease the lid and slip inside. Inside there is a ladder which'll take you neatly to the bottom. It's what the cleaners use."

"The tanks are *empty*?" asked Ilmar.

"Of course they're empty. Empty for the *outward* voyage to Finland. And come back full. It's some sort of business arrangement. Several Swedish firms buy crude oil in the West. They then sell it semi-clandestinely for God knows how much to the Finns. Who, in turn, send some of it over to the Germans, at a price. That's about the long and the short of it. You climb up into the tank and pull the lid over your head and wedge it. With whatever you like. So it stays open a couple of centimetres. That's essential. To have air to breathe. There'll probably be a litre or two sloshing around in the bottom. So you simply sit there on the steps with your nose in the crack. Though, it's not such a good idea to smoke. You sit and count – up to twenty thousand. Perhaps as little as eighteen thousand. And you climb out in Helsinki. There'll be no soldiers nosing around over there. You can walk off in any direction. There are no barbed-wire fences round Helsinki harbour."

I remember the mixed feelings with which Jaak's story left

me. On the one hand, it was a desperate fiction, on the other, suggestively tangible reality. We asked him whether the friends he had who had used that method weren't by any chance friends of ours. He didn't name them, but did say that we didn't know them. We asked how they had fared. Jaak said: just fine. We asked him how he knew. One of them, the one who travelled second, had recently sent a letter by courier where he wrote how easily everything had gone, and mentioned that it had gone the same way for his predecessor. We asked: how come – he actually *described* the journey? Didn't it seem rather risky to *describe* such an event in a letter which could end up in God knows whose hands? Jaak said: Of course he didn't describe everything *in detail*, not in such a way that informers would be able to gather how he had travelled!

It was already midnight by now, the anti-aircraft batteries in Lasnamäe began sputtering and a minute later the air-raid sirens began wailing. When the noise of the sirens had died away, you could clearly hear a whirr-whirr-whirr coming down out of the greenish moonlit sky. The windows of the neighbouring houses shattered. Hurrying footsteps could be heard on the asphalt. After the bombs which had fallen a month ago, when a number of neighbours had been killed or injured and some houses had been burnt to the ground, many people began making for the shelters during raids. The only large stone building provided with a cellar for the purpose was two hundred metres away.

On this occasion, at any rate, we remained where we were. For the house was empty. Only Anna was at home. She never went down to the shelter but, as she put it, held her breath under the bedcovers, prayed to God and thought of the third stone flag to the right of the pulpit in the floor of Pühalepa Church on Hiiumaa. And none of us three wanted to make any move in the direction of the shelter. Especially as somewhere out towards Kadriorg four clusters of bombs – as we could feel – had been dropped in close succession. Ilmar put out the lights. We sat for a short while in darkness. Then Jaak removed the blackout from the window and returned to the table. The room was now quite bright in the light of the full moon, and he said, raising his glass:

"Well, we've still got a drop of the elixir of life twinkling in our glasses. Cheers – as they say – to the freedom-loving peoples of the world!"

Ilmar did not drink to that. I did. For it was very necessary in spite of, or just because of, the bombs to carry on bantering. We put down our glasses on the table. We talked, what about I don't remember. Calmly. For such nights had become everyday occurrences. But I do remember Jaak speaking in a louder voice than myself and that this bothered me a little. As if by speaking loudly he might betray us to the bombs. The ack-ack guns fell silent. The whirr-whirring rose and fell. Somewhere between Narva Road and Tartu Road a number of houses were burning. Then the sirens sounded the all-clear and despite the familiarity of the matter (and the uncertainty as to the whether the all-clear was to be taken seriously) we were released from the inevitable chain of events. We went out on to the verandah and watched the glow of the fires. Ilmar said:

"No doubt there'll be dead and wounded out there."

I remember stating: "Lord knows how many personal tragedies – only –" and left my train of thought unfinished, but Jaak took it up and continued:

"Only – what is a catastrophe in these times? Now at least a whole country would have to go up in flames for the world to call it a catastrophe . . . and then one half would call it a catastrophe, the others a triumph . . ."

After a leisurely Sunday morning breakfast (Uncle Aadam and Aunt Ella sipping quietly at their hot chicory water – one had stayed the night at the theatre, while the other had still continued to play chess even after the air-raid), Uncle Aadam invited me into his study. He gestured towards a padlocked trunk by the wall and said:

"I put a number of my more valuable books in there. On account of the bombs. I brought it on a handcart which the Ardnas next door lent me. It's in the yard. Be a good chap and help me to load the handcart and take it down to the Kunsti-hoone.[7] There, a Mr Tilder will take charge of the trunk and put it down in the cellar."

When I inquired whether I could also take a look at the books, he replied tetchily that I could, of course I could, but later when they had been brought back up out of the cellar when things were back to normal. And just as I was about to grab hold of the handles, he uttered "Just a moment!", peered out of his study and returned saying:

"Let's wait till Ella has gone out."

"What for?"

"You know, it would only increase her fears of bombing raids even more – if she sees that I am – well – moving valuable objects out of the house . . ."

I asked *what kind of* books there were in there and he answered vaguely: "Several kinds. Medical books too. A first edition of Morgagni's *Anatomy*, among other things."

Ella went out a quarter of an hour later. Aadam and myself heaved the trunk on to the cart and pushed it along to the Kunsti-hoone, the House of Art. And I remember thinking, as Uncle Aadam and I were proceeding across the square pushing the cart, that Aadam always had been one of the more democratic Tallinn doctors of his generation . . . And later I thought: what strange times were these, where a trip across town with a handcart allows the pusher to draw a conclusion such as this!

Mr Tilder, a short, tubby, button-eyed man with a face more that of a rat than a *"tilder"*, an Estonian greenshank, met us at the entrance of the Kunstihoone, along with a younger man who was unknown to me. They carried the trunk down into the cellar without our assistance. Uncle Aadam said that the checklist was in the trunk with the books and Mr Tilder asked whether the Morgagni was among them. And when Uncle Aadam replied: but of course, Mr Tilder cried, still carrying the trunk and panting:

"Well, *in that case*, what are you worrying about – that alone will fetch a thousand marks . . ."

I had been advised to take a walk down Petrooleumi Street

before seven on Monday morning. To meet one particular crossing agent before he had gone to work. But he had already left
home. But since I was in the immediate vicinity of the harbour,
I decided to take a look at the spot at the beginning of Sadama
Street which Jaak had been talking about. And sure enough: a
few minutes after seven, a locomotive drove, before my very eyes,
out from behind the power station and shunted eighteen tanker
wagons into the barbed wire enclosure while the gate stood open
for the purpose.

After my fruitless attempt at finding a crossing agent, Ilmar
and I sat breakfasting alone. Aunt Ella had not yet woken up and
Uncle Aadam was already out and about. And had also left a note
on the kitchen table in his familiar curlicued crows' feet scrawl:
would I come and meet him at the hospital at around six. We
ate some potato cutlets fried in margarine and which could have
done with being half as big again. I told Ilmar not to be so
gloomy. I said that I would for sure find a carrier at a reasonable
price so long as Ilmar had the patience to wait, and it would all
be over in a matter of days. And that Uncle Aadam would as sure
as damn it get the money from somewhere. I had, admittedly,
not succeeded that morning on Petrooleumi Street, but I would
return that evening. So that Ilmar needn't seriously consider
using Jaak's method, ha-ha-ha-haa. I told him the story about
Jaak's "hare-raising" skiing activities as a boy. But I also mentioned, still laughing, that I had, that morning, nonetheless seen
Jaak's fantastical tanker wagons with my very own eyes: eighteen
of them shunted into the barbed-wire enclosure in the space of
five minutes . . .

For the sake of convenience, I jumped on my uncle's *Brennabor*
again, prepared to shout at the policeman, if necessary: Oh, thank
you for bringing it to my notice! The number must have *just*
fallen off – A-11873 . . . But despite having use of the bicycle, I
did not manage to make it to Uncle's place for dinner. I had
promised some lady that I would chop firewood for her at midday,
and had dinner at her place: cabbage soup, without fat, with
sausage-meat pasties whose filling she had put through the mincer

and on which she had used goodness knows what other tricks to make them more or less palatable. And by the time I had finished stacking the wood after the meal it was time to pedal up to the hospital. Uncle looked at his watch and cleared his throat. It was seven minutes past six and I thought to myself as always: pity he's such a ludicrous pedant . . . Then he tapped his pipe clean into the ashtray, locked the door of his surgery from the inside and pressed a bundle of banknotes into my hand:

". . . Go and take these to your Ilmar."

"Can't you take them yourself?"

"He said he wouldn't accept any money from me but he would from you."

"But look . . ."

"No iffing and butting. I'll be out for quite a while today. And I don't want to have them on me. There could be bombing raids, arrests, what have you . . ."

"How much is there?"

"Four."

". . . Four thousand?"

"Yes, yes, yes. I asked around. He really is reputed as being a clever boy. Let him go to Sweden. Joining the Estonian Brigade of the Finnish Army would hardly be any more sensible than joining the *Leegion*. They're all murderers of our lads, the lot of 'em. In a year, or let's say two, everything'll sort itself out. At least he'll get a good start this way. Now go and give it to him!"

"But – who lent you the money . . . ?"

"Oh . . . Nobody lent it me . . . That is to say – there was this man."

"Wait a minute – those *books* – you went and sold them, didn't you?"

Uncle Aadam yelled, almost falsetto, as was usual in moments of irritation: "Well, what of it? Haven't I even got the right to sell my own books? Well, have I or haven't I? Now skedaddle! I'm in a hurry. And keep your trap shut, will you!"

I came out of Uncle's surgery and weighed up whether I should give the money straight to Ilmar or do so by some roundabout method – and whether to go to him with not only the money but also instructions on how to use it . . . I rang from the phone in the hospital lobby just to see – it was past six already – whether Endel was still at the bank. He was:

"Yes. Come along by all means. I'm here and I'll be staying here. They've drawn up a rota for guarding the place at night for some daft reason. And I'm on duty tonight."

And in truth: Endel received me at the empty bank with pleasure and a willingness to be helpful. Yes, it was all arranged. A large motor-boat. Leaving Saturday night from the Noarootsi peninsula. You could even say – one quarter legally. OK – an eighth legally, then. The prelude to the evacuation of the villages of the Swedish-speaking area of Noarootsi. But paying four thousand for your berth. When it's a question of a friend from the university. Got the money? OK. That has to be handed over immediately. To be passed on.

I told him I'd pass on the message. And just then the air-raid sirens went off. A little ack-ack fire. The odd cluster of bombs. But it meant staying put for one and a half hours. Endel suggested listening to what the world at large had to say and switched on the large Philips bank radio. I remember that we heard through the detonating bombs: the Americans had landed at Salerno . . . London was playing Shostakovich's Seventh . . . Battles were being fought to liberate Novorossiysk . . . The 17th German Army had made a victorious retreat from the Crimea . . . On Corsica, a popular revolt had been raging for three days and somewhere an ecstatic choir accompanied by an ecstatic orchestra was singing:

> *Hac in hora*
> *sine mora*
> *corde pulsum tangite;*
> *quod per sortem*
> *sternit fortem,*
> *mecum omnes plangite . . .*

When I arrived back at Uncle's place, it was half-past eight. I thought, while taking the cycle down into the cellar: Ilmar will no doubt accept the money from me. If not four thousand, then at least two ... I went to his room. He wasn't there. Neither were Aadam or Ella at home. Anna didn't know anything about Ilmar's whereabouts – oh yes – only that he had picked up a pair of wirecutters from the kitchen about an hour before ...

I ran back into his room. One rucksack and some few things were gone from the cupboard. Had he – crazy that he was – not even left a message? But he had. It was a tiny note on the coffee table under the corner of the ashtray:

> Peeter!
>
> Try to understand and explain it to the rest: I don't want to cause you all any more expense or inconvenience. So why shouldn't I give this damned stretch of lead piping a try, since it happens to exist. Thanks.
>
> I.

Less than a month later I learned from someone returning from Finland: Ilmar had been found in the tanker wagon in Helsinki. Dead. Overcome by crude oil fumes. He was not discovered until he had, in effect, died a second time: when his corpse was drowned as they filled the tank with oil.

For a long time I was tormented by the fact. It has continued to plague me for years. But who would take an interest in my despondency? The leitmotiv of dreams I used to have was of me crawling through a dark pipe, my nails scraping against the black iron walls. My nightmarish drowning in liquefied asphalt. The split-second image before my mind's eye, right up to the present day: coffins transformed into giant lengths of lead piping ... For a long time afterwards, the stench of crude oil or petrol made me retch. And yet I have not succeeded in vomiting up my feelings of guilt. I have simply got used to them. As you can get used to almost anything.

The roots of events are truly endless. Also the crop reaped from the events is immeasurable. Thirteen years after the adventurous nights in the room under the eaves on Lepiku Street (and not ten years since the *word* that brought it all to fruition) I was making my way along Ülikooli Street in Tartu, when I stopped at the window of the bookshop on the corner and looked at the pillars of the main University building. A pretty, short and slightly rotund woman in a dress the colour of orange-peel approached me and asked:

"Excuse me, you must be – I haven't seen you for such a long time – you were a friend of Ilmar Timmas', weren't you?"

I said: "Yes, Piia. Only – I've been away for a long time . . ."

She asked: "Tell me – what became of Ilmar . . . ?"

I said: "He – won't be coming back. I'm sorry."

"Was he – killed . . . ?"

I clearly must have nodded. Piia asked:

". . . Fighting on whose side? Who killed him . . . ?"

I said: "That, I *really* do not know."

Then Piia turned and walked away. The breeze caught her orange dress and I understood that she was pregnant. For one fleeting second the perplexing thought crossed my mind: now how could that be possible . . . ?

1980

Translator's notes for "Lead Piping"

1. *Kristjan Jaak Peterson* (1801–22) is regarded as the first modern Estonian poet and, during his short life, managed to contribute articles to the fledgling press on Estonian philology and mythology.
2. *Nikolai Triik* (1884–1940) and *Ado Vabbe* (1892–1961) were Estonian Expressionist landscape artists and portraitists, the former influenced by Edvard Munch, and who made study visits to Åland, Norway, Leningrad and Paris. *Oskar Kallis* (1892–1918) was the Symbolist illustrator of the Estonian national epos, the *Kalevipoeg*.
3. *Colonel Utuste* was the founder of a pagan religious sect.
4. *Stockmann*. The Finland-Swedish owner of what is, even today, the largest department store in Helsinki.
5. *Zurückstellung* – having one's call-up postponed.
6. *Revaler Zeitung*. The German-language newspaper during the German Occupation. "Reval" is the German for Tallinn.
7. The *Kunstihoone*, or House of Art (built 1934) was the new centre for the fine arts in central Tallinn and contained then, as now, a picture gallery and flats for artists.

The Stahl Grammar

The Stahl Grammar

All manner of things have happened to me. I have been drowning in the icy sea, sinking into a sulphurous pool, been trapped by a flow of lava, under an avalanche, in front of an express train, soil has been thrown over me in a grave, I have sat in the electric chair waiting for the order to switch on, been infected with leprosy, been in a plane plunging down into the crater of a volcano – and have, on waking, always returned from my oppressive nightmares to the world of normality.

Now, in the spring and summer of 1944, I experienced for the first time that waking up in the morning did not bring any relief. Since the box-like single cell with its grey distempered walls which I saw when I opened my eyes did not fade into unreality. The bars across the windows, as high up as those across a cellar window, stayed put. As did the whitewash on the windowpanes (to prevent you from looking out of the window if you were to heave yourself up by your fingertips). The two hinged bunks, lowered from the walls at night, with their two occupants, plus the other two sleeping on the floor underneath all remained. As did the brown-painted box for the privy which had been provided with a lid and which served as a neck-rest in lieu of a pillow, and beyond that the odour of the privy itself floating up from the bumpy floor, a smell hardly discernible but undeniably present, giving the black air its distinct quality until it was time to rise. Then, in through the half-open window from the yard outside, the smell of chlorine would creep up your nose, which a breath of wind wafted in from the left, from the door of the mortuary which was situated on the lower floor of the old prison building. The strong smell of chlorine – mixed almost imperceptibly, but to a degree that could not quite be ignored, with the smell of corpses.

In those weeks, from amongst the four thousand prisoners in Tallinn Central Gaol, four, five, seven, nine, twelve prisoners died daily. The majority flecked with typhoid fever, which had broken out here at the height of summer. And Old Hoary, the old jade which had toiled for two decades under the blue, black and white, and then the black, white and red flags, was now toiling, staggering, reeling, knees trembling to cope with her heaviest burden yet. At around four in the morning, still in the darkness of the July night, from the purplish strip of gravel right below our window could suddenly be heard the creak of the mortuary doors as they were opened, and half-whispered, half-shamefaced curses ("How can skin and bones be so damned heavy . . .") as something heavy was dragged to the cart followed by Old Hoary's dull footsteps and the crunch of gravel under the wheels. And anyone who risked sticking his head through the open window, his nose pushed out through the bars, and looked down (in the worst instance he would earn the rattle of machine-gun fire from the perimeter wall on the other side and a shower of stone chippings for his pains), would be able to catch a glimpse Old Hoary's left ear and scraggy haunches and the long, dark box on wheels wobbling along.

A month previously, there had been five of us in a four-metre-square cell originally intended for one inmate.

Number One – an ethnic Russian from the Petserimaa Province,[1] Sofronov, forty years of age, slow, taciturn, smiling, whose face was like a village icon and whose back had been beaten black and blue, something undescribable. He was accused of being involved with attempts by the underground to free inmates from the prisoner-of-war camp at Pskov.[2] Three weeks ago he was taken away. But in broad daylight, not in the first instance the most ominous of departures.

Number Two – Lill, a signalman from Viirpalu Station, a pale lad with a brown moustache, who was accused of appropriating two crates of butter intended for the Germans from a train standing at the station. He had been sentenced to death in Tallinn for this crime and was waiting for a reprieve from Reichskommissar Lohse in Riga. Till he was taken out two weeks before and brought back a couple of hours later, his grey coat smelling of the sunshine of the yard and he himself trembling, dazed and radiant inside that coat – and, my God, alive, his sentence having been commuted to fifteen years of hard labour! What did fifteen years of hard labour mean in Estonia in July 1944? He was allowed to collect his belongings and was taken out forthwith.

Number Three was the farmer Johannes Kraav from the Räisa District of Viljandimaa Province. He was a man of around forty-five, serious, short and not especially downhearted, given the circumstances. He had been sentenced to death for hiding his nephew who had descended from a Soviet plane in the spring and had asked his uncle for assistance. The nephew was no doubt already pushing up the daisies. The execution of the uncle's sentence was taking its time, and he entertained the hope that he would be allowed to live. For he had a farm back there in Räisa which had been awarded him for services rendered in the Estonian War of Independence. He had nevertheless been in the wrong place at the wrong time, as he had been awarded the *Vabadusrist*, the Estonian Cross of Freedom, for fighting at the front against the *Landeswehr*. But hopefully, Herr Lohse did not know for what he had received the Cross and the farm. Towards the end, the nerves of this otherwise calm man were on edge owing to the hopes entertained. He was summoned one afternoon a week before. He left hopefully, but on his return the stubble of his beard had turned completely black. For his face had gone grey under the stubble. He had been refused a reprieve. True, his application for commutation of sentence had not actually been rejected. A lawyer had been waiting for him in the review office. He had been allowed to write his will. I tried to convince him of the fact that this did not necessarily mean that his application had been refused – though this was the only more-or-less logical conclusion. Apart from the suspicion as to whether a condemned man would actually be given the right to write out his will. Especially in the case of men condemned for political crimes under the current régime. I could not at the time imagine that it was a question of Herr Lohse being particularly receptive to argument . . . A concession had nevertheless been granted to the old freedom fighter! He had been given the exceptional right to write his will, which those sentenced to death did not otherwise receive! And his dishonourable hanging had been commuted to an honourable death by firing squad – *Heil Hitler*! . . . A couple of days later Johannes Kraav was led out at eleven at night by three blackshirts who were visibly drunk and audibly taciturn.

Number Four, the only one left sharing the cell with me after the others had gone, was Eduard Salu, a farmer from Taebla District in the western province of Läänemaa, a man thirty-three years of age. His wife was also on the third floor of the same building and sentenced to death like himself. And their three children, two, three and five years of age were at home in Võntküla being cared for by neighbours. Wife Virve's brother had come by parachute from Russia and had been concealed by them in their smallholder's cottage for a number of weeks ("How could I possibly have handed him over?"). Until eyes had begun to watch, and tongues to wag . . . One evening, the week before, they had come for Salu. I can remember his pale face and the beads of sweat covering it. And the quick, clammy handshake as he tucked his small bundle under his arm: ". . . Well, it's time to be going." I remember my decision to look him encouragingly in the eye. And the equivocal wonderment I felt when I heard him say: "See you." And I remember his glance, as he turned his head when already on the threshold – as the barred gate of the corridor opened and slammed shut again – and the look of naked fear extinguishing every spark of joy: ". . . Do you think they're taking Virve out now, too?"

After that, I was in the cell on my own. And it must be said that a couple of days later when they transferred me to another cell, again a single one, and still empty, but this time with a wide view of the harbour, I did have that well-known feeling of having turned collaborator but, at the same time, a feeling of relief. In those days, the world was experiencing death so widely and in so many guises that my own brush with death is embarrassing to recall. But the voices of those who had met an unnatural death and who had so recently occupied this boxlike cell with me, their footsteps on the floor, their contact with objects, with the tin bowl out of which we had all drunk, the brass tap where we had all washed ourselves, and with the night-table on which we had all broken bread were almost, on touching these objects again, physically painful to me. The new cell liberated me, to a certain extent, from this oppressive proximity. At the same time, there was a dangerously large amount of time for me to insinuate into my skull the lead bullet of my own circumstances.

I had, of course, not as yet been sentenced to death. I was still under investigation. My back had not, for the time being at least, been beaten black and blue. Everything could still turn out alright. But *could* also go wrong. Events could take a disastrous turn.

My most recent adventure, which had caused me to end up in Tallinn Central Gaol, had begun four months previously. Until March '44, I had been living in Tallinn with my parents. On 9 March, after the firebombing of that city, my parents had gone to stay with relatives out in Pärnumaa Province, while I had considered it necessary to remain in Tallinn. The apartment on Õuna Street belonging to my uncle, Doctor Aadam Veski, had been burnt to the ground on that selfsame 9 March and my uncle had gone to lodge with friends in a half-finished house right on the outskirts of town, on the banks of the River Pääsküla, a kilometre or two from the suburban railway station. And I had managed to get myself a room in that same half-built house, a room with the heating already installed and looking out over the garden. An iron stove. A tin chimney sticking out through the window. A few crates of books. A table-lamp. A blackout curtain, that went without saying. A typewriter. And I stayed there the most agitated six weeks of the whole Occupation. In the end writing nothing. Till I was saved by the phone which had, against all expectations, been installed in that half-built house. A Pääsküla police official, a friend of Uncle Aadam's, had phoned through the message: "Doctor Veski – if there's a certain Peeter Mirk living under your roof, he'd better make himself scarce right away!"

The fact that I had, technically speaking, been a draft-dodger those last two months could perhaps already have been sufficient reason for the authorities to take an interest in me. But on this occasion, the interest turned out to spring from the fact that the week before a number of people had been apprehended in a large razzia and in whose pocketbooks my address had presumably been found.

Six or seven minutes later, I left the house, a plywood suitcase in my hand and rubber boots on my feet. Three quarters of an hour later, I had made my way through the wasteland of spring puddles, so that tracker dogs would not be able to trace my route, to friends in the village of Alliku.[3] There I hid for several days while Uncle Aadam arranged for me to disappear from Tallinn. Former patients of his, an old man and woman, the half-Estified Swedish family by the name of Krüüdner, were one of the three families left on the island of Aksi.[4] One windy evening in April, I walked along the water's edge at Kalarand, carrying a bundle and the suitcase and found, at the quayside, a boat ready for departure. Both men on board knew of my arrival and cast off without delay. Not until we had passed the fishing harbour and the waves had begun to toss the boat about a good deal, did I ask on what I was actually sitting and was told that between the wheelhouse and the engine, under the tarpaulin, was an empty coffin, for on the island we were heading for there would be a funeral, and a wake, the next day. Old Krüüdner spoke so that the other old man sitting next to me would not be able to hear on account of the lapping of the waves: that man's neighbour's daughter had been a bit well – you know, different – and had hanged herself a few days previously from a nail in the shed . . .

And though I tried to avoid interpreting the fact in such a way that the hanged woman's funeral and wake would coincide with my trip, the thought still would not leave me in peace.

On the second day, I was invited to sail with the black-pennanted boat to the island of Prangli where the cemetery was located. I politely refused the offer and stayed put as I did not want to attract undue attention with my unfamiliar face. Instead, I wandered a number of times through the area of low juniper heathland used for grazing sheep, two kilometres in length and half a kilometre in breadth. In the afternoon, the mourners returned, the three families from Aksi, plus relatives from Prangli in two other boats. The wake was to be held at the neighbours' homestead but it could be seen that the mourners had also wandered into the Krüüdner house. So I decided it would be better to make myself scarce, disappear in among the junipers, and spend the night in a net hut on the northeastern shore of the island. But old Mrs Krüüdner cried in consternation: "What's the point! There's nothing to be afraid of here. Here they're all *our* people."

And both at the wake, where I was dragged to the beer table, as well as during the week I spent there, I certainly felt myself to be one of them. All the more so, considering the juniper hillocks and the gravelly beaches were so marvellously deserted and near to the sky and full of the liberating wind which felt particularly curative after the strain and agitation of my last days in Tallinn. But only for a week. For then the first boat arrived since I had been on the island, heading for Finland. It moored for a few hours in a sheltered cove on the northern shore and then continued its journey in the dead of night. But I made no effort to board that vessel. And then I suddenly grasped the fact that this was what old Krüüdner had actually expected me to have done. But I was loath to have it confirmed that my departure from Estonian soil – and this strip of land surrounded by sea was nonetheless a piece of that country – had become an inevitability. I still entertained the hope that liberation would come, well, not of course in a couple of weeks' time, but perhaps in a couple of months – so as to try to stay as long as possible on this speck of an islet. Soviet radio announced the major advance in the east, and Allied broadcasts told of their successes in Italy, and of the terrible destruction taking place in Germany, and such news had nourished these hopes for some while now, all the more so since I had been unable to sit by the wireless set uninterruptedly, and my ear tended to sift out the items of news which supported this thesis. Now, suddenly, the hours listening at the Krüüdners' old *Are* wireless set blighted the buds black once again. The Soviet advance had been repulsed at the River Narva,[5] Berlin announced that it would defend the Baltic states at all costs since they constituted an irrevocable part of the German *Kulturboden*, and the Allies admitted that they were not making any progress whatsoever at the foot of Monte Cassino. So the next months were not expected to bring any dénouement. And from the mainland came the news of the continuing arrests and mobilisation. Around that time, a police officer in a motor boat arrived from the Kaberneeme Naze: to make his regular check on the fishing licences of the islanders. As the boat approached, I had already long since made off into the juniper hillocks. But some while later, the border patrol boat and a trio of coastguards, two Estonians and a German, turned up on a couple of further occasions and searched three houses in vain – in effect begging for beer and a bite to eat. After such small tests of his nervous system, the creaky and toothless old Krüüdner became steadily more aloof: my stay on the island could simply not last for ever . . . His red-cheeked wife rebuked him on each occasion and would give me a wink: dearie me, their own boys were now spread all over the world, one in Russia, the other in Sweden, a third in America or wherever he might now be! In the present circumstances they could easily look after strangers! Especially as the young man happened to be Doctor Veski's close relative, and Old Joonas, that is to say the master of the house, had only managed to get his rheumatism under control thanks to the Doctor's ointments, so –

In these crosswinds of deliberation, it was Krüüdner's bitter and anxious air which most likely swayed me, so that I ended up taking the easiest way out: I bought myself onto the next Finland boat arriving from the Kaberneeme Naze for a thousand marks.

We had to leave in the middle of the night, but only if it was so foggy that the Keri lighthouse could not be made out. And in the late evening, it could not be seen. So the departure was on. But as I walked down to the shore, the moon had slid out from behind the clouds and the Keri lighthouse could be seen standing quite clearly on the horizon, across a stretch of sea still as a mirror. But the crew had meanwhile been at the moonshine and the gruff-voiced skipper explained that they were going to sail, come what may.

I thanked the Krüüdners for putting me up, bade them farewell and lugged my suitcase and bundle (the bundle containing Mrs Krüüdner's smoked leg of lamb and two huge loaves of bread) through the moonlit junipers down to the seaweed-strewn cove. I sat on a low rock at the water's edge, the boat being moored at an old fishing jetty fifty paces away, and waited for the dozen men, plus a couple of women, to assemble on the beach. Although one or two of the men had managed to get themselves tanked up, the people gathered more or less in silence, given the circumstances. Besides, such boat people consisted mainly of folk who were strangers to one another. All of a sudden, one of the crew came over, his feet crunching the gravel beneath him, sat down beside me and said:

"Hello, Peeter. I'm so dreadfully embarrassed to find you here. I mean to say – for you to find me. I'll pay you back right away," and he opened his neat leather suitcase, began rummaging around in it and asked while still fumbling: "Have you got your novel with you?"

This acquaintance, met so unexpectedly, was Lembit Tammo. A former schoolmate, slightly older than myself. A swarthy lad of medium height and a sharp profile, very resolute, very erudite, a very stylish soul. During my university days, I had kept his company on occasions, for he could be an interesting type in small doses. All the more so, since despite the lean times we were experiencing, his knowledge of literature and literary theory had already made him a respected critic among the younger generation. But as regards the embarrassment to which he was alluding, the repayment of a debt and the novel, that is what my story is really about.

We had last met a month before at the Nõmme home of mutual friends, the Kasks, out near the Valdek marsh, eating a supper consisting of beet stew in their small flat, and sipping *Mäe Pisarad* schnapps. Apart from the host family and myself, there were present only Lembit and his stately, beautiful and long-legged redhead Iira Vingissaar. I had taken Lembit aside and handed him the three hundred marks he had asked me for when I had rung him to invite him over to the Kasks. He was in desperate need of the money to settle a debt. And I had recently pawned some Meißen cups which Aunt Anna had left me at Pastarus's for five hundred marks. His present embarrassment stemmed from the fact that he had now wished to rush off to Finland without having settled his debt with me ... He said, rummaging among items of clothing:

"This is no doubt the finger of God. That we should happen to be sailing together. Here ..." and he handed me a book. In the darkness of the night I could not see what it was but had the feeling it was something quite ancient. I protested:

"... Listen – why go and give ..."

"No, no!" he said with his characteristic resoluteness –" Keep it! Since I don't have any money. But it is Stahl's Estonian Grammar. Anno 1637. In Helsinki you can get around six hundred marks for it. Well, let's say five hundred, let's say four. As one or two pages are damaged. And it's got my *ex2olibris* in it. Anyway, not less than four hundred. So it covers my debt to you, at any rate." And he asked once again: "Have you got your novel on you?"

The people who could ask me anything at all about my novel, people who knew of its existence, amounted to no more than those four: Toomas and Taimi Kask, old friends of mine and literature buffs through and through, Iira Vingissaar, a woman who, as far as I was aware, had taste – though I had heard that she was busy being tastelessly unfaithful to Lembit with a certain

Puustagu – and Lembit himself. I had, that evening at the Kasks', showed them my newly completed manuscript. I had told them of its contents and read out substantial passages to them.

I understood that bringing up the topic of my novel right now was, to a certain extent, a way for Lembit to avoid having to talk about the debt. That too. But it was nonetheless typical of him: to start talking about a novel at just such a time, in the agitation of departure, under the bare heavens, with the toes of one's boots already in effect in the sea . . .

I opened my plywood suitcase there and then on the bare frosty mattock and pushed the Stahl Grammar in on top of the lambswool jumper.

"OK. So long as you're not fleecing yourself by doing this. But there's no Uncle Rockefeller waiting over there for me either. But the novel – is right here." I tapped the cover swathed in the jumper.

"Haven't you left a second copy behind?"

I shook my head.

He said: "Well. You'd run less risk of losing it altogether. That would be such a damned shame. Though over there I suppose you'll . . ."

He rattled on for ten minutes about my work – which he had never even read in its entirety – about its vices and virtues, the genre, about retouching parts of it, its place in Estonian literature somewhere between Gailit[6] and Hindrey, one or two stylistic elements it had in common with Tuglas, the aspects that could basically be attributed to myself, that is to say being trammelled by the ponderousness of the beginner, the cheap glitter of a political tract which certain passages exhibited – so that the work should under no circumstances fall into the hands of the German authorities, at least not while they had any power over the author – and then he went on to talk about – as he put it – the great precision and intensity of the flow of inner life . . . All this seemed, sitting there on the rock, a little absurd. When, instead, he should perhaps have been trying to grasp what was actually happening to us. And even more absurd when Tammo, on being called by the skipper, rose to his feet and walked beside me towards the boat, and as he got into it stumbling over rocks and getting water in his boots he continued to talk unabated. And I remember that when, with one foot in the boat and the other on the stone of the jetty, he looked over his shoulder at me and said the manuscript reminded him of something by a Charles de Coster[6] with a Joyce-fixation, I could not hold back a stab inside me, for however far apart these authors may appear to be, I realised my work to be hovering somewhere in between *Ulysses* and *Til Eulenspiegel* . . .

Our boat was a former spirits smugglers' hull and could still manage her twelve knots, and it was this which no doubt made our gallant boatswain so especially confident. Though the boat could take many more than the fourteen people, especially as some seemed to have full-sized suitcases with them. When we had left the cove and the captain let the engine turn at full revs, the prow stuck proudly out of the water, while the stern, where I had found a place with my suitcase and my bundle, hung alarmingly near the surface, the wash dashing itself noisily and frothily against both sides of the vessel.

Despite the twelve knots, it felt as if we would never get away from the shore at Aksi and as if we were almost at a standstill on the leaden sea. That we were clearly asking for trouble – a black snail crawling across a silver salver in the moonlight. That we expected at any time the swiftly approaching Germans to turn up in pursuit of the pop-popping chug of our engine. Tammo had made for the shelter of the wheelhouse and I had nothing to say to strangers. So that in the maddening anxiety caused by the mirror-smooth and odiously bright sea where we lay exposed, as if in a moonscape, it seemed that I simply began recalling the contents of my so-called novel out of sheer defiance.

It had been written, it seems to me even today, as follows: a mixture of life, hearsay and invention, difficult to separate, and where both public and private aspects, as well as both perceptions and action were more or less freely (and more or less recklessly) added to, and exaggerated.

Two hundred closely typed pages. A young man (present-day readers of my stories will recognise a certain percentage of him) has moved to Germany with his parents on account of his father. He has married a half-Jewish woman who dies there. In the spring of '43 the man comes, or rather flees, back to Estonia – and here, unlike in *Til Eulenspiegel*, it is not the Klaas of the story but his Nele whose ashes are carried in a pouch close to the heart. The novel, if that is in fact what it was, consisted of the diary jottings of this young man for one year of the Occupation of Estonia. A diary of both his thoughts and actions. What was noted down ranges from autobiographical self-torment right up to the most poisonous commentary on the era, while the diary of events presented a certain amount of documentary detail and scenes against whose background Tammo's comment that the diary was dangerous from the point of view of the authorities rang all the truer. No doubt on account of those pages which described the hero breaking into the store at the Jägala[7] camp where items confiscated from the prisoners were kept, into the warehouse full of the belongings of those murdered, a warehouse housed in an old building on Karja Street right in central Tallinn, and the scene with a certain Herr Enckell, a Swedish journalist, who is staying in Tallinn to comment on the current situation to the international Red Cross – who refuses to take with him clothes of a hundred prisoners, obtained off-the-peg in Prague, Vienna, Brünn, Riga, Tallinn and Warsaw, also children's clothes – good Lord – how he not only refuses to take them with him: but even refuses to touch them with a bargepole . . . Until my protagonist flees to Sweden as the Red Army crosses the River Narva into Estonia – for as a person who in 1939 was regarded as a German, there was very little good to be expected from the East – until he flees, carrying his manuscript, to Sweden – and submits the German version of his manuscript to a publishing house and the well-educated man who accepts it turns out to be the fateful Herr Enckell.

"Look out! Look out! Here they come, the bastards!" – "We're all buggered!" – "Fucking hell!"

I was wrenched away from my meeting with Herr Enckell right back to the present. My luminous watch said twenty-five to two. Ahead lay Keri Island, a couple of sea miles distant, slightly to port. From the western shore of the island a German patrol boat was approaching. It was doing three times the speed of our boat and was heading almost straight at us so that we seemed to be flying towards one another.

"Turn to the north! To starboard! Northwards!" someone was shouting. I thought that we were going to go down anyway. The captain was bawling: "Keep off the reefs! She's going aground."

Our boat, loaded down to the gunwales, changed course so abruptly that the deck almost touched the water, then righted again. But our manoeuvre had been spotted at once. We were given a rocket signal ordering us to stop. We pressed on in a northerly direction. Then the patrol boat changed course – it had now passed the island sufficiently to be coming in our direction – to starboard and sped towards us along our new trajectory, emitting a burst of machine-gun fire at the distance of half a kilometre.

I am unable to describe in retrospect either the lacerating feeling of failure or the agitation at coming unstuck, stunning and petrifying at one and the same time, which I of course felt. One or two of the passengers huddled in a mass under the protective cover of the upper deck and clung to their places, others began to clamber over the luggage into the wheelhouse while others again were crawling out over that same luggage. Someone was shouting: "Death and destruction – I said so right from the start!" What I myself was doing I cannot rightly say. Then someone shouted:

"Anybody with compromising stuff – overboard with it!"

Ten seconds later two briefcases flew from the stern into the water. A couple of lighter objects followed; I imagine a couple of the passengers had thrown away their revolvers. And I rummaged in my jacket, anorak, and trouser-pockets in search of the key. So that I could open my suitcase and throw the manuscript into the sea. But the key was nowhere to be found. I had no doubt lost it in the dead grass of Aksi, or among the pebbles along the shore. I rammed the blade of my pocket knife into the seam of the suitcase and prised away so that the lock might give, but the damned case (Uncle Aadam had obtained it God only knows where after his house had been burnt to the ground) would not give an inch. And in the relative calm in which our boat was now rocking now that the engine had been cut off, the approaching throb of the patrol-boat engines could be heard – my God – it could only be fifty metres away now! So I threw my whole suitcase overboard.

I shall not attempt to describe how the patrol hove to, how we were taken aboard, how we sat in silence on our luggage in the juddering hold, our early-morning arrival in black despair at the sunny harbour of Tallinn, nor the SD lorries which transported us to the church hall of the Kaarli church. There we were separated at once. But the less anyone knew anyone else there, the better. All the grim natural laws of universal tyranny seemed to apply in our case especially. And I remember how I felt a certain relief when Lembit and myself were assigned to different cells. For I had already committed one thoughtless, but blatant, *faux pas* as far as he was concerned. As we bobbed up and down Tallinn-bound in the patrol boat, I had not observed his particularly depressed mien in time, and had asked:

"Iira didn't come with you then?"

To which Lembit replied "No!" as sharply as if struck by an axe – and added, as if the shaft had been broken by that "no" – "Iira moved in with Puustagu last Tuesday."

Nor shall I attempt to describe my first interrogation, insolent of course, and yet perfunctory and formal, or my quick removal to the Central Gaol then, during the first days of May along with Sofronov and Lill, of whom I have already spoken.

At first, I was, at least, optimistic. Of course the German Army awaited me and the punishment battalion. But *some* way would surely be found to sneak off underground, or even get to Finland. So that compared to Sofronov with his bruised back and the changeable moods of Lill with his death sentence, my fate was a shamefully easy one. My only concern was to aver – as I had done during the first and only interrogation – that I had been hiding for three weeks in the vicinity of Õuna Street among ruins and in cellars and that I had left Tallinn for Kaberneeme Naze by bus and boarded a boat which happened to be waiting there. About the three weeks on Aksi Island and the Krüüdner family I was as silent as the grave. So that the first month in the cell – Kraav and Salu came a week or so later – was quite embarrassingly comfortable. Soon, the days nevertheless turned into weeks, the first second, third and fourth, which led to an element of unease. And not only that. Also hunger. Only for the first three days did the two-hundred-and-fifty-gramme daily bread ration seem ridiculously generous and the stories of hunger in the prisons, a malicious fiction. But when it transpired that this, along with a drop of soup and a little porridge was the only fare, hunger made its presence felt within a week, and old mother Krüüdner's loaves and legs of lamb obsessed me to a quite ludicrous extent. But in the growing hunger and worry I found one solace: every day spent in prison was one day nearer to the final solution, whatever conditions may have to be faced on the road which led there . . . And what conditions could they be? Some commission or other sending me to the punishment battalion . . . Three leaden-eyed types with SS-epaulettes who would rap out questions in my face as to why had I betrayed every Estonian's noble duty to join the German Army at this time, and tried to flee to Finland . . . ? What difficulties would it cause me if I were to allow the doglike voices to graze past my ear, look them all in their blue eyes and say: "Gentlemen, I was acting in the steadfast belief that my exchanging the armed forces of the Führer for those of his friend General Mannerheim[8] could under no circumstances qualify as betrayal." But why to Finland? Because the latest Berlin Radio broadcasts had given me the impression that, as regards the front of Greater Germany's dreaded struggle, the southern thrust of the Finnish front was most under threat and the application of my efforts *there* would consequently be of most use . . . They would then bawl me out to a greater or lesser extent, depending on what they had had for breakfast, but there would be no question of my being shot. They would simply send me, at best, to the Lavassaare camp, to the peat bogs, from where a good many had managed to escape, or, in the worst instance, to the punishment battalion – on the road to which opportunities for escape always presented themselves ... So as far as I was concerned, there were no particular problems for the time being. Until one blindingly bright July morning I was led through the prison gates to a car (my God, how fine that summer of 1944 seemed to be!) and was driven sitting between two uniformed men in an open Mercedes through the kissably beautiful city to Kaarli Street where I was taken into a bright dusty and half-empty office where I was told:

"Take your things!"

No, no, this could not mean I was going to be set free. I cast that delusion aside immediately. But neither was I expecting what awaited me. In the middle of the floor of the room lay a heap of suitcases and packages. Presumably, the luggage from our boat. And there among it all, fantastically, by chance, unbelievably – not in the middle, not at the edge, not exposed, nor too hidden by the rest of the luggage – lay my plywood suitcase which I had thrown into the sea. I recognised it at once. And sensed at the same time how the two officials in the room were scrutinising my actions and reactions.

It was, in fact, a foolish surge of conceit lasting a mere second, which came over me at that moment. I was horribly shocked. I felt the fear of death clutching at my heart: all is lost! My manuscript, everything that was said there, is in their hands! I have absolutely nothing to look forward to now. And yet at the same time the stab of rage of the desperate gambler seized me: So be it! But I must do everything in my power to prevent *them* from having their way. I must *play along*, as long as I possibly can ...

I did not delay for more than three seconds. I stepped up to the heap of luggage, moved aside a few bundles, eyed the suitcases. I said, as neutrally as I possibly could:

"I had a sailcloth bag ..." and added with light irony – I do not know where I summoned it up from, presumably my almost total entrapment summoned hidden resources – I added with light irony: "There were two loaves of bread and a smoked leg of lamb in the bag – I could have done with it now, but I can't see it anywhere."

I was sure that the SD had already laid their hands on all the eatables.

The senior of the two officials said: "The food supplies were mouldy and had to be thrown out." Following my light irony, he said this with slight nervousness – and then asked in a very matter-of-fact voice:

"But why don't you take your suitcase?"

And I answered, with slight surprise and as much casual aplomb as I could muster:

"I didn't have a suitcase."

"I see."

Strangely enough, they did not insist any longer. I was taken out of the room so that I had the opportunity to think: the suitcase must clearly have drifted on the surface and been fished out of the sea as the patrol boat caught up with us. And as there was at first glance nothing of any particular value in it, it was taken along with the rest of the luggage to SD Headquarters. Here it would, of course, have aroused interest: *one* of the refugees had tried to get rid of it. So the SD, of course, opened it. And found my manuscript, without the name of the author, thank God, but intact, wet with the seawater, thoroughly soaked perhaps, but fully and fatefully readable ... Thank heavens there was nothing, absolutely nothing, which could link the suitcase to its owner with any degree of certainty. Apart from the nameless manuscript, I had packed a couple of woollen jumpers, several pairs of socks, a pair of handkerchiefs without a monogram (I have all my life considered monogrammed handkerchiefs as something atavistically petit-bourgeois) and some tins of preserves. It could be imagined that they carried out the same experiment as they had with me with all those who had been on the boat. So that *up to now* no one would have admitted to being the owner of the suitcase. No one after me would do so either – so that it would be *most interesting* to see what happened next . . . And then right there, five paces outside of this experiment room – the thought struck me that in the case there was also the Stahl Grammar with Lembit Tammo's *ex libris* in it . . . ! So that the suitcase could immediately be linked with Tammo. I did not know whether right away. Since I do not know whether the *ex libris* included his full name, which was of course most likely, or only his Christian name or simply his initials. But at any rate one would only have to open the said publication and make some professional enquiries . . . So it would lead to Tammo in any case. And had presumably already done so. And then? Tammo would deny that the suitcase belonged to him. That was clear. But *what* would he say? Would he yell: "It's Peeter Mirk's suitcase! I remember: he opened it on the shore at Aksi and pushed the Stahl Grammar I had just given him inside. Take a look for yourselves!" – Or would he remember the deadly nature of my manuscript and tell them: "The suitcase doesn't belong to me and I haven't a clue whose it is" – ?

I felt, while I was walking down the corridor towards the exit, a strapping fellow in a dark blue suit on either side: now the most fantasy-filled combinations of hope and hopelessness are bursting alternately in my head . . . At the same time one of my warders steered me into a room and shut the door behind him so that we were just the two of us in the room. He allowed me to take a seat at the writing desk, sat himself down behind it, took a sheet of paper out of the drawer, laid it in front of him and said:

"We are going to note down the fact that none of the items on display belong to you. OK?"

"OK!" I said.

He wrote a one-sentence report and let me sign it. Then he put the pen back in the drawer and looked me in the face with a certain perplexity (or very well-feigned perplexity) -a sturdy white-haired man with deep-set grey eyes, a broad, slightly weather-beaten face of that exceedingly national type, behind which I had learnt to discern not only sheer heartfelt boorishness,

not only a sense humour like sawdust, a ready touchiness and
mute enmity, but also the potential for unreasoning brutality. He
looked up from the faded greenish paper of the writing desk and
looked me straight in the eye:

"... You know – I will do all in my power on your behalf ...
Tell me – is there anything I can do for you?"

I remember with great clarity the confusion I felt on hearing
those words: This is a provocation without a doubt! And, incidentally, from this point on it has become quite clear that I am no
longer being regarded as simply one of the lads who had tried
to make it to Finland – unfortunately ... And maybe it is not
simply a dirty trick ... Even *here* in this building such men do
exist ... Perhaps this white-haired chap really is offering to help
me. The chances are ten to one against, a hundred to one ...
But even in that case he's not treating me like just one more
failed Finland escapee. But has read my manuscript and realises
it to be mine (hmmm ...) – but is positively inclined towards
it ... But I just *can't* go and tell him: if you agree I'll show you
the ruins and cellars where I spent the last three weeks in hiding.
And then give me a chance to escape. And then do so yourself
too, of course. Since after letting me go you won't be able to
hang around any longer ... No, no, no, I simply can't ... But
should I then go and tell him: "Go to Dr Veski's and let him
get rid of my typewriter – before any search of the house takes
place!" (For the authorship of the text would then be an irrefut-
able fact.) Or could I say to him: "And let Aunt Ella, that is to
say Mrs Veski, burn up the contents of the rag bag." For similar
reasons of house-searches. An ordinary bag of rags. Which for
some ridiculous reason was saved from the fire. Cut into small
pieces with scissors. To stuff cushions with. Instead of feathers,
as the geese and ganders of this country had been plucked bald
by the master race for their eiderdowns ... (For into that bag I
had stuffed those hundred patches of cut-up off-the-peg clothing
from Prague, Vienna and Brünn which the prototype for Herr
Enckell had refused to touch with a bargepole ...) Can I? For
God's sake.

"No. I'm afraid there's nothing special you can do for me. You know best what you are able to do. If only you wish to."

His colleague entered the room: "Ready?"

"Ready."

We got up and they both escorted me out of the room without a word. And then, as we had descended the stairs and walked along the corridor towards the outer doors – I do not know whether it happened by accident or design – Lembit Tammo was led past between two uniformed men. He looked unexpectedly ghastly. Quite grey. But perhaps I looked the same to him. We exchanged glances. In silence. We were unable to say anything to one another.

I was again driven through the sunny town which had become even more unreal in its sunny, friendly disposition – an unreality, as I now suddenly understood, which had already been so characteristic of the city that morning. And when I had arrived back in the murky Cell 36, smelling as it did of chlorinated lime, I attempted to systematise my most recent impressions and draw conclusions as to how I should react.

The answers to some of the questions had been quite elementary.

Until I received proof to the contrary, I would regard my conversation with the white-haired officer as a provocation.

As far as Lembit Tammo was concerned, everything depended on whether he told them the suitcase was mine or that he hadn't a clue as to whom it belonged.

Was there any point in my denying that I owned the suitcase if Tammo had told them it was mine?

I came to the conclusion: presumably not. And did not for the present consider *what* the consequences would be.

Was it likely that Tammo would say he didn't know to whom the suitcase belonged?

I came to the conclusion: at least to begin with. For he was not a blabbermouth by nature. Despite his profusion of erudite expressions. And he knew what his statement would mean for me. But how could he explain away the fact that the Stahl

Grammar with his *ex libris* in it happened to be in the suitcase?
He couldn't . . .

I climbed up on the stool and, on account of the fug, squeezed
my face into the triangular gap between the window, which stood
ajar, and the frame.

The sea was washing leisurely up at the gravel of the embankment under my window. The majestic silhouette of the city was
mirrored in the peaceful lilac pink of the bay. In the sea roads,
two dark-grey landing craft were moving in the direction of the
Paljassaare peninsula, the chug of their engines barely audible.
Beyond the battery at Vana Patarei, a white boat with two sets
of oars was sailing, presumably to haul in the cod lines . . . One
hundred metres to its right, on the other side of the barbed-wire
entanglements, a number of naked brown-skinned Kalarand boys
stood argy-bargying and sprang with a crunch of gravel into the
turbid waters of the nether reaches of the fishing harbour . . .

Tammo *could*, of course, explain it away! More or less convincingly at that! He could explain that he was in financial difficulties.
He could pay back his creditor with that I.O.U. – worth three
hundred marks. This would not be dangerous and would add
weight to the credibility of his story. For he could say that he
sold books to pay off his debts. The Stahl Grammar among
others. To a stranger. Obviously, a book speculator . . . Where?
Oh yes – in the café of the House of Art. At the back behind the
right-hand table. (Such details might seem superfluous but would
raise credibility.) When? A couple of days after the March bomb-
ings – when it transpired that book prices could fall *even lower*.
What did the buyer look like? Small. Rotund. Clipped moustache, slicked-back ginger hair, parted in the middle. And wire-
framed glasses. He, Tammo, knew nothing more about the
business. Nor how that book, his *former* book had ended up in
that suitcase, nor to whom the suitcase belonged . . .

I grew tired of hoisting myself up by the bars to breathe the
sea air and stepped back down from the stool. And understood:
what *naïveté*! They will deal with all fourteen of us from the boat,
one by one. My manuscript is so criminal in their eyes for them

not to do so ... God – those disciplinary beatings of railway
workers (the brother-in-law of my protagonist is one of those
beaten) – those ribald anti-Führer jokes by the boys in the Leegion (my protagonist hears them with his own ears and scoffs
along with an untameable glee) – the excesses of those little,
timid, cruel and greedy home-front Führers with their dreams
of the manor houses they would obtain (my protagonist observes
them on many occasions when staying with his grandfather in
the country) – and those transports to the Jägala polygon (my
protagonist observes them from the window of a roads' inspector
with whom he is acquainted at Raasiku Station, and also listens
to the bursts of machine-gun fire in the pine groves behind the
camp, his heart pressed to the ground). And the break-in at the
stores (my protagonist takes part himself ...).

They will deal with everyone one by one. And arrive at the
conclusion that there never was any book speculator on the boat.
Nor anyone else capable of writing literature. Apart from Tammo
and myself. And then they will soften us up to a sufficient degree.
Not necessarily Germans. Oh no, those doing the dirty work,
those whose job it was to make us confess, will not only be
Germans. Oh yes: it was Estonians who had smashed in the nose
of my schoolmate Jüri back in '41 – on the suspicion of having
Red sympathies – although his father was one of the founders of
the blue-black-and-white Republic and he himself religious from
his early years on. So that Estonians could well be let loose on
us. In their number there might be, say, that kindly white-haired
chap ... Maybe even some personal acquaintance or other: I had
indeed seen one of them in the building already! And got an idea
of his attitudes. While Whitie was writing his report, someone
wearing the greenish uniform of a police officer opened the door
and stuck his head inside. And recognised me. And I him. It was
one of those hundreds of boys and girls who, along with myself
some six years before during the period of our matriculation, had
shaken hands with President Päts on receiving our final results.
The son of an officer and a soldier from the time of the War of
Estonian Independence. Now with his own officer's stripes.

Those belonging to this building, admittedly. And a pointed moustache under his nose. He stuck in his head, recognised me – it was possible that he already knew of my presence there and was looking in merely to express his disdain – and said:

"Aha. So we're *so* far apart now, are we . . . ?" shook his head with indignation and shut the door again . . .

. . . So they are beginning to soften us up . . . And if we nevertheless do not own up, either Tammo or myself, that the fateful suitcase and the fateful manuscript within are mine – then they will go along to Pääsküla and drop in on Uncle Aadam and will find in my room (my former room) my old *Continental* and will then be quite sure of the provenance of the manuscript. They would not even need to bother tipping out the contents of Aunt Ella's rag bag onto the table and rummaging through them . . .

And all this will happen if Tammo does not tell them that the suitcase is mine. But if he does . . .

I took the aluminium spoon from the shelf in the cupboard and knocked on the water tap: *tap-tap-tap-tap-tap*. My neighbour responded and I tapped out: *dot-dash-dash-dot dot-dash-dot-dot dot-dash dash-dot-dash-dash dash-dot-dash-dot dot-dot-dot-dot dot dot-dot-dot dot-dot-dot dot-dot-dash-dash-dot-dot.*

My neighbour replied: *dash-dot-dash-dash dot dot-dot-dot,* and I set out the chessmen, which consisted of buttons, without further ado.

By way of tapping we managed to telegraph throughout this wing of the building. It seemed incredible but it really was so: flawless Morse Code contact could be maintained with the neighbouring cells by way of the water pipes. Knocks from beyond the walls, ceiling and floor could not only be heard quite clearly but even quite loudly. So that even messages from the neighbours on the floor above could be heard, more faintly, but nonetheless audible. How such a system of plumbing came to be installed in this prison which was specially intended for the preliminary investigation of political prisoners was truly hard to explain. That this had been done with the very intention of inciting the prisoners to make contact and then to monitor them just did not correspond to the inventiveness of the authorities that had ruled this country for the last twenty years. Though you never could tell . . . The piping and its strange qualities was, at any rate, a fact. And the fact that *right now* the system was simply not used by the SD for obtaining intelligence, that is to say, that there were no investigators here and there who were busy noting down the information conveyed by means of tapping on the pipes, was just too good to be true. But a game of chess with one's next-door neighbour was an entirely neutral affair. It could only be regarded as dangerous by the ill-willed and vengeful idiots of the guards. They would come running if they heard water-pipe-Morse tapped the slightest bit too loudly, usually rushing up to the door of the cell, whipping open the peephole cover and pouring into the tiny box of the cell a rank mouthful of Feldwebel's invective. The most evil among them, such as the doddering seventy-year-old groucher, the black-as-night Veiman, would naturally report the whole business and put the cells in question on short rations. I have to say that during the first month to six weeks that wouldn't have disturbed me particularly. Though from the time that Uncle Aadam had traced my whereabouts and Aunt Ella had begun sending me packages, prohibitions would have hurt. And yet in a more critical and fundamental way, a game of chess with one's neighbour was harmless, even if you did not altogether know who he was. As was the case here. I knew that in Cell 35 there was a man from Rakvere by the name of Jalakas who had telegraphed as his reason for being interned: the events of nineteen-forty-one.

So I set up my chessmen – we couldn't manage to play without both board and pieces – and we struggled through four games. Till we were worn out – a state clearly reached by my partner at the same time as myself. Usually the number of games won was roughly equal. That evening, despite every attempt at concentration I was *somewhere else* and it was all I could do to force a stalemate even in the fourth game. It seemed that just that night the blazing streak of the July dawn cut into the ashen distress of my sweat-drenched dreams like some blood-drenched omen. And

I had the impression the very next morning, or it may have been a couple of days later, that the doctor whom I had not seen for a week or so was there, the old querulous Vicar of Bray doctor, neither humanist nor sadist, who had sweated away several stone on account of the two-month-old epidemic of typhoid fever; though he himself was guilty of neither the epidemic nor the horrible theatricals staged by the SD later to "account for" the epidemic. Three medical orderlies, political prisoners, were hanged in the prison yard, accused of having spread the disease by having lice. From the individual prison cells no one was taken out to witness the drama but from the large communal cells prisoners were ordered to stand and look on. Anyway, on the threshold of my cell stood the doctor and asked:

"Have you got lice?"

"I have."

"Why the hell don't you kill them then?"

"I do. But every day there are another five of them in the seams of my underwear."

"So why don't you use the powder?"

He pointed to the drum on my bedside table. It contained a soup-spoon full of German Army issue louse powder which we had been ordered to sprinkle into our collars. I opened the drum and thrust it under the doctor's nose.

"I do. It works marvellously. See for yourself. I've got ten lice in the powder itself for the fourth day running. And they seem to be thriving on it."

"Hmm. Any complaints?"

"Yes. Lack of sunlight. Lack of exercise. Lack of freedom."

"Hmm." He turned to the orderly who was standing behind him with a notebook: "One Vitamin B injection for Cell 36."

An hour later old Veiman took me along to the prison sick bay. It was situated in the same corridor in a one-man cell, with a sign over the door instead of a number. Veiman shut the door behind me and the badly shaven medical orderly put a swab in a bottle of ether:

"Roll up you left sleeve."

I thought: well, I hope he's not going to do what they are rumoured to do in Dachau and elsewhere.

But I had seen this orderly somewhere before – seen him before. He dabbed my left biceps with the ether and whispered in my ear:

"Doctor Veski would like you to know. You'll be set free if you admit to where you went into hiding. The Krüüdners are sailing shortly for Sweden. Don't admit to anything yet. Wait till they've gone. Look out towards the barbed-wire enclosure this afternoon. If you can see a white coat then you can tell them where you were hiding. Because they will already have left." And then aloud: "Sodding thick skin this young bloke's got, can't even push the needle in."

I wrestled with my feelings a short moment – but this time it just seemed too convincing! And I *had* indeed seen this orderly at Uncle Aadam's place. And so I whispered back:

"Tell Doctor Veski to get rid of my typewriter! And let Mrs Veski burn her rag bag."

"Well – *there we are* – at last . . ." The injection had already, of course, been given and the needle was already out and I felt a stab of fear while this orderly, with an angular face as if hewn from wood, was hamming his lines. Which turned into a stab of joy which I felt once back in my own cell. For the fact that Uncle Aadam had managed to contact me and that I had been able to convey to him the words of redemption – if it was only not too late . . . Relative redemption only, of course. For even if my words had not come too late, even if they managed to get rid of the typewriter and the rag bag, these were only the first and most immediate items of evidence. And the real state of affairs compared with Uncle Aadam's naïve hopes in me almost made me laugh . . . Good Lord – I had already been asked with whom I had been in hiding after Pääsküla and my story about the ruins and cellars of Sibulaküla in central Tallinn had already been scoffed at. For where someone who wanted to escape to Finland spends three weeks of his time was not particularly important.

Not now, at least, in comparison with the question of my manuscript.

And this last fact brought my thoughts back so fatefully to present reality. I seem to remember that a few days later, or perhaps it was a week, I was driven back to Kaarli Avenue. This time in a green sailcloth-covered lorry and through the grey pouring rain. I remember how the raindrops which I got in my face through the back and sides and through the roof, and which I tried to catch with my lips, felt strangely depressing and refreshing at one and the same time.

A man of medium height and around forty-five years of age, and with a small moustache and a shiny bald pate who seemed dangerous not so much on account of innate cruelty but on account of his experienced and insistent manner, sat waiting for me behind a desk. He opened an attaché case in silence and placed my novel, in the temporary binding I had given it, before him on the desk. I recognised both the unmistakable cover, the flyleaf and the ink blot on the top ends of the pages. The official looked me full in the face and said, prolonging his words slightly for theatrical effect:

"So, you deny that this work is yours."

I decided: admission can come at any time. Now it was a question of *playing for time*. I said – I hope I succeeded in saying so in as lightly a bored tone as I could:

"No – how could I go and do that?"

"Aha!" He was immediately pleasantly surprised. "So you do admit it's yours! Very well. That will make things a lot easier for us."

"I'm not admitting anything," I said with a peevish sigh of being in the right. "How could I have concealed, or lay claim to, something, if I haven't a clue what it is?"

"Ahaa . . ." sighed Baldie, and I saw his little grey eyes grow malicious. But he kept himself under control.

"Well, remind yourself."

He handed me the work and gave me time to leaf through it. Oh yes, it was the same work alright. The very same as I had dreaded. Without even a blemish. Not soaked through in the slightest. The writing quite clearly legible. Fatefully identical to itself. And I naturally thought at that moment: Why did it have to fall into their hands ... But – now at least it strikes me that I was not thinking: Why did I have to write things such as these in the first place.

... The world, I knew, had never before experienced a grimmer moral pandemic. But would anyone have any use for my experiences of it? Only, maybe, if I could put them down on paper ...

This country will be fine. When we have pacified it – conceded the Untersturmführer, placing a chewed crust neatly on the edge of his plate in the manner of someone well brought up. You, we'll send East, get you from under our feet. Stalingrad will be renamed Hitlerstadt. And you will, let us say, cart shit for the municipal flowerbeds. Or even become a policeman. It is up to you. He spoke in German, so that the host would not be able to understand. Only the remarks he smilingly tossed over his shoulder at the host were understood by the latter. But here, he continued, your former house will become my manor house. Here you reared ten head of cattle, but I will rear twenty. That is the difference. And if you like, the justification ...

... Bright green, transparent pine trees against a bright blue sky. Like tall notes in Bach's *Toccata*. Underneath on the heather – from another horrible world – the stench of petrol. And in the sand the snakelike imprints of tyre tread. I did not dare to venture up to those pines, whose trunks had been chewed at by bullets ...

... Wooden poles from wall to wall. Nails sticking out of both sides. Eight nails per metre. On each nail three overcoats. Lighter ones, darker ones. In the moonlight, the colours could not be distinguished.

> With fur collars and without. Twenty-four overcoats
> per metre. Sixty metres of overcoats. Each coat like the
> skin and plumage of a flayed bird. The skins of the baby
> birds on a separate pole . . .

I suppressed my feelings as best I could, and said with as much
aplomb as I could muster:

"It seems to be a work of literature. I am a lawyer, as you
know. I have written a couple of small specialist treatises. But
never any literature. That you may also know."

"You mean to say – this is not your work?"

"Of course it isn't."

"And you don't have a clue whose it might be?"

"Not the slightest."

I expected that the heavies were now going to enter the room.
Or rather – I didn't. But I feared that *now*, maybe . . .

Baldie said quite quietly:

"Look, let me tell you something. This manuscript was found
in a plywood suitcase. The patrol boat fished the suitcase out of
the water. Twenty or thirty metres from the deck of your boat.
The suitcase had been thrown overboard. To get rid of it. Not
on account of the socks and the sweater, but on account of the
manuscript, of course. Presumably the owner couldn't find the
keys in the rush. So that he could throw away only the manuscript.
We checked: in the boat there were only two persons who could
have been the owner: you and Tammo. And you do, after all,
know Tammo. The rest of them are out of the question. You
understand. Primary education. Half-completed secondary education. Blue collar professions: lorry driver, building-site foreman, shop assistant, a few schoolboys. Too lightweight a bunch."

I countered with the most obvious question:

"But why do you imagine that the person in whose suitcase
the manuscript was found must be the author? One of the poorly
educated men or one of the schoolboys could very well have
taken it for somebody else. God knows for what reason. He
wouldn't necessarily have a clue as to the contents. He'd just

been told that in case of trouble throw the manuscript in the sea. So against Tammo or me, you."

"Look, there are some things you can leave for us to decide, if you don't mind!" he yelled quite sharply, then growing pleasant again with unexpected rapidity: "I'm telling you: *either* Tammo *or* you. And what's more: we have reason to suspect Tammo a whit more than yourself. But only by a hair's breadth. For the time being. And now it is beginning to look as if it was you all along. Listen, I can tell you this: I understand people's protective instinct. But you must understand that every argument you use in your defence *throws suspicion* on Tammo! So – if it was you all along, then I must ask you, young man, *where is your moral fibre?*"

I have to admit that I had suspected the existence of such a question. The question as to what I should do in the event of their starting to suspect Tammo as having written my work. But I had rejected that particular version of my defence in insisting: of course it wasn't me! And of course it wasn't Tammo either. Simply one of the other twelve who had been acting as courier. Investigate who it is – and the author will soon be revealed . . . But although having this said right in my face did confuse me, I nonetheless managed to see the tragi-comic aspect of the situation lurking in the background: that Baldie with his thin, moist and pinched lips was asking me in this most amoral of buildings where my moral fibre was . . .

Baldie spoke: "Naturally, the consequences of the authorship of this text will be particularly unpleasant. *If* you happen to be the author, you will know this yourself. But a fully grown man must take the responsibility for his actions. You *cannot* just toss your responsibility over your shoulder so someone else gets punished. Especially in the case of a *friend*. And Tammo is almost a friend of yours."

At all events I was silent for a moment. Then Baldie continued:

"I said: the consequences will be particularly unpleasant. This manuscript is no joke. So only a straight confession will give you a chance. A physical chance, so to speak. I will leave aside the ethical side of things."

This time, I succeeded in opening my mouth and said:

"Tammo is quite capable of speaking for himself. And I did not write that manuscript. You have twelve more people to investigate. Why shouldn't some shop assistant or schoolboy have been able to write it? Or is it perhaps too *good*. When all's said and done, Bornhöhe[9] was only a schoolboy when he ... And besides: how do you know that you caught everyone who was on the boat? Who can know how many there were? The boatswain was completely drunk! Who could be sure that one of the number didn't jump overboard when we were stopped? Keri Island was only half a kilometre away. Kagusäär Reef even nearer. After a hundred metres a swimmer could touch the bottom. How can you know?"

Baldie looked me straight in the eye:

"So – it's Tammo?"

"I have been trying to tell you all along that I think it's someone else!"

"So you think it's more morally acceptable to let suspicion fall on a third party?"

I did not reply. Since I would only have been able to reply with a piece of insolence. Then Baldie said:

"Alright. I'll give you until tomorrow to think it over. And in the meantime, I'll be having a word with Tammo."

When I was back in Cell 36 – the rain had passed and the afternoon sun made the bay glitter – came the reaction.

The idea of the man who jumped overboard had popped up in my head and had seemed my salvation at the time. And while they were taking me back to the prison I had developed it to such perfection that it almost became the only convincing story. God, if none of the occupants of the boat were suitable as the author of the manuscript and they were all (and *had* all to be) innocent of being a courier for the manuscript – then the theory that the guilty party had been present but had escaped had a compelling logic of its own! That is to say: jumping overboard the very moment the patrol boat arrived. A panic reaction. Or a more or less impulsive attempt to get away. The man could have thrown the suitcase into the sea or jumped in with it. The man could have drowned. Most likely, incidentally, that he did. But he could have managed to get to Keri Island. He at least jumped into the sea with that in mind. And no one noticed him. It was night, after all! *How* light or dark it really had been – whether the moon had been obscured by cloud for a moment – no one would now be able to say for sure. It was, at any rate, half past one in the morning. And whether the island was a couple of hundred metres nearer or further away – that would be hard to establish with any certainty . . . If they checked with the light-house or the radio station they would say that they hadn't seen anything suspicious, no boats had sunk, no corpses washed ashore. And hiding on an flat islet of only a few hectares was impossible . . . Or perhaps a boat had really been carried away by the current. Perhaps some drowned man had been washed ashore. Then they would start to check – and time would pass . . . The proximity of the island did at any rate seem to me to give my variant a definite air of credibility. And everyone on the boat would be beyond suspicion . . . And I thought that Baldie had been genuinely surprised at my idea.

The stale air of my boxlike cell sobered me up within a few minutes:

Childish fantasies . . . No one will take the story seriously. No one will even begin to check. No one will even get to know of it. Since Baldie will brush it aside, preferring to entertain his own hypothesis. And even if it isn't all nipped in the bud and an investigation does take place, everyone will be obstructive, in the first instance the crew of the patrol boat: How could it have happened? Right there under the very noses of the patrol! No chance of anyone having jumped overboard! . . . And our own skipper will surely mention (and has surely already done so) a definite number: the boat contained fourteen people. So it was pointless to continue with this fantasy. Pointless even to think it . . . And furthermore, that appeal to my moral fibre . . . I felt myself breaking into a cold sweat . . . Wasn't twice two still four, even if a bastard or a murderer said it was? And now *he* will be

busy interrogating Tammo ... And since they suspect Tammo
slightly more than myself (on account of the *ex libris* in the Stahl
Grammar, of course) they might let the bruisers loose on him
... Right now, Tammo could be lying face down on the concrete
floor of the cellar of the church hall while they rain blow after
blow on his back ... And if Tammo still doesn't confess – or if
he does it will be my turn tomorrow – It is beginning to look as
if I myself will have to confess ...

I climb back up onto my stool and thrust my face out through
the window on account of the lack of air. The bay and the city
are there far away and are no concern of mine. Even that indifference is somewhere far away, but that makes me a little afraid.
And then I see it: on a strip of ground beyond the hundred-metre
long barbed wire enclosure a woman steps out from between the
low buildings by the shore, walks in among the empty net-drying
poles and is now over by the nearer boats which lie upturned on
the shore. And now I can see: she has long free-flowing black
hair, brown legs, white shoes and a white dress which lifts in the
wind. And now I recognise her. It is Doctor Veski's wife. It is
Aunt Ella. She walks over to the strip of land fifty metres beyond
the barbed wire, puts a towel on the ground, takes off her shoes,
turns her back to the prison and for a minute does warming up
exercises. Then she unbuttons her white smock and takes it off.
Standing there in her bright red bathing costume she lifts for a
moment her dress high in the air so that it is caught by the wind.
Then she puts her dress down on the bank. No one has as yet
run up to stop her or shouted at her. And with her calm, well-
trained step she walks over the gravel into water stained by the
oil of the boats and smelling of fish guts. Up to now, the only
swimmers here that I have seen have been dirty Kalarand urchins.
And now here swims an actress who is considered outstanding,
at least in the eyes of the theatre critics of her generation – I am
grateful and feel sorry for her at the same time ... A minute or
two later she climbs out of the water. Still no shouts or noise
from the guards, as usually happens with the urchins. And I can
see: Aunt Ella does not begin to dry herself off on her towel but

raises her dress in the air as if to dry it in the wind. Ten seconds, twenty, thirty. Only then does someone begin to shout from the prison and a green-grey young *Untersturmführer* comes rushing up to her on the far side of the wire. By the time he arrives she is sitting on the bank putting on her shoes. She stretches out her hand in the direction of the peaked cap of the officer and you can bet your life that she is saying: "Young man, be a dear and give me a hand. I'd like to get up." For the boy extends his hand. And they are walking along on the other side of the fence. The boy is explaining something and Aunt Ella seems to be smiling. They disappear out of my field of vision and I cannot tell whether Aunt Ella is taken to the guardroom of the prison or not. But it makes no difference. For she will no doubt get home from there. Get home safely. She will travel in the overfull goods truck triumphantly all the way to Pääsküla, triumphantly as she has carried out her risky little mission. Now I can own up to where I had been hiding. In a few days I will at least be out of prison and will think something up ...

I realise with depressing clarity what a pitiable lie it all is. I step down from the stool back into the cell. And suddenly, during one wave of anxiety, the knowledge hits me that I really do not have a hope. Neither physically, nor morally. As Baldie had so eloquently put it. For the truth will be beaten out of me. While, were I to remain silent I would undoubtedly be the death of Tammo. For the longer I remain silent, the more suspicious he grows in their eyes. Up to the point where he denounces me, at least. And if I succeed in remaining silent, my fate is sealed nonetheless. For they could still tolerate my leaving the place – though I had felt the scabbed weals on the back of the icon-faced Sofronov for myself – but they couldn't send me back into the world with such a back ...

And then I made up my mind.

Now, several decades later, it nonetheless seems that it was not a difficult decision to make. Quite the contrary – it was a liberating one. I sat on my stool, planted my elbows on the edge of the bedside table, held my head in my hands and said to myself:

tomorrow when Baldie summons me I will admit to having written the manuscript. And after that, it felt as if the whole of my body was that hand held convulsively against the wall or jamb of the door and suddenly released, rising, rising, rising as if to take wing.

I remember how I sat there on my stool in the corner, my shoulders against the wall. I felt that my shirt was soaked through but that I was neither hot nor cold. I had – I can say so *now* – I had the feeling a bottle of mercury would have as it shattered, its contents running out all over the floor . . . And I thought: I shall not now think about what I shall feel after having owned up to being the author . . . Now I will simply relax.

When I had come to my senses, my neighbour was knocking agitatedly on the pipe and, looking back on it, I imagine the knocking had been going on for some time. From the strength of the knocking it could be heard quite clearly that it was my neighbour. He telegraphed:

Thirty-three calling thirty-six.

I was not really expecting this. But I tapped out a reply:

Thirty-six listening.

And then came from further away:

Give your matriculation number.

I did not immediately grasp what was meant. Then, suddenly, I did. God! Me and Lembit, Tammo that is, noticed while at the Kasks' that our matriculation numbers happened to consist of the same digits: mine 16835, his 15368. So Cell 33 was Tammo's! He was trying to contact me and wanted to be sure that it was me who answered . . .

Very well. His attempt at contact was already useless. Not only on account of the walls in between. But also because of my decision which had come in between. But I naturally tapped out the reply:

16835.

And he answered:

15368 here. Listen. I won't be leaving after all. I have my reasons.

*Won't even try. Because of Iira. So the suitcase and the manuscript
are mine.*

And then, with eerie rapidity:

*Dot-dot-dash-dot dot-dash dot-dash-dot dot dot-dash-dash dot dot-
dash-dot-dot dot-dash-dot-dot.*

Silence.

I would have been equally confused had I received the message
written in normal handwriting. Then too, I would have read it
over several times. But this cursory tapping, gone a moment later
without leaving the slightest trace – as if it had never existed,
shook me right out of the indifference caused by my resolve to
confess:

What? He couldn't! What did it mean? What had I in fact
heard?

For the next hour and a half or so I kept trying to make
contact again. He did not answer. Then our evening tea water
was brought round. The sound of the hatch opening, bowls clink-
ing, water sloshing began to be heard, advancing from the left,
and arrived at my door – I carried my aluminium bowl with the
drop of warm water over to my bedside table and heard: footsteps,
Jalakas', my neighbouring chessplayer's, hatch being opened and
then shut again. His neighbour's also opening and shutting. The
next one should be Lembit's. Then someone yelled:

"What the fuck's he gone and done now?"

I heard old Veiman's dragging step as he ran, opened the hatch,
swore, phoned. Then Veiman's hissed words as he happened to
pass right above my half-open hatch: "The cunt would have to
do it during my shift . . ." Someone said: "No. A doctor won't
be necessary." Unknown officials walking along the corridor.
Then something heavy being carried past my door towards the
stairs. Someone whispered: "Yes, sir. With a strip of shirt. On
the lavatory pipe."

Three days later I was taken for interrogation in that same
prison. But it was no longer Baldie. Now it was the same one as
had asked whether he could be of any assistance to me. The only
thing he asked me this time was: *where* had I been hiding those

three weeks? He wrote down Aksi Island and the Krüüdners and said I should have said so right from the start. Two days later, I was taken to the office and a soldier was assigned to take me, along with my papers, to some major at the recruitment point for the *Leegion*. The fact that I was never handed over to him is another story. But my years of meeting Kraav, Sofronov and Salu when dreaming are part of this one. And my stepping into a single cell where on the privy box Lembit Tammo, who almost became my friend, is sitting and up to whom I step – up to whom I step to ask for forgiveness for some forgotten matter – is sitting – isn't sitting! – is hanging, his feet on the ground, his backside suspended in mid-air some five centimetres above the seat, and who turns towards me, friendly, silent, weightless in the draught, looking beyond me in a strange crooked sort of way. These entrances too, belong to this story. And to me. Unfortunately. And luckily.

1980

Translator's notes for "The Stahl Grammar"

1. During the interwar years of Estonian independence, *Petserimaa* was a part of Estonia. A province populated almost totally by native-speakers of Russian, it was given to the Russian Republic after Soviet annexation in 1944. *Läänemaa* and *Pärnumaa* are the northern and middle provinces on the Estonian west coast, while *Viljandimaa* is in the south of the country. During Soviet times a system of smaller oblasts was created in line with the Soviet system elsewhere, but in the early 1990s the old system was re-introduced.

2. Pskov (Est. Pihkva) Centre of a large Russian oblast sandwiched between the Estonian, Latvian and Belorus borders, plus that of the former Leningrad oblast. The city, which sports a huge kremlin, and which was occupied by the Germans 1941–44, was badly damaged in the fighting.

3. *Alliku* – a village to the southwest of Tallinn.

4. *Aksi* – an island in the Gulf of Finland to the northeast of Tallinn and near the larger island of *Prangli*. The *Kaberneeme Naze* is the nearest point on the mainland and the *Keri Lighthouse* stands far out to sea to the north. The Krüüdners belonged to the Swedish-speaking minority (*Estlandssvenskar*) who inhabited some of the Estonian islands.

5. The *River Narva* forms the present border between Estonia and Russia. During the interwar years, Estonia governed a strip of land on the Russian side of the river, which meant that both Narva itself and Ivangorod (Est. *Jaanilinn*) across the river were on Estonian soil.

6. *August Gailit* (1891–1960), *Karl August Hindrey* (1875–1947) and *Friedebert Tuglas* (1886–1971) all represent a somewhat aestheticising aspect of Estonian literature. *Charles de Coster* (1827–79) was the Flemish author of the archaic picaresque novel "Til Eulenspiegel", written in French.

7. *Jägala* – an Estonian arms storage area near Tallinn during Estonian independence, turned into a concentration camp by the occupying German forces. Another such concentration camp was *Lavassaare* in the Pärnumaa Province.

8. *General Mannerheim* (1867–1951) the Finnish Chief of Staff who skilfully steered Finland through World War II and is still held in great respect in more right-wing circles even today.

9. *Eduard Bornhöhe* (1862–1923) was a writer of patriotic novels set in feudal times, the Walter Scott of Estonia.

The Conspiracy

The Conspiracy

Picture a stone culvert twelve metres long, five or six metres in diameter, and distempered a greyish pink on the inside. It is bisected along its full length by a colourless, *ergo* ash-coloured, wooden floor. And we live on the part above the floor, in this vaulted corridor, walled up at both ends. At the sea end, there is a large barred window some of whose panes are missing, so that the biting sea air lashes straight in from time to time. And on occasions, pigeons fly in onto the stone sill to peck at bread-crumbs strewn by someone who has saved them up from his six-hundred-gramme ration.

In the wall opposite the window is a door lined with sheet metal, and supplied with a hatch and a peephole. Along both sides of the room, propped up against the curve of the walls, are iron-framed bunks. In the corner stands a stove with black metal facing, next to the stove a water ewer and in the other corner a privy. Along the length of the room a row of open lockers which forms a long table beside which stand benches for four or five men apiece. High above the table, completely encased in concrete lest someone tries to hang himself from it, is a huge iron hook which has been fixed there two hundred years before to take the strain of the strap used to hitch up a large cannon when aiming.

This is the nineteenth cell of Section Four of Tallinn Central Gaol. At this moment in time, i.e. the last days of October 1946, the cell houses twenty-two men. Twenty-two cases under investigation.

*　　*　　*

Art maintains its right to *select* its objects of study; the nature of this right may be debated but the right itself is indisputably valid. Let us therefore simply leave aside the more peripheral figures from among these twenty-two, and so look at those in the fore-ground in that most neutral of ways: by the order of their bunks. Thus we have:

Aaro Ahven. Sixteen years of age. A vocational school pupil from Kuressaare or Kärdla. A small fair-haired, bird-faced boy. His reason for being here was, of course, by his own admission (practically everything said here regarding such reasons is based on personal accounts): About a year before, in October 1945, Ahven had gone for a smoke during break at school. In a rarely used and dimly lit corridor. Then the bell went. Even in everyday life this blond lad was a little nervous, a bit of a worrier, and had a slight complex about tidiness and order. He stubbed out his cigarette against the heel of his shoe but did not actually throw it away. He looked around for somewhere to dispose of it. Ahaa – the door right by where he was standing led to the lumber room under the stairs. As it was unlocked, he tried to find an empty sardine tin, or some other suitable receptacle, for his fag-end. He lifted the latch. The door opened. And there in the half-darkness, amid the dust and the school lumber waiting to be thrown out or mended, he saw a picture. A black-and-white portrait in a dusty brown frame. Whose portrait, he did not know. But a portrait for which they had hammered a nail in the wall of the assembly hall and which had then hung there. Until the fly-specks and bleaching sunlight had done their work. And unfortunately this picture was not behind glass. No doubt never had been. Or the glass had been removed to cover the new por-trait. Unfortunately, because if the glass had been in place, the idea would never have struck the boy. He would have thrown his cigarette-end away into some old rusty washbowl or other. But now he took out his penknife. Not one of those useless blunt ones you could buy in the shops, but one his father had made him, and razor sharp. The sort with which he could whittle Daisies and Dobbins for his cousin Teet out of the hardest spruce as if it were mere clay. He thrust the blade into the corner of the mouth of the figure in the picture. And cut open the lips of this self-assured man. Drew the knife back to the middle (a whim lasting three seconds), twisted the blade enough to part the lips slightly – I can imagine that this action unexpectedly caused the smooth-jowled man to grin a little – and pushed the fag-end in between his lips. He then stepped back, stood admiring his work for a couple of seconds, went back out into the corridor, closed the lumber room door and went off to his class on Stalin's Constitution or Woodwork, or Locksmithying. A fortnight later he was arrested. Someone had seen his jest through the half-open lumber room door. He did not know whether this someone, secret observer and secret informer, was one of the pupils or one of the masters. Which made me strongly suspect it was one of the latter, some feeble old groveller who had prostrated himself face down in the mud under some burden of guilt or other, rather than one of the pupils, still almost children, the young workers of tomorrow and the days beyond. At any rate, Aaro was now here. His charge: Criminal Code, Paragraph 58, Section 8 of the Soviet Russian Federal Socialist Republic. That is to say with carrying out an act of terrorism. Even now, he still did not know on account of whose portrait this had occurred. Judging by the description he gave, it was likely to have been one of Beria.

The second man, in the neighbouring bunk to Aaro Ahven, was Ilmar Elken. Thin, swarthy and dark-haired as far as could be seen from the shorn heads we all had, he was around forty years of age but looked over fifty. In the eyes of nineteen or twenty of the inmates of this cell he was an extremely taciturn, somewhat maladroit man in glasses who, his hands trembling, would make roll-ups from loose *makhorka* shag and the tiniest of cigarette papers, and in whose bright gaze there stirred something strangely impertinent, but who seldom looked you straight in the eye, and only took part in the conversation of the cell sufficiently to avoid becoming conspicuous among the nineteen or twenty

others. For the other two or three inmates, Elken was an accomplished poet with the profile of Dante, and was, as someone once
put it, an almost prophetic bard who, on the strength of his two
small collections of poetry, had risen to these heights in the eyes
of the narrow circle of poetry lovers who, at least in their own
opinion, were of a high ethical standing and of discerning taste.
And was a man who was sitting here – as I saw it – almost of his
own volition. Eighteen months ago, he had been arrested and
in the first instance on a trumped-up charge which, even compared to the average level of charges at the time, seemed
ridiculous. One of the things he was accused of was that he had
listened to enemy radio broadcasts from abroad. Elken's first
investigator had deduced this from the utterances of the
neighbour in the flat next to Elken's. The dialogue between the
investigator and the neighbour will have gone something like this
(Elken saw the written report of the meeting on a subsequent
occasion):

INVESTIGATOR: Did Elken listen to enemy broadcasts from
abroad?

NEIGHBOUR: How should I know?

INVESTIGATOR: How could you not know when everything
can be heard through the partition wall! It has been checked.

NEIGHBOUR: Maybe, but I didn't understand them –

INVESTIGATOR: What do you mean you didn't understand
them? If you could you hear them clearly.

NEIGHBOUR: But they were in foreign languages, weren't
they?'

INVESTIGATOR: In foreign languages? Then they must surely
have been enemy broadcasts! And you are trying conceal the fact.
Don't you feel ashamed of yourself? You yourself work in a comb
factory. And yet you are trying to cheat the workers' authorities.
For whose benefit? For the benefit of the anti-Soviet intelligentsia!

On top of this, works by Nietzsche were found on Elken's
bookshelves. Which he had not rushed to burn in, as he put it,
the great and spiritually liberating bonfire of joy.

With these and similar accusations against him, Elken was
brought to Tallinn a month or so later – and here he happened
to get quite a different investigator. It seems that different types
also happened to exist.

The new investigator had said that Elken's Tartu file was useless (for which reason he had shown it to Elken) and had started
from scratch. Elken's decent knowledge of Russian, which the
Tartu investigator had derided as being intentionally inadequate,
was, according to this new man surprisingly good and Elken
derived great benefit from this opinion. Furthermore – the new
investigator had exhibited a certain amount of interest in poetry.
And Elken's knowledge of Russian poetry was even more
propitious in the eyes of the investigator. Elken had even been
an outstanding exception in these matters. For he had not
only thoroughly perused Pushkin and Lermontov, but also
Bryusov and Blok as no one else of his contemporaries apart
from a tiny handful of the youngest ones. At any rate, the new
investigator compiled a report which put Elken's explanations
from the three interrogation sessions in a particularly positive
light:

"So there we are. And now we just have to add: '*I hereby confirm
that I will in every respect support Soviet rule.*' And then you sign
it, and I think we can count on the outcome being the best
imaginable."

Elken said quietly: "But I can't sign that."

"Why not? From all you have said so far, it is quite clear
that . . ."

"No, no. You can see clearly from this document that I have
never consciously done anything against Soviet rule. Nor intend
doing so. That I can, of course, set my signature to. But something which says that I *positively support* Soviet rule – You see,
supporting one type of rule precludes the support of the other
types. Making a decision of that kind requires a good deal of
time and consideration. A good deal more, at any rate, than these
rather perfunctory chances for comparison which I have been
given. And I have to admit: a number of the principles, or at least

the practices, of Soviet rule are *so* alien to my way of thinking that I fear that I will, for a good while yet . . ."

"Listen here, my good man – can't you understand what you are doing to yourself?"

"Yes, I suppose I can. But what I can't do is sign this paper."

"Elken – don't be absurd!"

"I'm not being – Just think: in our report there is as yet not one syllable of untruth. Do we have to go and spoil it all now?"

He did not spoil it all. And was now awaiting sentence. In the best instance, judging by experience, he could expect, shall we say, five years of exile. For only those who *supported* Soviet rule were allowed to get off scot free – those who if not fervently, then warmly, if not warmly, then tepidly, or coolly, or icily, but at any rate to some extent supported Soviet rule! Not those who said, even when under investigation, that they needed time to think the matter over, nor those whose decision, even when this thought process had taken place, was still not entirely predictable . . .

The third man was SS Hauptsturmführer Joachim Gerlach, around forty-five years of age with a huge chest, a deep unbridled voice and a sallow face. He had escaped from a POW camp somewhere in the province of Viljandimaa and had been caught in the forest making his way southwards. In the shank of his boot he kept a knife, a whetted piece of bayonet, which he would, as likely as not, have used if necessity and opportunity had coincided. In private life before the war he had been the owner of a pottery workshop. Four employees. Making flowerpots and bird whistles. And although he lacked a talent for philology, he tried tenaciously to learn Estonian. Even before, he had been able to ask for bread, water, meat and milk. And now, he had picked up a number of new words which he repeated in his curt German accent: *dze Vest, dze East, dze Norß, dze Sauß, Roat, Taun, Hauß.* His interest in languages was too much part and parcel of his illusions of escape for me to be particularly keen on kindling these. Instead of teaching him the vocabulary of the countryside, I taught him poems. And these too he learnt by heart:

> In dze Scale, dze Fate of dze Vörlt
> Only veighs vonne Gramme.
> From Lecture Teatre to Madhauß
> A mere Schtepp for a Mann.[2]

But when, during the last days of October, a copy of the Soviet Estonian daily *Rahva Hääl* dated the 16th of that same month happened to find its way into our cell, and when I translated the execution of the sentences at the Nuremberg Trial (Ribbentrop hanged, Keitel hanged, Rosenberg hanged, Kaltenbrunner hanged, Frick hanged, Frank hanged, Streicher hanged, Sauckel hanged, Jodl hanged, Seiß-Inquart hanged, Göring poisoned himself) Gerlach looked through me at the white-washed wall beyond and said faintly but clearly enough:

"*Das ist nicht wahr. Das kann nicht wahr sein. Das ist eine sowjetische Desinformation.*" (Loosely: "Rubbish! Soviet disinformation!")

The next man, counting along the bunks from the window to the door, was Doctor Viktor Kuurmann. Sixty years old, fat, with a pock-marked face that once had been red and had now turned grey and who wheezed. He was here, as far as could be made out, on account of being informed on regarding his activities during the German Occupation in some provincial hole, whether Mustla, Mustvee or Mudila, I cannot quite recall, where he worked as the town doctor. From what we were given to believe, he had been accused, as a member of the local Recruitment Board during the Occupation, of declaring the perfectly healthy sons of some true-blooded blue-black-and-white Estonian businessmen and rich farmers unfit for national service, while sending some consumptive Red schoolmasters off to be mobilised. On this subject he would wheeze:

"Of course it's all old wives' tales. If I'd have slept with Manni more than Mari instead of the other way round, I would now have the cleanest record in town, wouldn't I?"

Before coming to Tartu to run a doctor's practice, Doctor Kuurmann had attended a seminary in Riga and spoke Russian with relish, maybe even more pithily than he did Estonian, brightening up life in Cell 19 no end with his improvised sketches involving quick changes of character, from a police officer of his youth, to a mayor or a rag-and-bone man; but he had his greatest success as a drunken Orthodox pope, necking with the wife of the deacon, while at the very same time the deacon is canoodling with the pope's wife. And when we asked him to tell about the most strange and inexplicable event of his years as a doctor, he related the following:

"Well, you all *znayete* what a ganglion is, a dead man's bone as it is called in these parts, and what the doctors call a periostic tumour. I had one myself for ten years or so – right here on the back of my right hand. Not a particularly large one. But rather a nuisance on account of where it was located. When I balled up my fist, or carried something in that hand, it always hurt a little. Anyway, one day I was told that one of my patients, an old alcoholic here in Tallinn, had been found dead. Without any ID papers on him. So I was called in to go to the mortuary and identify the body. And when the formalities had taken place, the duty doctor went off with his assistant to the adjoining office to write his report, leaving me alone for a moment with the corpse. It then struck me – things rarely strike me at *such* an opportune moment: why do they call a dead man's bone a dead man's bone? It is so called because from time immemorial people got rid of one by touching it with the hand of a corpse. During the washing of the corpse you touch the hands several times when applying the soap. And now here I was *in camera* with the dead man so to speak ... Well, as you *znayete*, twenty-five years' practice as a doctor doesn't exactly make you superstitious. But now – I stepped up to the bier and pressed my dead man's bone against the back of the right hand of the deceased. By the way, if my profession hadn't accustomed me to it I would have been surprised at just *how* cold the hands of a corpse can be. Pressed it once. Twice. Thrice. So that even I couldn't help smiling. And then I washed my hands, signed the report and stepped out of the mortuary at the Tallinn Central Infirmary, walked down to the tableware shop on Liivalaia Street, bought my wife some new teacups and had to hurry off with them to the station to catch the night train back to Tartu. Since my right hand would tire after about five minutes. Twelve cups and saucers and fruit bowls too. But as I was walking home from the station the next morning – I had to walk about one kilometre from the station – I suddenly remembered, just as I walked through the garden gate of my house: I had been carrying the package in my right hand all the way – without noticing any difficulties ... I remember putting the package down in the dark of the entrance hall, turning on the light and standing under the lamp: the dead man's bone had gone! It had vanished during my seven-hour train journey as if it had never existed. Well, I didn't exactly run off to the doctors' club to tell them of my discovery, but *here* I can admit to what happened. A fact is a fact."

And as regards the intimate theatre of the pope and the deacon, the doctor then played both roles by turns, rolling his eyes and spraying spittle in his enthusiasm. The lazy, smutty, gander-like, somewhat lisping pope and the voracious, jumpy, precipitate deacon – and, subsequently, both the pope's better half and the deacon's woman. For these latter roles the doctor had taken a straw pallet and panted and whispered as now the pope's wife, now the deacon's, played hard-to-get and sighed passionately. In the space of three months, I had occasion to see this performance three times. It can be supposed that the old man had played this charade dozens of times over the years, and yet never once did the act lack – how shall I put it? – creative improvisation. On each occasion he would modify his playlet. Each time, he would leave aside some of the less apt lines and add new comic asides and put ribald remarks into the mouths of his characters. And he enjoyed his own performances so much, forgetting himself and, as mentioned above, spraying so much spittle, that not even the most humourless spectator could avoid sharing the enjoyment.

*　　*　　*

The next man was August Karp, a lathe-operator from Kraamer's Machine Tool Factory. Fifty-five. Greyish blond hair. Wiry. Quite pale now but in the sun his face of a Red Indian would easily become a reddish brown and even more weatherbeaten than now. Gradually, during the fourth month of our acquaintance as neighbours in adjoining bunks, the facts trickled forth by way of his tart irony: he was in here because he had, along with the Kraamer's electrician, prevented the Germans from blowing up his factory. The two of them had both cut through the leads to the mines which had been placed in the factory workshops.

"So what are you doing in here? You should have been given a medal for what you did!"

"I very nearly was. The paper had been signed. When we got the factory back in our hands in October. But *that* was when all the trouble began."

"I don't follow."

". . . You see, it was then that some of the men began to recall how, three years previously, before the arrival of the Germans, the factory hadn't been blown up either . . ."

"Had it been mined in 1941, then?"

"Huh-huh."

"I mean to say – by whom?"

"On that occasion – by the Reds."

"And what happened that time?"

"The same thing."

"You mean *you* cut the leads then too?"

"Well, I suppose you could say that."

I remember how we were conversing in a whisper, lying on our bunks. The rest of the cell was asleep. I looked over at Karp's face – he might have been an old inscrutable Navaho chief – in the light of the electric bulb that burned throughout the night. God damn . . . I asked:

"But tell me, *why* did you actually . . . ?"

He was silent a short while: "You see – they came – young lads, complete strangers. They laid their charges all over the shop and went their way. If they had only *taken a look* at what a fine

state the workshops and workbenches and the floors were in . . .
I had put in thirty years of my life into that factory. And the
other one-hundred-and-fifty or so working there, heaven knows
how many . . . And if it had all been old Kraamer's property –
but it was now supposed to be the property of the *people* . . ."

"But – but you at any rate saved it for the Germans, in fact,
didn't you . . . ?"

"Do the Germans own it now?"

"Well – if you hadn't saved it the first time round, you wouldn't
have been able to save it the second time round, would you?"

"That's what I told the tribunal – "

"And what did they say to that?"

"They said: we're giving you your whack for what you did in
'41. You'll serve your ten years, and then we'll see what you get
for what you did in '44."

As a rule, Karp would be tinkering around with something,
his back turned towards the peephole in the door. Something
forbidden, that goes without saying. As raw material he used the
handle of his own toothbrush and those of his fellow-inmates.
When there did not happen to be any of those he would get
bakelite ballpoints or some such objects from men from the workshops whom we passed in the corridor during exercise. Using a
strip of tin as a saw and with incredible patience, he would slice his
raw material into white, red, blue and brown discs, a millimetre or
two in thickness. With a piece of wire, and the same patience,
he would bore holes through these. From the men in the workshops he would occasionally receive tiny pieces of aluminium
sheet metal or wire. He would wind the sheet metal around a
three-inch nail into a tube. And slid the coloured discs from the
piece of aluminium wire so that they alternated with the rings
made of aluminium. Knocking with endless patience and using a
small hammer without a handle which he had hidden behind the
skirting board, he riveted the rings and the discs together. Then
sandpaper would come into play and, finally, a piece of woollen
cloth. He rubbed, polished, burnished – whereupon the nail was
taken out of the tube and he was left with a smooth, glinting,

multi-coloured, slightly conical cigarette-holder – which made you think of decorative baubles you could find in bric-à-brac shops or on the market all over India or Africa. Usually, Karp would make them for those who gave him a chunk of bread in return but, as often as not, he would make them anyway, as in the case of young Aaro Ahven on his seventeenth birthday: "If you do have to smoke at all – and you're inside for smoking, aren't you? -then, here you are: so that you don't have to go around shoving your fag-ends into the Devil knows whose gob instead. But can smoke them up in a decent prison mouthpiece."

From time to time Sergeant Kõuk would make a foray into the cell in search of such forbidden items. They passed unnoticed during usual inspections with no trouble at all. But those of Sergeant Kõuk were rather special. As it happened, the moral standards of all the lower ranks of prison warders were lower than average. These men were dense, clay-headed, often quite shabby individuals. But among these lower ranks there were nonetheless no really pathological cases. Except, that is, for Sergeant Kõuk.

Sergeant Kõuk was a tall, thin, fresh-faced lad, whose jaw was slightly too large, and whose neck slightly too scraggy. He always entered the cell with a crash, always storming in, always pouncing, his face always blotched red as if angry at some personal affront (at times we imagined he might have been suffering from galloping consumption – I'm damned if he wasn't). Asking around during my time there I must have spoken to a hundred prisoners who had, during their collective century of experience of the Central Gaol, never heard Sergeant Kõuk do anything else but hiss, his words tumbling out in a barking snarl:

"Whtthfcksgngnhrthn!"

Ratch! A coat hanging against the wall was torn to the ground, so that the loop snapped. From bunks, here and there, a straw pallet was dragged – raaap! seam ripped open, paws inside. Rarely did he find anything there: in one month no more than an old scrap of newspaper or a strip of metal sharpened into a knife.

Karp had evidently caught Kõuk's attention during one of the latter's surveillance stares through the peephole and the sergeant had got wind of his anti-state cigarette-holder manufacturing activities:

Tramp, tramp into the cell. Karp's hinged bunk down from the wall with a *karpartsaki*. A bench kicked aside. The straw pallet, his coat, hat, kitbag, all rummaged through and left in a heap on his bunk. Nothing whatsoever. For Kōuk knew nothing about the tools behind the skirting board.

"Jcktvrhr!"

Karp took off his jacket with measured slowness. The sergeant snatched it out of his hand, held it by the tails and shook it. From the pocket, or between the lining, two cigarette-holders clattered to the floor, one of which being the half that Karp had just been working on. Kōuk tossed away the jacket and jumped onto the cigarette-holders. Hopping on his left foot, he stamped on them with his right – gasping in rapture, almost orgasmically – stamp-stamp-stamping them to smithereens – stopping to catch his breath and panting:

"Fckng-sddng crftsmn – fckng-sddng crftsmn – Thrdyssltry –"

When Kōuk had gone and before the warder had come to take Karp to his solitary cell, someone said:

"He's a real dog . . ."

Karp muttered as he struggled into his jacket: "Even dogs sometimes get the shits –"

Aaro Ahven swept up the bits of the trampled cigarette-holders with a brush and put them on the table in front of Karp on a scrap of paper. Shaking with fury he said between his teeth:

"Submit a complaint against the cunt . . ."

"To whom?" asked Karp and looked at us all in turn. Longest of all at me, it seemed, since I had read the basics of Soviet Law at university. He then looked at the bits of the holders in front of him and said:

"Half of the discs survived, at any rate."

Following the order of the bunks, I would now have to talk about myself. For to relegate myself to the role of a peripheral figure and to remain silent about myself would be rather peculiar in the circumstances. And so: a tall young man with an inquisitive face. Almost twenty-seven years of age. Tried his hand at various things: writing poetry, bragging, searching for the truth, conspiracy, and most recently a bit of lecturing. And nabbed that he might come up with an explanation for this surfeit of activities. There exist pseudo-entomologists who are incapable of examining anything unless it is stuck through with a pin ... And who would be obliged, following the order of bunks, now to speak about themselves. But I simply cannot. The reason is simple. For if I were to go by the relative level of knowledge of the study material (even though this may be inaccurate knowledge) then I ought to remain completely silent about all the rest. On the other hand, if I speak about myself in proportion to what I say about the rest, this would consist of an inordinately larger proportion of silence than of storytelling.

So anyway, my left-hand neighbour was Filip Ivanovich Alexeyev. When he was pushed into Cell 19 two months before, he had been a thin man of average height and sixty years of age with a small neat grey moustache, a top-quality bluish-grey raincoat, a blue velour trilby and I decided: here we have a refugee from Soviet Russia whom they managed to arrest somewhere or other. He turned out to be an engineer, a *polkovnik*[3] in the Red Army and a Leningrad man. After being demobbed, he had become the Director of the Tallinn Electricity Board or something of that order. But had been around a bit in Tallinn and Paldiski[4] even before the First World War. While he was still a midshipman on the Imperial Russian yacht, the *Standart*. And it transpired that this bitter and witty old gent had been quite a lad in his time. Dancing in the summers with the girls of the burghers of Paldiski, while the yacht stood off in the sea roads.

"*Oo jaa*! Many's the Paldiski beauty I can still call to mind ... Ha-ha-haa ... And one in particular – Ellakene. Ella Johannovna. A girl from a Böcklin painting. And what a dancer she was too! Mmmm ... Her father had a strange villa covered in honeysuckle outside town, down by the shore."

"What sort of villa?" I asked suddenly.

"Do you know, it was really three or four tiny summer cottages, which had been connected up by a series of glassed-in galleries. Quite a weird hotch-potch. Painted a dark red. Window frames white. Thatched roofs. Like some sort of Carolingian royal castle from a children's story book."

"And what did the father of this Miss Ella do?"

"He was a lawyer in Tallinn. Johan Petrovich Toim. I visited them in Tallinn too. Ella and I almost got engaged. But then came the war. And so on, and so forth."

I remember jumping to my feet roused by the smallness of the world and the flood of memories:

"Filip Ivanovich, do you know what happened to your Ella? You don't? She became an actress! A famous actress. A Merited Artist since last year. And, for the last twenty-five years, the wife of my uncle, Dr Aadam Veski!"

Filip Ivanovich laughed a long, dry and hearty laugh. Given the context we almost became close friends after that.

In a way, this proximity bothered me nonetheless. For in our cells there were always a number of informers. Tappers as they were called, translating the Russian term стукачи. For from time to time they would tap on the cell door and would say something to the guard who opened the hatch, that they had toothache, for instance, and wanted to see a dentist, while in reality they went off to report to their boss. The tappers, or "milch cows" as they were known in pure Estonian, were invited out to be milked now and again. They reported on the general mood of their respective cells and of course what the prisoners who were of especial interest to officialdom said and did. To the more intelligent milch cows, the task was given to provoke conversations on given topics, spread rumours, register the reactions of prisoners, et cetera. Their actions would often bring prisoners a spell in solitary or in some instances, less luckily, a new round of interrogation plus extra years on their sentence. The administration tried, by moving their eyes and ears from one cell to the next, and by other means at their disposal, to protect them from the conflicts which their activities would create when they were discovered by their fellow cellmates, or when suspicions became too great. In prison, these conflicts amounted to no more than sending milch cows to Coventry or, at the most, giving them a thrashing. But in the camps, among prisoners who had received the maximum sentence, the milch cows had to be that much more careful, since there they would simply be rubbed out. But here there were always enough unstable and petty criminal elements who could be talked round with the promise of an extra portion of soup or early release. I tried to defuse conflicts between informers, or suspected informers, and the rest of the cell in a semi-humorous manner. Within earshot of everyone I would go on as follows: My dear cellmates – why all this animosity against informers? Let us think clearly: we are all here quite without justification, at least in our own estimation. Since we have done nothing, or almost nothing, against the state. And we think and speak as loyally to our country as ever we are capable of doing. The only thing is: we now have quite a difficult time informing the authorities of the fact. The only people who we have to help us out a little in our plight are our comrades the informers. So: instead of beating them up – let's make use of them! . . . Now, in the presence of Filip Ivanovich, this tactic became hard to maintain. Since Filip Ivanovich was desperately blunt in his speech, not only with informers but also with the prison authorities. Above all, he made no secret in the cell of why he was here in the first place – or at least how he understood the situation himself. He explained quite openly for everyone to hear: he was inside because his secretary, plus one or two of his subordinates at the power station or wherever, had been informers and run a race to blab to the authorities to the effect that he, Filip Ivanovich, had, for instance, at the first anniversary meeting of his assuming the post, said the following: that when developing our power grid we could learn a thing or two from the Germans, among others. That in itself would have sufficed to have him arrested. I felt that in this last judgment Filip Ivanovich had been a trifle naïve. For his engaging, but nevertheless slightly dandyish, urge to speak the truth was so great that if he had subordinates who were at all ambitious, his file was bound to be pretty thick already. And after his arrest, a trump card was indeed played against him: in June 1944, during the advance near Bobruisk, he an erstwhile Czarist officer and thoroughly rotten recidivist had arbitrarily freed some German officers who had been taken prisoner! Filip Ivanovich had explained: eight German officers, a Major, two Captains and a number of Senior and Junior Lieutenants had been brought to HQ at the moment when all units were being sent forward and were just about to set off. So that he as Head of Section had no one to escort the prisoners to the rear. So he had allowed the Germans to hand in their arms, had explained to them carefully (he had a good command of the German language) which route they should take for the twelve kilometres to Reserve HQ, and demanded they give their word of honour as officers that they would comply.

When asked: "You mean to say that you actually admit to having given Fascist officers the opportunity to escape?" he had cried: "Whatever do you mean – how could they possibly escape when they had given me their word of honour!" He was then told: "Listen, since you are not a complete idiot, then you must be a very cynical man, if you went and believed such feudalistic twaddle in the case of Fascist officers!" He had asked: "Can you prove that the officers escaped?" The reply he received was: "We are not obliged to prove anything! And if you, Mister Imperial Midshipman, could prove that they did not escape it would not make any difference. Because you gave them the chance to do so!" He had cried: "I did not give them any chance – they gave me their word as officers!" And he was told: "So you *are* a complete idiot, after all. But that fact won't help you either."

By way of our comrades the informers, the authorities got to hear of what Filip Ivanovich thought of Tallinn Central Gaol and its administration – how our window had no panes of glass in it, how we were not given needle and thread on the specified days to mend our clothes and underwear with, and how our fish soup, a greyish gruel smelling of fish innards which we refused to eat, was considered as *normal*. So one day – rickety-rackety-rickety-rackety praukh-praukh-praukh – in marched the Prison Governor in person, a man of the rank of major, into Cell 19. We, of course, jumped up and stood to attention in a line while the little red-faced Governor marched in front of us with his short stiff legs and poked us in turn in the chest with his thumb:

"Name? Name? Name? Name?"

"Alexeyev."

"Ahaa. So *you're* the one who they tell me thinks that Tallinn Central Gaol is not a prison but a brothel?!"

Filip Ivanovich, a *polkovnik*, stood demonstratively to attention in front of the Major and said with deadly seriousness as far as could be seen from his expression, but with an inner joy at the sting of the retort:

"It is a patent lie, Citizen Major, that I ever could have said such a thing. A brothel has a Madam, and order holds sway. Here there is neither the one nor the other."

I had once asked him: "Filip Ivanovich, tell me, considering your way of thinking and your big mouth, how come you've managed, up to now, to remain untouched?"

He replied: "Up to '34, thanks to Sergei Mironovich Kirov.[5] He knew me personally. Then up to the war, I'm not rightly sure. A miracle perhaps."Now Kirov was dead, the war had been won, and Filip Ivanovich was given a fortnight's solitary forthwith.

So that for two weeks, my left-hand bunk neighbour in practice was: a small erstwhile tippler with a wrinkled face and a vodka nose, a lad from the Province of Valgamaa near the Latvian border who had started out as a conjurer and impersonator at a fair and perhaps really had ended up treading the boards at the Säde Theatre in Valga itself to become what he introduced himself to us as --- Timmermann the Actor. Timmermann the Actor who was beginning to get over the shakes occasioned by one year's forced abstention from alcohol. (Incidentally, is not being remanded in custody while under investigation the most effective enforced treatment for alcoholism?) Timmermann's withdrawal

symptoms only manifested themselves in one form: verbal diar-
rhoea. And since he prattled on happily and at a certain, shall we
say, artistic level, and while one could hardly imagine a better
set of listeners than prisoners under investigation, he succeeded
in marketing a number of good stories, half-spiced up with folk-
lore, as personal experiences.

"When I joined the Guards, they sent me off on sentry duty
to Toompea Castle,[6] just like that. I had already clocked up a bit
of experience treading the boards as a secondary school pupil.
Life was a doddle up there for the young soldier lads. You got
leave to go into town at the drop of a hat, which made sentry
duty on the ensuing Monday morning a pretty grim business, as
you might imagine. Sleep would weigh heavy on the sentries like
a sack of flour. And the Commandant, Colonel Reisberg, was a
real cunt. On his feet from six or seven every morning. Going
around checking the sentry posts. If he'd at least done it in a
civilised manner. But, oh no. He would sneak up on you. So
sodding quietly that if you had but one grain of sand in your
lugholes you'd hear nothing. And if you'd rested your rifle butt
on the ground and hadn't wound the cord round your hand, then
whoosh, gone would be your rifle. Then he'd take it off to his
office and kick up a hell of a fuss. Sometimes there would even
be a court martial. And this happened to me too. The Toompea
garrison was also responsible for guarding the residence of the
Riigivanem,[6] the Premier. There, where they've now got the
People's Commission for Health, or is it a Ministry nowadays?
The façade of the building looked exactly the same as it does
now. Except that the plaster and the paintwork were fresh in
those days. The sentry post was on the Orthodox Cathedral side
beside the main doors, under the overhanging balcony. If you
remember – there were Grecian stone pillars, a couple of Carrier-
Tits, or whatever they call them, holding it up. And one Monday
morning there I was on duty. If you want to know in detail – it
was January 1932. A quiet early morning. Snow was falling softly
as if sprinkled by the Sandman. And two hours before, I had
arrived back from painting the town red. My eyes closed little

by little and – dunk, dunk – I kept nudging the stone knockers of the stone lass with my fur cap-"

Here I couldn't help saying: "Here, Timmermann. There aren't any caryatids there. They're just ordinary rounded pillars."

Timmermann was not to be put off. "Well, they haven't let me out to go and have a look at what's there *right now*. I'm talking about what they had there then. I mean, Christ, it was fifteen years ago, after all. You're so much younger, so you wouldn't know. Anyway, as I was saying – dunk, dunk – against the afore-mentioned. When suddenly I awoke and could see in the light of the lantern the Colonel, that bloody creeping skeleton, walking away from me, lifting his feet in the fresh snow like a cat in mud – my rifle in his hand! I felt as if a barrel of cold water had been poured down my neck. I came to my senses. What the hell was I going to do now? For I knew what would follow. At the end of my watch when I went back to the guardroom, I would be summoned, bawled out something terrible and sent off to Central Guard Headquarters on Tartu Road. There they would put me on bread and water for a month and it would only be by God's grace that I would get off that lightly. For if I were court-martialled, they would slap a year on right away. That for sure. It would have been OK if I had just been guarding let's say some potato barn – but this was the *Riigivanem*'s residence. Anyway I thought my number was up. But then I had an idea. One floor above the guardroom was the Colonel's office. And in that office my rifle, wasn't it? And twenty paces further on Captain Vender's room. He was some sort of economic manager there. I had been in all these rooms tidying up and stoking the stoves and keeping my ears open, too. So that I knew: Captain Vender was the brother-in-law of the Colonel and a relative of the Estonian Chief of Staff, General Laidoner. And I had met General Laidoner on a number of occasions. He would often stamp through the guardroom and say something to the boys in there, sometimes grumbling, sometimes raging, sometimes rebuking. So that his *voice* was quite familiar to me. And I had no better plan than to play my trick. Five minutes later, when I had entered the guard-room without my rifle, someone shouted:

"Timmermann – the Colonel wants to see you!"

I said to the lads over my shoulder: "I'm in the bog. Back in a minute!"

The messenger disappeared and I – like greased lightning – into the vestibule to the telephone booth. Via the switchboard I asked for Captain Vender's number and when Vender answered, I asked in a different voice:

"Erm – hm – Colonel Reisberg there?"

Vender replied: "No, this is Captain Vender."

"Vender? You? Good morning. Laidoner here. I'm calling from Viimsi. Those confounded Viimsi operator chappies gave me your number instead of Reisberg's. Wait till I get my hands on them – I'll give them a lesson they'll never forget! But anyway – to keep things simple just call Reisberg to your phone. I'll hold the line."

Vender of course replied: "Understood, sir! I'll get him right away, sir!" and I could hear him clicking his heels under the table. Half-a-minute later a familiar crusty voice said:

"Colonel Reisberg speaking, sir!"

"Reisberg? Morning! This is Laidoner. Artur, listen. First, I happened to get hold of a few packs of jolly daring French playing cards and second, some rather fine bottles of French bubbly. So I thought that perhaps this evening. . ."

At this point I covered the receiver with my hand and began puffing and calling "Hello, hello, can you hear me?" through my fingers and said in the NCO telephone operator's voice: "Sorry, General. I'll put you through in just one moment, sir. *One* minute, sir."

Then I left the phone dangling on its lead and left the booth. If Reisberg thought it was Laidoner on the other end he would stand there till lunchtime if necessary. So I had a few minutes: whizz, to Reisberg's door. Whack – into the room! The rifle – it was, of course, there – behind his desk in the corner! Down the stairs! Whizz! The rifle into the pyramid in the guardroom!

Back into the vestibule! Into the phone booth! Into the half-covered receiver: "G-g-general – hello – hello – lost the connection – we've lost the connection, sir –" Plop – receiver back on the hook. Caught my breath in the booth for a minute or so. So that the old man would have time to get back to his office. Then up the stairs: knock, knock, knock.

"Mnyes."

"Private Timmermann reporting, sah!"

The old man was already sitting behind his desk, his jackboots poking out from under the table: "Timmermann? What damned Timmermann –? Eh? –" but then he remembered and shouted like a cracked cannon: "But where's your rifle, Private Timmermann, what?"

"In the guardroom in Pyramid Number One, Colonel Reisberg, sir."

The old man glared at me and motioned with his left hand in the direction of the corner behind his back:

"Then what's *that*?"

"An empty corner, sir."

The old man wheeled round, chair and all, and stared into the corner. I saw his crop grow red. He then turned back round and grunted:

"Inform the Head Guardsman: For your prank, I'm giving you three days." And I thought: if I get off with only three days' solitary I really couldn't grumble. And he completed his sentence: ". . . for your prank I'm giving you three days' leave of absence!"

Why exactly, or approximately, Timmermann was now in here with us remained unclear to me. Sometimes he seemed to wish to give the impression that it was not for political, but rather for criminal reasons, sometimes he mentioned something about expressions he had used on stage at some constituency meeting during the previous year's elections to the Supreme Soviet.

Next to Timmermann along the row were a number of serious men from the countryside, sceptically sniffing farmers from medium-sized or larger farms who had, by their own admission, guarded haystacks, shotgun in hand, as part of the Omakaitse[7] self-defence force during the German Occupation. Among them, by the way, was a very quiet old man of almost eighty who had been the *Vallavanem*, or parish elder, in Pärnumaa Province for thirty years and went into history for the immortal last words he said before the tribunal: "Since the most respected tribunal has sentenced me to ten years – since they won't get any more out of me, and less they would not consider – then I would ask, that when in the camp I finally kick the bucket, could I please be buried *in a sitting position*. So that after my escape into the nether world I may not have to re-appear before the tribunal, but can *sit* out my sentence with honour."

A further addition to our cell was the informer of that period, Siimo Kink. A twenty-one-year-old boy, pretty and pink as a chocolate box, with a small ginger moustache, a tiny mouth and blue and innocent eyes resembling fly-buttons. He went off at times to the sick bay to have ointment applied to the itching rash on his throat and chest and the rash was real enough. Only that when others also went to get ointment it did not take more than five minutes, while in Siimo's case it would take an hour or even one-and-a-half. Siimo made no bones about the fact that he had dropped out of the second year of militia school, and in on us, and this is supposed to have occurred on account of the fact that, on entering, he had understandably concealed the fact that he volunteered to join the German Army. And now he was not only staying here to have his crimes investigated but to enable him – inconspicuously, it must be said – to investigate those we had committed. Or, Lord knows, maybe he was here only for the latter reason, to get a little more piquant practical experience.

Siimo did not break the rules himself, or invite others to do so as milch cows otherwise did. The only thing he did that was against regulations was to make himself a tube out of brown packing paper and bread-lime, cut with the tip of a blade (there was a knife made of a strip of metal hidden in a crack in the wall and he did not feel it his duty to inform about that) – cut finger-holes with the point of the knife in the tube, rig up some reed or other, and perform songs by blowing through the tube in a low drone. For instance, "Kalevite kantsi" – *The Fortress of the Kalevs*. But when Doctor Kuurmann winking an eye at the rest of us asked why the hell he was playing such a nationalist song, he began instead to play "Я другой такой страны не энаю. где так вольно дышит человек" *I Know No Other Land Where Folk So Freely Breathe* – so that Filip Ivanovich yelled at him: "Young man! If you don't play something else, I will come and ram your teeth down your throat, personally!" Whereupon Siimo hastily changed over to playing "Ema südant" – *Mother's Heart*.

To Siimo's left, in the bunk nearest the privy, slept an NCO from the German Army by the name of Robert Raik. A tall, long-legged swarthy man of about thirty-five or forty with a tragic Spanish horse-face. He reminded me of a stiff-legged grasshopper who had hopped into the shower bath and clambered out of it again, while at one and the same time of an old Orthodox painting of the Road to Golgotha by an artist whose name slips my mind. Raik too was an innocent, or almost entirely innocent, man. He had admittedly been an NCO in the German Army, but had only joined up some months before he would have been called up in any case. That was all he was guilty of and was now in here waiting to receive his ten years ... I saw him again fifteen years later at an open court session at the Naval Officers' House. Where he had been brought from the depths of Siberia after his ten year sentence plus five extra of voluntary exile. But the session treated his defence counsel no less harshly than it did him. Since for him everything was predictable, corresponding to the worst nightmare. But for the honourable old defence lawyer, one episode did come as a surprise. While the people were swarming out of the hall during a break in the proceedings, an old, grey woman with an almost expressionless face, stepped up to the lawyer out of the throng and said: "Anyone who defends *somebody like that* should get what he deserves," and spat in the lawyer's face. For she had received the ineradicable impression that Raik had been one of those who, in the Jägala concentration camp, had thrown infants up in the air by the legs with his left hand, then shot them through the head with the automatic in his right.

But then, one morning at the end of October, or the beginning of November, the locks on the door of Cell 19 rattled in that characteristically neurotic and angry way (they could only be opened in that way – as if always on behalf of Sergeant Kõuk). The steel-plated door swung open and in came our twenty-third man and in that familiar if curious way as if falling into water. And once again the locks rattled as the door was shut behind him.

Of above average height. About thirty-five. From his reddish face it could be seen that he had not as yet spent long in these buildings. A fair crew-cut. Quick grey eyes with white eyelashes. Even a slight paunch under his white shirt. But his clothes, a black winter coat, moleskin trousers and half-length boots without laces into which darned foot-clouts were pushed showed that he was nevertheless no complete newcomer.

He eyed us, squinting slightly, and put his soiled white linen kitbag onto our table, threw off his coat, took a seat and released the drawstring of the kitbag:

"I can see that there are no *blatnoi*s[8] in here so I can take out a bit of bacon."

Timmermann asked: "Does a chap have a name?"

The new man sunk his teeth into his bacon sandwich:

"Lehtpuu, Eero, if you please."

"Who are you spying for?" asked Timmermann.

"What the fuck d'you mean – 'spying'?"

"Well, I mean, are you spying for the Germans, the British, the Americans or the Estonians – whose side are you on? Everyone in here spies for somebody. So who are *you* spying for?"

"Look here, I wasn't born yesterday! I've been here four months now. And before that fifteen years looking after the parish farm. From the time my old man kicked the bucket. Over the whole of Arujõe Parish. Ninety hectares of land. Two farm hands. Three girls. Twenty head of cattle. Eight farm buildings. Pubs, fairs, markets. Hell, Lehtpuu's Eero hasn't let himself be cheated out of one shitten cent!"

"Well no – if you run *such* a big farm, then I suppose you haven't," conceded Timmermann, winking at the rest of us.

Lehtpuu tucked into his bacon sandwich, wiped his chops with the back of his hand, pulled the drawstring of his kitbag to, and began to roll a cigarette using a scrap of newspaper. Timmermann politely but firmly raised his own cigarette paper to the mouth of Lehtpuu's tobacco pouch:

"The owner of *such* a large farm does, of course, support those working in the field of culture." Whereupon he gave a reverential nod of the head accompanied by the words: "I am Timmermann the Actor."

Lehtpuu looked at him through his pale eyelashes and decided that the friendship of such a windbag in a new cell might just be worth a roll-up. "Ah," he replied – "I have seen actors on stage in the village hall. Thinner and fatter ones than yourself –" and sprinkled a little tobacco into Timmermann's palm, but such a quantity as if to imply Timmermann to be one of the very thinnest. Timmermann thanked him profusely, rolled himself a cigarette, asked Lehtpuu for a light, drew on the fag, inhaling the third-rate tobacco smoke into his lungs and, screwing up his eyes all the while, said with profundity:

"Ve-e-ry nice and smooth. You did, of course, produce this yourself?"

"But of course. I have a few beds of it over by the garden wall. Linda sends a packet of it each time."

"Aaaa," said Timmermann through a cloud of smoke, "how does Linda-the-Missus manage to cope all on her own? Doing all that heavy autumn work on a large farm. Sending packages to her farmer husband. Must be a clever girl."

"Clever she certainly is," said Lehtpuu with conviction, "otherwise I wouldn't have taken her on."

While Timmermann's sucking up to Lehtpuu had remained a form of scrounging – or playing at scrounging – it left the rest of us cold. The slight minus of cadging, or the slight plus of ribbing, on the part of Timmermann left us cold, at any rate. But I did notice how several of us began to pay heed when Timmermann went on to ask:

"And how does a farmer like yourself set about *taking on* a wife?"

"What do you mean 'a wife'?" grunted Lehtpuu and exhaled his smoke.

"Why shouldn't I call her 'a wife'?" asked Timmermann unabashed. "The lady running *such* a large farm must of course be the farmer's wife."

"My wife is whom I choose to be my wife."

"Oh, undoubtedly," conceded Timmermann, "when you've got *such* a big farm back there."

Karp pushed the remaining half of his cigarette holder into his pocket and looked up over his fingers, grown grey with polishing the aluminium:

"Ah, so you've got a mistress, then."

"I can see you don't come from Mulgimaa,"[9] said Lehtpuu. "A mistress is someone who you've lived with for God knows how long. So that she's well on the way towards becoming a crone. Not, you know, someone who's hardly turned twenty."

"Oh, I see." said Timmermann meekly. "And who is it who's hardly turned twenty?"

"A *bird*, you understand," said Lehtpuu irritably.

"Right! What a beautiful old-fashioned expression," said Timmermann, now satisfied. "Of course, a bird who's hardly turned twenty and pretty as a picture, to boot."

"But of course," grunted Lehtpuu.

"Well, that's clear enough," stated Timmermann, "otherwise the farmer wouldn't have taken her on."

"Oi, oi, oi." Dr Kuurmann suddenly walked up to the table, his hands clasped behind his back, a worried frown on his brow. "This is a serious business. I'm not talking about the farm. The farm will go to pot, anyway. I'm talking about the bird. Leaving a *wife* in that fashion – no problem. Simply a bit of a holiday from her. A mistress, even less of a problem. When you've lived with her for twenty, thirty years. But a *bird* . . . A beautiful young bird – mmmm . . . What a terrible shame. Just think of it: here you are sitting in front of your dry crust of bread and your putrid fish soup, subjected to the spite and bawling of the Kōuks of this world – but you still get a hard-on at night. You can't fool me. I'm a doctor. I know. But just think what that bird can be up to. You're not so young any more, for one. And what's more: there are no temptations for you in here. But she's had a month or two – you said so yourself – for her mouth to start watering, not to mention other parts of her anatomy. And now you have gone and abandoned her."

"Sod off, I didn't abandon her!" yelled Lehtpuu furiously.

"Oh but you did, you did. Only, not of your own free will," wheezed Doctor Kuurmann, "and she's all alone out there in her role as mistress of the manor, you can imagine, fresh, randy, excited – surrounded by fleshpots, churns of cream, cider flowing in the bedroom, splish-splosh, and willing young men trying to get in through windows and doors. How long will she be able to hold out?"

"Linda won't be tempted," cried Lehtpuu vehemently, "or I'll show her!"

"Like shite you will; and you'll hardly be showing her round Siberia if you're out there for ten years," said Doctor Kuurmann.

"For fuck's sake, who's said anything about ten years?"

"Or five, then. No one in here's ever gets less than that," wheezed Doctor Kuurmann, relentlessly.

"How many years do *you* intend getting then, mister farmer, sir?

". . . Fuck knows," grunted Lehtpuu, "but not ten anyway!"

"But we got our info from a – how d'you put it? – legal counsellor, first-hand. We've got some sort of Professor of Law in here with us. Present your case to him and then ask him what he thinks. He'll tell you straight."

These last words were uttered, in a voice which was just breaking, by Aaro Ahven who had just moved over to the end of the table where the conversation was taking place. And the professor of whom he spoke was myself. I had soon noticed that in the cell, where occupants went unchecked and facts could not be, people would boost their own reputations in two different ways. The most common way was self-promotion by wish-fulfilment: corporals made themselves out to be full officers. The more daring and more painfully ineffectual plodders among them would raise themselves to the rank of lieutenant. There was talk of a poor *veltveebel*, a sergeant major, who had received a sentence of seven years for being an NCO during the German Occupation but then, when already in the camps, whispered abroad so often the fact that had actually been a captain that he was subsequently given the full fifteen years in accordance with his rank. Clerks would present themselves as departmental heads, cobblers as shoe manufacturers, bicycle sales agents as car salesmen – diametrically opposed to their real interests in their present place of residence. The second type of promotion was achieved by boosting the value of themselves, and the cell as a whole, in the eyes of their cellmates. I had lately been effortlessly promoted from junior lecturer up to the rank of professor and had simply grown tired of denying it. (Some zealous Adlerian will perhaps claim that my recalling this is as a result of my own unfulfilled ambitions. Ha ha haa. Let it go.)

And so I did not go and start explaining to Lehtpuu that I was *not* a professor, since I had explained it sufficiently to everyone already. Lehtpuu eyed me most sceptically, but his desire to get some explanation as to when he would be able to get his bird back brushed aside any scepticism. He asked, almost angrily:

"What's it going to cost?"

"What?"

"Look, if I tell my tale and you give your opinion, what will I owe you for it?"

"It doesn't cost anything," I said dismissively. "How could you think it'd cost you anything?"

"Well, if you don't pay 'em, people don't tend to think either," he said hastily and took hold of the buttons of my shirt. I tried to wriggle free and said:

"Listen, I'm not a fortune-teller, looking into the future!" But young Ahven was eager to explain:

"No, no. Professor Mirk knows about such things. I'd already have seven years round my neck if it wasn't for the fact that he told me what to say during the investigation. And now they're reviewing my case and you never know."

I screwed up my eyes and persuaded myself that Siimo Kink had not been paying attention to what Ahven had just said. But Lehtpuu dragged me over to the stone windowsill and said, breathing garlic into my face:

"I'll tell you all about it. The rest of them needn't bother listening."

I tried to position myself so that the draught from the broken window blew away the smell of the garlic. And he told me his story, rapidly in a half-whisper so that it was hard to hear what was being said against the rushing of the sea in the background. His was quite an ordinary story, but with one or two unexpected twists.

Half of his farm had already been confiscated in 1941 to form the grounds of some agricultural college or other. Three settlers had been sent to farm the other half. Two of them were no problem, as he put it. One of them had gone off with the Reds to Velikiye Luki[10] in the summer of '41 and stopped a bullet there. The other had disappeared after the Germans came to town. He had been recruited into the German Army and had stepped on a mine in the Sinimäed Hills in '44. The third had worked for Lehtpuu during the German Occupation and had died of pneumonia in the early spring of '44. And it was with this third man that the problem lay. For his widow had blamed Lehtpuu for the death of her husband. That her husband had been taken by the Germans – as a new settler and fellow-traveller of the Reds. And that they had threatened to shoot her husband. And then Lehtpuu, the influential farmer that he was, had intervened and talked the man off the hook.

"But what do you then mean when you say you were *blamed*?"

Yes, blamed. The widow had said: Lehtpuu was supposed to

have set conditions for Oskar while he was still in the clink: I'll rescue you from your impending diet of soil *if* you come and work for me at Laaspere for your keep as long as your strength holds out. If you start shilly-shallying, I'll have you cleared away. And Oskar had agreed and slaved away at Laaspere until he grew ill and died.

"But how can you be blamed for his pneumonia?"

"The woman says that her husband had gone log-hauling on my orders when he was a sick man. I had threatened and Oskar was supposed to have been afraid that if he hadn't gone I would have had him arrested and that he would get the bullet for what had happened in 1941. And he would most certainly have done."

"And how did the widow know of the threat?"

"Oskar is supposed to have told her."

"No other witnesses?"

"No."

"But did you – threaten him, I mean?"

"I wouldn't be so daft as to admit to that! I didn't threaten him!"

"Ahaa . . ."

I didn't press matters any further. For I knew that if the whole truth were to come out, it could hinder my proffering advice. But I trained him in what to say as best I could. As a pastime, to a certain extent. For the vanity involved in proving to myself, to him and to those who happened to be listening that I had potential as a defence lawyer – although I had no experience whatsoever in this field. But, to a certain extent, I took on his defence out of defiance. Defiance against Stalin's, and Beria's, and God knows who else's sentencing machine. Did we not – all the Lehtpuus of this world and myself too – possess the right to present our case from its most attractive angle to that mechanistic Moloch? Even if the Moloch did not care about anything in our case, did not take anything into consideration? Apart from its own blind egocentrism? I did not announce this right to Lehtpuu. But as to how he should conduct himself at the tribunal, that I did at least try to drum into his head. Yes – he had just said that his case would be coming up soon before the war tribunal. So they would at least have to listen to him. Not like in the great majority of cases, where a so-called "troika" pronounced sentence behind their backs. He, Lehtpuu, would also have to have an official defence lawyer at the tribunal. So I told Lehtpuu what he should stress in court and to what he should principally draw the attention of his defence counsel:

Oskar Juhanson had never had the slightest quarrel with him, Lehtpuu. Despite the fact that he, Lehtpuu, had been a farmer and Juhanson a settler on his land. That was also testified to by Juhanson's widow who had explained: "When me and my husband moved onto the land, Lehtpuu had merely said: 'Take what you're entitled to'." And I taught Lehtpuu to explain especially why and how such indulgence was possible. Because he, Lehtpuu, had become the master of Laaspere farm on his father's death when he was but an eighteen-year-old boy. And at that age he had regarded this not as a gift or a privilege, but as a burden. Because what Lehtpuu had actually dreamed of was not the farm but an *education*. But the fact that the responsibility for the farm fell on his shoulders meant that he had already had to drop out of secondary school. So that the arrival of Juhanson had not been in any way a loss for him, Lehtpuu. It had in fact come as a *relief*.

Lehtpuu listened to me, shut his eyes with the white eyelashes and exhaled in a whistle. And I taught him the explanation:

Juhanson had really been a most clever and quiet-natured man and his widow had accused Lehtpuu of threatening him out of sheer spite. For Juhanson did not have to be goaded into doing his work, and certainly not threatened. Juhanson himself understood what was necessary in those shamelessly lean times. And understood full well that Lehtpuu had saved him from being shot and did his work without any compulsion being applied. And I also taught Lehtpuu: if, however, they happen to ask *why* he, Lehtpuu, had bothered to rescue Juhanson from captivity, he was to look down at his feet and admit: "Well, I can't deny the fact that I once was the owner of a farm and thought that in such hard times such a hard-working chap would come in useful for my farm . . ." But having said that (I taught him), he was to raise his eyes from the floor and look the chairman of the tribunal straight in the eye and say: "But the main reason I saved him was because I knew Oskar very well to be a good chap and deserved a better fate than a German bullet." And I also advised Lehtpuu to stress in his own defence statement that Lehtpuu had never been in the German Army nor – *nota bene* – the Omakaitse Defence Force. Running the farm had kept him out of the army (since farmers were responsible for their quotas), and he had avoided joining the Omakaitse. And he also explained to me: "I wasn't so daft as to become a dogsbody for some jumped up lieutenant." And what prevented him from saying to the tribunal: "I didn't join the Omakaitse because I didn't want to have to hunt down my own men on the orders of the occupying powers. For what else did the Omakaitse spend its time doing?"

And I also recommended he let his defence counsel explain to the tribunal:

The concrete accusation against Lehtpuu was so disproportionate and so in conflict with the statements of others, that the tribunal should not take it seriously. The actual and, in essence, more significant issue at stake was of quite another nature namely: was, or was not, Lehtpuu a *kulak*? It should be noted that Lehtpuu was not at any rate a kulak in the literal sense of the word. On account of the fact that already as far back as '41 half his land had been taken away from him and incorporated into the grounds of the Voonaste Agricultural College, and also on account of the fact that by the time the Juhansons and others had received their settlers' plots, Laaspere only consisted of thirty hectares of land, which by our new standards was the most average of farms. But the material content of the matter was formally of more significance, of course. Crucial was the matter of *who* Lehtpuu was in word and deed. The defence will ask the court to take into consideration the fact that the defendant had in his explanation mentioned the farm as a *burden* which had been placed on his shoulders while still a boy, and his unassuaged thirst for education is something human, telling and moving. And what is more, during the three-and-a-half years of the German Occupation, when thousands of kulaks of the same age had rushed off to join the German Army along with their sons, Lehtpuu stayed put. At the very same time that the majority of kulaks of a suitable age had at least joined the Omakaitse quite voluntarily, Lehtpuu had kept out – he had himself explained why: because he did not want to hunt down his own men on the orders of the occupying power. And at the same time that the physical annihilation of activists in '41 was, to a great extent, the work of the kulaks, Lehtpuu was busy getting – by using his good name, but really to a greater extent the weight of his father's name locally – Oskar Juhanson out of prison and preventing him from being shot . . . And I continued: here the counsel for the defence should add – "Even for any citizen regarded as loyal by German Occupation standards, there were risks attached to taking such a step. I will tell to the honourable members of the court of an instance (the lawyer could say) – from that very same Province of Viljandimaa. From Räise, the very next parish to Arujõe, that is to say in the same police district as Laaspere, and Lehtpuu's own. There lived in Valgvälja, in his own house, a man who, by Occupation standards, was a well-respected farmer, one Aleksander Kraav. The farm was a so-called Farm of Honour. Received, that is, for services rendered during the Estonian War of Independence, over twenty years before. And the aforementioned Aleksander Kraav kept his *Vabadusrist*, his Estonian Cross of Freedom medal, in his desk drawer at home. I do hope that the honourable members of the court are aware of what precisely such a medal signified and for what the bourgeois government had given it him. Anyhow, this Aleksander Kraav had a nephew. The nephew was conscripted into the Red Army in '41, and was dropped back into Estonia by parachute in '43. And where else had he to go but to Valgvälja farm? And what else could the uncle do but take in the boy and hide him? But the enemy has always, alas, no shortage of bootlickers: a couple of weeks later both men were arrested. And both the nephew and the uncle, the Red parachutist and the blue-black-and-white Knight of the Cross of Freedom, were shot without further ado. Of course (the defence lawyer should say), Oskar Juhanson had not arrived by parachute from the Soviet hinterland. But he had nonetheless been a Soviet activist back in '41 – even the plaintiff can confirm this – and was, in the eyes of the occupying German forces, likewise a doomed man under sentence of death. To which I may add that Lehtpuu had no Farm of Honour, nor did he have a Cross of Freedom in his desk drawer. So that in the climate of senseless brutality of the occupying forces, this was a risk of which Lehtpuu was very much aware. And yet Lehtpuu went and took that risk."

And I acted out for him how I would sum up before the tribunal if I were his defence counsel:

"Members of the court! The charge brought against my client under the Criminal Code Paragraph 58, Items 1 A and 3 lacks concrete proof. Furthermore, my client does *not* – although a perfunctory examination of the facts might suggest the contrary – he does *not* represent a class inimical to Soviet power. As regards his class allegiance he is – thanks to chance factors of his personal history, due to his own way of thinking and his cautious nature, and especially owing to what I would call the helping hand of historical development – one of the most diligent and willing middle-class farmers, the likes of whom in fact constitute a very large proportion of agricultural workers of the Republic. With his nine years of schooling, Lehtpuu belongs to their most educated stratum. With his faultless fulfilment of republican quotas he belongs to the category of those most clever and economically efficient. And on account of his behaviour during the Occupation, he would seem to represent what I should call the most humane stratum of our middle-class farmers. For this reason I would ask the court to treat the accused, my client, as we treat most middle-class farmers and drop charges against Eero Lehtpuu and free him forthwith since the charges laid against him are ground-less and without foundation."

"Bloody hell!" said Lehtpuu, "it's a good job you've got to the end of that. I was already beginning to think: if he goes on much longer, he'll have dragged me like a rag through a kettle of Red dye ..." He swallowed and asked: "... But, I mean – will a speech like that get me off the hook?"

I said: "It is at least the only tale which does not make it quite impossible for you to be set free. As likely as not they'll still give you ten years. So – go to court, present these points in a cogent and confident manner and then let's see what happens. But don't start *hoping* for anything."

"Hope would be pretty stupid, of course," said Timmermann hovering around us, "hope in this building is just to keep babies sweet. Pap with sugar. Do you know what hope's called in here. It's called *The Murderer*."

"What d'you mean, Timmermann?" said Doctor Kuurmann pouting his thick lips and screwing up his eyes, "you should never abandon hope! Or do you think that Mr Lehtpuu should give up hoping that, for instance, Sweety Pie Linda is staying faithful to him? One can but hope. However many seducers there are knocking around ..."

"They must have been around the missus like horseflies," said Timmermann, creeping up and again pushing his cigarette paper under Lehtpuu's nose.

"Well, they got bugger-all out of it," said Lehtpuu, nonetheless sprinkling out enough *makhorka* for Timmermann's roll-up. "Daughter of a cotter. From next the dung heap. Who would notice her? Nobody. Till a man comes along who's got *eyes* in his head. *Nowadays* she's got no shortage of admirers. Now she wears silk stockings bought her by yours truly, while Asta down the village has gone and given her a perm in exchange for a side of bacon."

"But haven't there been any – shall we say – *serious* suitors?" asked Doctor Kuurmann with grand neutrality coupled with sympathetic interest.

"Well, of course there have," said Timmermann in a matter-of-fact manner, getting the boot in, "there's always a thrush in among every flock of sparrows. How could it be otherwise with such cherries, ripe for the picking?"

The fact Doctor Kuurmann joined in the fun again with such

gusto rather surprised me. They were sitting, Timmermann and the Doctor, so close on either side of Lehtpuu and were so involved in his affair that I could not help smiling. I was thinking: if I'd have been in Lehtpuu's boots at this moment, I would be beginning to feel decidedly uncomfortable. Lehtpuu muttered:

"There was one slimy toad of a schoolmaster. Our schoolhouse burnt down during the War and the school classes took up half of our living quarters. Then this chalk-grinder thought he was well in there, and began to play Linda "Viljandi paadimees" – "The Viljandi Boatman"[11] on his damned piano accordion."

"Well, I suppose her hubby put a stop to that pretty sharpish?" conjectured Timmermann with a glad sigh.

"I certainly did that," said Lehtpuu calmly, "I boarded up the door to the hall from the kitchen side telling him: 'Kaarel, if you set so much as one foot in here, I'll chop off your toes with an axe. Is that clear?'"

"But how did the missus take it?" asked Doctor Kuurmann, his lips moist.

"It wasn't up to her," grunted Lehtpuu, "she sulked alright, but she just had to knuckle under. For I told her: 'You know something, if I see that slimy toad in here again, I'll chop his balls off!'"

Whereupon Karp said quite unexpectedly, while continuing with his polishing:

"What are you on about? You've been to secondary school – and you don't even know that toads don't have balls."

Ahven burst into laughter and Doctor Kuurmann, who had moved away by this time, brought Gerlach over to us:

"Listen, Mr Lehtpuu, our German here wants a word – he was caught in Viljandimaa Province a couple of months ago. About fifty kilometres to the south or southwest of Viljandi itself. On some large farm or other."

"In which parish?" asked Lehtpuu.

"That, of course, he doesn't know. He doesn't even know the name of the farm. But he says it was a big farm, where there was

a young and pretty farmer's wife. And the farmer's name was
Karl," the Doctor turned to Gerlach – "*der Besitzer hieß Karl,
nicht wahr?*"[12]

"*Der, den ich für den Besitzer hielt, hieß Karl.*"[13]

"That's the whole point," said Doctor Kuurmann, "it turned
out that this Karl, whom our German thought to be the farmer
himself, wasn't the farmer at all. The farmer himself had been
arrested. And this here Karl was with the farmer's wife in his
stead. So it seemed. And this Karl got the militia onto our
German here . . ."

"And what was the name of the farmer's wife?" asked Lehtpuu,
agitated already.

The German shrugged his shoulders: "*Das weiß ich nicht.*"[14]

"He doesn't know," clarified the doctor.

"What colour hair did she have?" asked Lehtpuu hastily.
"Blond?"

"*Ja, natürlich blond. Alle Estinnen sind blond.*"[15]

"How old?" Lehtpuu wanted to know.

The German answered and the Doctor explained: "He can't
really say. He only saw her very briefly by the light of a lantern.
But *young* at any rate."

There were tiny droplets of sweat on Lehtpuu's brow:

"Hm. Was she slim or plump?"

The German replied and the Doctor translated: "He says she
was rather plump."

"But my Linda is so perfectly slim!" yelled Lehtpuu triumphantly and looked us all in the eye, one by one.

"Fine, then what have you got to worry about? Otherwise,
you might have started thinking that since –" muttered Doctor
Kuurmann. "Only that –"

"Only that what –?" asked Lehtpuu.

"Only that –" said the Doctor drawing out his words, "what
a German considers as plump could be considered as perfectly
slim out there in Mulgimaa. Possible, isn't it? Though don't ask
me."

"But what did this Karl look like?" asked Lehtpuu hoarsely.

The Doctor asked and translated: "Of medium height. On the thin side. About thirty, fortyish. Ordinary."

"But the farmhouse?" asked Lehtpuu. "Was it on the edge of the woods? Did it have a verandah? Looking out over an orchard? The orchard across from the fields?"

"On the edge of the woods – yes, it was. But the rest he doesn't remember."

"But what colour was the house? Green? Or not?"

"Hard to say. On account of the darkness. Maybe green. Maybe grey."

Lehtpuu was silent for a moment. Then he put his hands on his hips and said:

"Know something – why don't you just go and fuck off!" (This was directed towards Gerlach but was more widely intended.) "Fifty kilometres to the south of Viljandi – or to the southwest – or the southeast – Ha – the countryside around there is full of large farms! Half the farmers have been arrested! Somebody like Karl – God damn, I'm not such a fool to begin supposing that –"

Just then, the door hatch swung open and the soup orderlies began ladling out the fish and cabbage skilly into our tin bowls. When the clatter and rattle had finished the hatch was shut once more and we sat around the table and took our morning bread ration from our lockers and begun eating lunch. Those who had extra rations took something out of their private rusk bag or a piece of meat from their latest parcel. Lehtpuu pushed away his soup bowl:

"I'm not eating this prison swill. Anyone who wants can lap it up. Today's parcel day, after all."

"Have to see whether the missus is going to be sending the master a parcel every time," said Timmermann appropriating Lehtpuu's portion of soup.

"There's no question of there not being a parcel," said Lehtpuu confidently. "When I had to leave, I told her to send me food. And so she shall."

Parcels could be received every fortnight by those on remand, where a sender could be found. Forbidding parcels as a

disciplinary measure was a rare occurrence for those under investigation in Tallinn Central Gaol. The contents of the parcel were
wrapped up in a piece of paper or cloth and pushed in through
the hatch. Whatever there was – a loaf of pumpernickel, bread,
a chunk of meat, a jar of dripping, a pat of butter, a bag of rusks,
tobacco, cigarettes – all this after a diligent checker had gone
through it all, prodding things, cutting open the loaves, poking
holes in the butter and dripping, sometimes even stamping on
things in a fit of pique since any one of them could conceal
objects subversive of the system – metal files, hunting knives,
submarines . . . Cigarettes were broken open since experience
had taught the authorities that the papers could contain messages
telling the recipient Lord knows what. Finally, a form containing
a list of the contents of the parcel was pushed through the hatch
for the recipient to sign.

Half-an-hour after the oat porridge which we also received as
our lunch had been eaten, the parcels began arriving. For Doctor
Kuurmann. Elken. A couple of the farmers. For Alexeyev whose
parcel was taken back as the recipient had been in solitary the
last couple of days. And then for Lehtpuu.

"There, what did I tell you!" bragged Lehtpuu and rushed up
to the hatch. He triumphantly accepted a bag of rusks, a hunk
of bacon, a jar of dripping, a dish of cereal mix and a pouch full
of tobacco, grumbled at the Russian orderly in Estonian about
the fact that the piece of pork with fat weighed barely two kilos, then
handed Timmermann over his shoulder a pair of grey woollen
socks, a pair of large grey patterned mittens, a black sheepskin
fur cap with earflaps and finally a very decent pair of top boots.
He then took the list of contents and brought it to the table. We
were not allowed pencils in the cell, so he borrowed one for a
moment from the postman. I was sitting at the same table and
followed Lehtpuu as he checked the list with the eye of a business-
man. Then I looked at the list written by Linda, Mrs or no, in
pencil on the ruled sheet of paper taken from an exercise book:
2 kg bacon, 2 kg white rusks, 1 litre jar of dripping – in an
ordinary hand though one unfamiliar with writing, in even letters,

though the *t*s were crossed in a rather unusual way with their long and delicate cross-stroke which began on the line to the left leaving three-quarters of the stroke to the left of the upstroke and only one quarter after it – which according to graphologists denoted someone who thought more about the past than the future . . .

I have naturally asked myself what were my actual motives for joining the conspiracy against Lehtpuu, and to what extent I was driven by private ones: my over-readiness to teach him how to prepare his defence – while at the same time strongly suspecting that he had nevertheless threatened Juhanson – my embarrassing readiness which in some way needed balancing out. There was certainly the game of chivalry as regards the unknown Linda (by humiliating her humiliator), that too. And the fact that Lehtpuu had more or less slipped Doctor Kuurmann's noose. But principally, because of Lehtpuu as a type, with his loathsome and intolerable insensitivity.

God knows to what degree Lehtpuu's attitude to his private possessions during the next few minutes steeled my resolve to act – Lehtpuu sitting at the table rapidly stuffing his recent haul into his linen pillowcase and mixing his cereal mix with sugar in an aluminium bowl turning it into a dessert . . . Putting the rest of the mix back in his bundle and producing from there the very last piece of crackling. And after a struggle with himself handing it across the table to Ahven saying: "Here, my lad, have a munch of that!" (Perhaps this is his fee for lining him up with a defence counsellor.) Ahven is always hungry, he is a growing lad. And the crackling has not as yet started to moulder. Ahven cannot refuse. Perhaps he has never learnt to be proud in the face of overbearing superiors. But nonetheless he does not begin to gnaw hungrily at his gift or hide it in his locker. He leaves the crackling lying before him on the table. Nor does he make any audible attempt to thank Lehtpuu. He simply gives a slight nod in his direction. Karp is silently following this with interest from his workbench. Timmermann hovers to starboard and larboard of Lehtpuu, praising his masterly qualities and his wife Linda's kind concern over his shoulder. He has already received some tobacco from Lehtpuu (though not from the latest batch to arrive), quite enough to make a thin little roll-up. He strokes Lehtpuu's grey socks ("Such confoundedly soft wool . . .") and the boots ("In there, your feet'll feel like between the wife's legs . . .") and then says:

"But I can see that Linda's been stocking the master up for a long journey."

Doctor Kuurmann has put his own parcel (oven-baked bread, sugar, half a kilo of butter and a some home-made meat loaf) into his locker and is washing his hands at the washbowl with his newly acquired cake of perfumed soap. When he passes Lehtpuu to go back to his own place, the latter says, his nostrils a-quiver, his mouth full of sugar and cereal mix:

"That soap don't-half smell nice. But you can't eat soap."

And Doctor Kuurmann admits (winking at the rest of us):

"There are four times as many calories in your parcel as in mine. That's the difference between a gentleman farmer and a towny like me."

"Quite right there," says Lehtpuu, "that was how it was when the Germans ruled the country, and so it is now."

Gerlach is lying on his greatcoat spread out on the area of the floor onto which his hinged bunk is lowered at night. He sniffs the contents of the parcels, swallows his saliva and pretends to be asleep. Siimo Kink does the same but his mouth waters less noticeably since, although he does not receive parcels, he no doubt gets his extra portion of porridge during his visits to the doctor's to have his eczema painted. The farmers from the Pärnumaa Province are sitting on the floor on their bunk-spaces, conversing in low voices and smoking tobacco from a parcel sent by someone from their parish. To the right, in the bunk-space nearest the privy, squats NCO Raik, with his bony cheeks and his stubbly chin, on his rolled up greatcoat, his brown eyes now open, now closed, darting with fear, his pale face sweaty with apprehension, as usual. To the left, where the snow wafts in through the broken window sits Elken. He has just asked Ahven for an empty white laundry bag, put half of the ration of crackers he received in it and handed the bag back to the blushing Ahven. Now he is gazing out of the window, pulling bits off the soft piece of bread he has just received that morning and feeding the most courageous pigeon who has flown in onto the windowsill. It has wafted its way into the cell along with the snowflakes and is now eating out of the palm of Elken's hand. It is now that I do what I did. I go and sit at the window end of the table, with my back to the cell. Even Elken cannot see me since he is observing his pigeons. I take a slip of ruled paper from out of the lining of my jacket. I turn to face the cell, catch Doctor Kuurmann's eye and beckon him over. And then Timmermann. And then Ahven. And then Karp. Karp as well. I tell them all my plan in a whisper. They give it their blessing. Doctor Kuurmann with a wheeze of delight. Timmermann choking on his laughter. Ahven chuckling. Karp, the corner of his mouth a-twitch, his eyes narrowed with intensity. And at the same time I write with my stub of a pencil, which I have kept in the folds of my jacket, on that ruled paper – in those commonplace letters with the low-swinging cross of the *t* – hell, I'm no worse at forging handwriting than Timmermann is at imitating voices:

> Dear Eero,
> I have received word of the fact that they have given you at least five and maybe ten years. You will yourself understand that this is too long to wait. It will hardly come as any surprise to you that Kaarel sawed the doors to the hall open last week and we have now pooled our resources. I will try to send you parcels in the future, Kaarel agrees. He is a kind-hearted man. All the best!
>   Linda

I fold the slip in two, four, eight, and push it into Ahven's palm behind me. Lehtpuu's boots are passed from hand to hand accompanied by words of admiration. The men try the shanks, the heels, the seams and the insoles. They stroke the outsides and grope around inside – "Damned fine footwear." Then they are in Timmermann's hands again. And then Timmermann pulls the letter from out of the left-hand boot from under the insole:

"Hello, hello, what's this then? By gum, sir – it's a letter! A letter from our Linda! Here, look, it's even signed "Linda"! No, no, I'm not going to read it! Here you are, sir – read it yourself and see –"

Lehtpuu snatches the letter out of his hand. He stands right under the yellow light bulb. Timmermann stands behind him and reads along with him. Ahven, Kuurmann and Karp gradually move closer to Timmermann and peer over Lehtpuu's shoulder. I sit at the table and see: Siimo Kink getting up from the floor, with the stealth of a cat uncoiling as always, stretching out his hand behind his bunk and producing his paper flute. He has no doubt observed everything through his golden eyelashes and taken everything in through his little round ears and understood everything with that little pussycat head of his. Or is it by sheer devilish coincidence that Kink now raises his paper flute to his lips and begins quietly to play "The Viljandi Boatman"?

Lehtpuu puts the letter on the table. At least judging by our source of light his face is a yellowish grey. We, the conspirators, look one another in the face. I brace myself, open my mouth to tell him: Lehtpuu the letter – it's all a – then Lehtpuu mutters through his teeth:

". . . The fucking bastards."

We, the conspirators, look at one another again. I can read it in their eyes: hang on one moment longer, just one more moment – then we'll release him from his torment . . . *If*, that is, he's worth releasing.

Then the locks rattle. Two guards come in. Karp snatches Lehtpuu's letter off the table and stuffs it into his mouth. Lehtpuu himself doesn't even notice it has gone. In a flash, Siimo Kink has whipped his paper flute behind the bunk.

"Lehtpuu! Out with you!"

Lehtpuu looks with the look of a drowning man at us – lingers for a moment.

"Быстро! Быстро!"[16] As always.

Lehtpuu leaves with one of the guards. He no longer turns round to look in our direction. The other guard says:

"Pass over his things!"

We hand him Lehtpuu's overcoat, his fur cap, his boots, his bundle. And while we had momentarily hoped, while he was being taken away, that he might return to the cell, now we realise that he is not likely to be coming back here. That he is most unlikely to. That he will be put in solitary until he is sentenced tomorrow to isolate him from everyone else, when he will be taken to court, and after that, the "unknown". Far away, to the first or second section with which we have no contacts. And thence to the transport point. To Komi. The Urals, Siberia, Central Asia, to God knows where.

"We can't just let him go like that!" says Karp, when the door has been shut and bolted and we have looked at one another for a moment in stunned silence. Karp has most surely become the spokesman of our unuttered thoughts, since he himself has had the least feeling of solidarity vis-à-vis our conspiracy.

"But what are we going to do?" I ask, choking, and I can *see* how my thoughts, seeking a way out, dash themselves against the bars of the cage and fall back to the floor. (Do something to get you solitary? But Lehtpuu is surely somewhere else than where they usually take rule-breakers to, even if he is in solitary at all . . . Or ask those who bring the tea water in the evening to convey a message to Lehtpuu . . . ? But those men are recruited from the criminal or half-criminal elements with the shortest sentences who would not dare to do anyone a favour for fear of losing their extra bread ration – and who could hardly do anything even if they wanted to . . .) And so we decide – after such a long time it is hard to say to what extent we actually believed in our variant, and to what extent we worked it out merely to console ourselves: soon, presumably the day after tomorrow, Lehtpuu will be back in the building. After being sentenced, he will spend some time back here in the prison. From experience we know this to be a fortnight. Maybe a week, but even that would be time enough. We will find out where he is. We will quiz the soup orderlies, the tea-water orderlies, the breadmen, the workshop people whom we meet during our periods of exercise, we will call through the plank fence, we will whisper, ask through the planks – and will in any case find out where he is. And we will send him word: "Lehtpuu! Linda's letter, which was found in your boot, was just a joke hatched in our cell. Linda hasn't left you. Do you understand? It was all a joke."

I imagine that I myself entertained hopes of contacting Lehtpuu more than anyone else. Firstly, of course, since it was I who had got us into this impasse and bore a greater measure of guilt than the rest. Secondly, because I genuinely entertained a hope which I could not say openly to the others, at least not without Filip Ivanovich's permission. Filip Ivanovich had whispered to me: a certain bilious old *starshiná*, a captain who had been stripped of his rank, who had from time to time been the Head Guard of our section had conveyed a number of letters from Filip Ivanovich to his wife. Not, of course, out of any idealistic thoughts about helping the prisoners, but because he was rewarded handsomely by Filip Ivanovich's wife. The starshiná *could* have a look in the card index without too much difficulty and find out where Lehtpuu was going to be in two days' time and get a letter from us through to him. And Filip Ivanovich would be out of solitary by Thursday, i.e. the morning of the day after tomorrow.

I remember how, the Wednesday night, I woke up in the yellowish rheumy darkness of the cell, actually only one quarter darkness, since the Ilyich lamp burnt all night long. I woke to the uneasy breathing of twenty-two men, the air heavy with the night fug and the cold sea mist. Everyone, apart from Elken and Raik, was asleep. Elken was standing at the window, his back to the cell, looking out into the darkness. Raik was crouching on his bunk and having a fag, as if on some never-ending watch. And I suddenly realised that I had been woken by *fear*: what would happen if Lehtpuu never returned to the prison? What if Lehtpuu was released (on account of the defence plea I had taught him!) by the tribunal and charged off home – chopping off

Kaarel's toes with an axe and doing goodness knows what to Linda?

Just before reveille, I managed to convince myself, during the consolation of a light sleep, to imagine, believe in, hope for, dread that Lehtpuu's release, be it for other reasons or on account of my plea, would be in vain . . .

Before breakfast, Filip Ivanovich was released. That is to say, he was allowed to return to Cell 19. He looked even thinner, even sallower, even greyer than before, and the ends of his moustache had grown more pointed. Before we had even had the chance to say anything to him he asked:

"Listen, was there a new man here? Who was taken out to the tribunal yesterday?"

". . . Yes, there was – what of it?"

Filip Ivanovich told his story: the day before yesterday a man who could speak pretty good Russian was put in the solitary cell next to his, and he had managed to have a conversation with him through a hole in the cell wall. The man had asked Filip Ivanovich what he had got his solitary for, and Filip Ivanovich had replied "For complimenting the Prison Governor". When Filip Ivanovich reciprocated the question, his neighbour had answered that he had been put in solitary for what he had seen an hour or two before. He had been brought to the tribunal that same morning in a Black Maria. In the vehicle there also sat a man whom he had seen for the first time, a fair-haired Estonian, a farmer from the Viljandi Province, who said that he had been for a short while in Cell 19.

"But what was his name? Had Filip Ivanovich asked the man his name?"

"Lord, when do Estonians manage to remember Russian forenames and patronymics? How do you expect a Russian to remember the surname of an Estonian – through a hole bored with a piece of wire through a wall three-quarters of a metre thick. And then heard only once?"

Filip Ivanovich had heard the man's name. His neighbour in solitary had mentioned it. But it had gone right out of Filip

Ivanovich's head. Nevertheless – it had reminded him to a certain extent of the Russian word летун, *letun*, a fugitive. And that farmer had proved to be one too. For when the vehicle stopped in front of the tribunal and both of them were walking between the guards along the pavement, the man with the fair hair and the black overcoat made a run for it. He was presumably hoping to disappear in the crowd or get round the corner. But there were few people on the street, the corner was far away, and scared guards are boys with quick reactions. They shot down the fleeing man a few dozen paces away on that same pavement. Yes. Stone dead. Simply because the guards had had a scare. For according to the book, they should have only shot him in the legs.

I have, during the decades that have passed since that time, more or less managed to shake off the relative depression I felt when walking in deciduous woods, compared with the feeling of pleasure I felt while walking through evergreen ones.[17] But when last summer I saw, in the Alutaguse Forest, a flying squirrel, itself a летун, darting among the forked branches of a old linden tree under the blue sky, an unexpected pang of guilt struck me on account of the fate of that relic of a creature, and after giving the matter a good deal of thought, I realised why.

1980

Translator's notes for "The Conspiracy"

1. The irony here is that one of these "foreign languages" could well have been Russian, a language as foreign to the average Estonian as are English or German.

2. These lines come from a poem by *Betti Alver* (1906–90) written in 1935; the original Estonian is similarly "Germanised". Her earlier poetry was concerned, appropriately for this story, with the triumph of the lightness of spirit over the heaviness of substance.

3. *Polkovnik* (Russian) – the rough equivalent to the rank of colonel, making Alexeyev, further on in the story, of clearly superior rank to the Prison Governor.

4. *Paldiski* (old German and Russian names: *Baltischport* and Балтийский порт) – Estonian port to the west of Tallinn and Soviet naval base 1945–1994.

5. *Kirov* – pseudonym of Sergei Mironovich Kostrikov (1886–1934), a Soviet revolutionary assassinated in 1934 and after whom the town of Vyatka was renamed in that same year.

6. *Toompea Castle* (built 1922) – the building housing the Estonian Parliament. The *Riigivanem* was the Premier until 1934 when the post was fused with that of President. The present façade dates from 1935, hence Timmermann's attempt to browbeat Mirk about the "carrier tits".

7. *Omakaitse Defence Force* - the Estonian sections of the German Army which, in 1941, helped the Germans to flush out Communists and the residue of the Red Army. In the heat of war, they often behaved cruelly towards minor recidivists and totally innocent people.

8. *Blatnoi* (Russian). Common criminal.

9. *Mulgimaa* – an area in south-central Estonia between the towns of Viljandi and Valga on the Latvian border. The region was known in the nineteenth century for its rich farmers who also bought up farms in other parts of the country.

10. *Velikiye Luki* was where Estonians, recruited into the German and Red armies, were obliged to engage in battle against one another. *Sinimäed*, or "Blue Hills" near Narva in eastern Estonia where there were large-scale battles in August 1944 between advancing Soviet and retreating German forces.

11. *The Viljandi Boatman* (Viljandi paadimees) – A sentimental song about a romantic river ferryman, one of whose passengers is a beautiful girl with whom he falls in love. When Estonians meet socially, this tends to be one of the first songs to be sung.

12. The farmer's name was Karl, wasn't it?
13. The man I took to be the farmer was called Karl.
14. I've no idea.
15. Yes, blond of course. All Estonian women are blond.
16. "Hurry up! Hurry up!"
17. This cryptic last paragraph hinges on untranslatable puns. The Estonian surname *Lehtpuu* means "leaf-tree" i.e. a deciduous tree, and the Russian word летун means a flier, or refugee. The *Alutaguse Forest* – an area of mixed forest south of Kohtla-Järve and near Lake Peipsi in north-eastern Estonia.

The Ashtray

The Ashtray

Shall I tell you a most improbable story, one I know from personal experience?

Several quite different types of improbability exist. For instance, intrinsic improbability and statistical improbability – I do not, of course, know what professional probability theorists would think of my classification, but that is their problem. A sufficiently high level of intrinsic improbability would come into play if I were to start telling about my encounter with a UFO. In terms of statistical improbability however, this encounter need not appear especially improbable – judging by all those typed pages of ufology, giving the impression that every third, or at least three-hundredth, open-minded person round here has spotted UFOs with his own eyes, whether on the island of Saaremaa or in the Sayan Mountains.[1]

Although it is possible to prove anything you like with statistics, statistical probability or improbability has one important facet: it conjures up the illusion of measurability. In other words, in the case of statistically improbable occurrences, it would seem to be in some way possible to get a feel of *how* improbable any given occurrence becomes. For that reason, I have chosen to tell my story at the level of statistical improbability.

It was late November 1947, and our train was travelling along the Vorkuta[2] line, first due north from Kirov, then north-east. And that event at least was far removed from any type of improbability, be it intrinsic or statistical. Not even our senses took it for improbable any longer. Quite the contrary, it was all too damnably real.

The historic Twentieth Congress of the Communist Party of the Soviet Union has, in the meantime, been superseded by so many even more historic ones, that it begins to be almost improper to remember what was said at this most historic congress of its time. It was, at any rate, at that congress that the subject of illegal repression affecting millions was first aired at such a gathering. Repression was a catch-all phrase meaning anything from being sacked from one's job to being shot. But in the main it meant the illegal despatch of millions to prison camps, plus an incalculably smaller proportion of executions. Legal executions and prison-camp sentences were undoubtedly carried out against criminals hand in hand with what occurred illegally. And for a number of reasons, certain years enjoyed a veritable boom in both legal and illegal acts of repression.

The year 1947 was, in any case, one of these boom years. And although I will gladly leave any research into the more immediate causes to historians, I am obliged to mention at least the most significant events for the sake of those interested in my story. Obliged, since such people can be under the age of forty, and therefore able to make out *even less* from consulting existent official sources than those who have personal experiences of the events in question. Anyway, one of the main reasons for the boom taking place in 1947 but stretching back a couple of years in time and continuing a couple of years thereafter was the shift that had taken place on the map of Eastern Europe. A gigantic tract of land from Leningrad to Stalingrad, Petsamo to Beltsy and, to a certain extent, Berlin to Sofia had – according to taste – moved over to, ended up under, fallen to, or been returned to Soviet power. At the time, this meant to the power of Stalin and Beria. And with all the mental intransigence of these two, with all their wooden imaginings devoid of logic, investigations were instituted into how the millions of people from these regions had lived and fared before the arrival or return of Soviet power. *Investigations,* not in the sense of collating psychological data and drawing tactical conclusions, or using it for the sake of human progress, but investigations with a view to punishment. And this unfortunately occurred all the more naturally, and in the manner of an avalanche, that there were simply *bound* to be small-time crooks or big operators among these millions, whatever criminal code was being employed as a yardstick.

Seldom have the inquisitors worked with such smooth efficiency as during this period, where attaining formal results is concerned. Seldom in a civilised country, or one which purports to be, has the division made by the inquisitors, by way of illustrating their work, been as telling as then, that is to say seldom has the percentage of those declared innocent or freed by the courts been so minimal as to be virtually non-existent, and those subjected to punishment so well-nigh omnivorously huge. The inquisitors had become ideal in their infallibility!

For at that time, no one had as yet divided up those deserving punishment into those punished legally and those punished illegally. No one other than those who were punished themselves, that is. Which made such division a highly subjective affair.

The mass of those to be punished, quite undifferentiated in this respect, were pressed through troikas and tribunals and were then allowed to trickle, quite unhurriedly it must be said, through the various transit prisons and camps, moving in a mainly easterly and northeasterly direction, into the realms of wood and coal, ensuring a new base for the enrichment of the new and ennobled society. If not in their millions, then at least in their hundreds of thousands.

Thus the statistical probability of finding the young internationalist (ha-ha-ha-haa) Peeter Mirk in a train winding its way from Kirov to Vorkuta during late November 1947 was just high enough for me to be on such a train.

The train journey was, on the one hand, endlessly tedious but on the other, simply delightful. Kirov Transit Prison, to which we had been moved a month previously from the large mill on Konstantingradskaya Street in Leningrad, was a pathetic Noah's

Ark of wooden barracks surrounded by a wooden fence, drowning, during the rainy season, under its burden in the mud and
filth beyond the railway line and the outskirts of the town. The
room in which I had spent the month seemed to be typical of
the average cells in this building. Owing to the lack of space, life
went on day and night on the two-level bunks. Because of the
low ceiling, the top level had, at best, sitting room only. So that
days and nights were spent either lying down or crouched. Of
the forty to fifty men, about one quarter could manage to stand
between the bunks and the only exercise consisted of making
one's way to the latrine. The far corner of the room was hot and
stifling, while by the window it was cold since the glass panes
had been knocked out back in the time of Arakcheyev[3] and since,
during the second week of our stay, the temperature outside had
reached around twenty or so degrees below zero. All of this –
crouching in the cold to the left, dripping with sweat to the
right, the turfy bread and the slop-like skilly, a naked Ilyich-bulb
covered in flyshit hanging from the ceiling in a constant battle
against the smoke and gloom-filled stench of the latrine, the lack
of close personal contact owing to the fact that the politicals were
mixed in among the common criminals and the fact that some
of the politicals attempted to adopt the tone and manner of the
blatnois[4] to mask in some way the accursed fact that they were
intellectuals and so as to provoke less derision – all this was
quite within the bounds of statistical probability. Even the only
eccentric in our cell more-or-less kept within these bounds: Nikolai Nikolayevich. A fellow-prisoner. A former field surgeon's
assistant. A large man with deep-set burning piggy-eyes, who had
rapidly lost weight and who was already, or on the way to becoming, mad. From morn till eve, and at times even through our
fitful night's sleep, he could be heard preaching: "Comrades –
surely you knew: when you're on the job it is absolutely *forbidden*,
do you hear, the most absolutely evil thing you can do is to knead
a woman's tits! Kneading a woman's tits amounts to killing her!
A slow death, admittedly, but you'll kill her in the end nonetheless. For instance, you over there Vassili Vassilievich – come on,

now – admit how you've kneaded your wife's tits or those of any other woman you may have gone to bed with? No doubt about it! All men knead tits. Because they simply don't know any better. But there are those who do so perhaps just because they do know: that's the only way women get breast cancer. I know it's a scientifically proven fact: sooner or later every woman whose tits have been kneaded gets breast cancer. And it kills them . . ."

Even Nikolai Nikolayevich with his mania was within the bounds of statistical probability. In so far as field surgeon's assistants are represented in any society, they must occur to the same extent in the repressed portion of that society – since you could say that absolutely every type from society-at-large was also represented here. And in so far as they, surgeon's assistants that is, have any medical knowledge, this knowledge must, given the circumstances, be transformed into something of a phantasmagoria. In another tale I would be quite prepared to tell of how I myself, and not in such an exotic location as now in Kirov but in the almost homely surroundings of Tallinn Central Prison, managed to work out a grammatico-logico-social world order. But let us return to Nikolai Nikolayevich. Everything in what he said was within the bounds of statistical probability. Despite undernourishment and depression, erotic imaginings kept stirring within us and many of us had, thrashing about in the cellars of our mind, a guilt complex about what we had at some time or another done with our own wives, someone else's, or with God knows with who or what else. In a word, Nikolai Nikolayevich's *idée fixe* and the Kirov Prison as a whole had an oppressive influence on us. Even an unbearable one. And if you could stand it, this was only because you knew that things were so short-term. In so far as you could, in our circumstances, speak of *knowing* anything about your prospects. So let us rather put it this way: you could stand it because you hoped that things were so short-term. For we were always unfailingly ready to spin together all manner of infallible hopes for ourselves, realistic or unrealistic.

*   *   *

Oh yes indeed, I can remember how, some time before the commencement of this train journey I have begun describing, back in Leningrad in the large transit prison on Konstantingradskaya, quite a civilised place in comparison with Kirov, we used to hope for the most favourable things to happen in the near future. I mean my God, the Thirtieth Anniversary of the Great October Revolution would soon be knocking on our door! To celebrate such anniversaries there had always been amnesties, had there not? Indisputably! Well, you know – mumbled those more experienced fellow-convicts who tried to cover up the surge of hope within themselves with words of prudent scepticism – such amnesties exist but they're bound principally to affect criminals, being of rather limited compass as regards politicals. OK, be that as it may. But hitherto none of those anniversaries had been the Thirtieth! Nor has the next one followed so closely – how long is two years, really – on an event so liberating mind and spirit as the victory in the Great Patriotic War! The only possible conclusion: an opportunity for announcing such a widespread amnesty, one embracing political prisoners *as well*, had never before presented itself! Under the terms of such an amnesty as was now imminent, a good half, well, almost half of the prisoners or perhaps one quarter, were almost certain to be released. But among this half, or almost half, or this quarter, or even one tenth who were dead certain to be amnestied, there was room for each and every one of us. And, painful to relate, for a while there was even room for me! My short but rather compact life experience and a little legal training notwithstanding. For owing to my relative professionalism, I should have seen things in a wider context than many others did and could have kept myself aloof from childish hopes. And at the same time, looked at from a purely professional angle, I could see with my relatively well-trained lawyer's eye that, considering the crimes I had been accused of, I had got off with a toddler's sentence of a mere five years, making my case appear one of the more hopeful ones.

*   *   *

Of course the amnesty, news of which finally reached us by way of scraps of newspaper, affected only criminals, pickpockets and minor recidivists, only the "friends of power" as we immediately began to call them ironically, and even they from that margin whose misdemeanours were of the least gravity and then only to an almost negligible extent. Or perhaps a little greater, God only knows. But it has to be said, by and large, that the ensuing disappointment was out of all proportion to the hopes so recently raised. Soon we were hoping for other things. And in the Kirov we were hoping that we would leave the place as soon as possible, to enjoy conditions which simply had to be incomparably better than those we were living under at the time.

And then, one morning, it really happened: column close ranks, Mirk, Pyotr Ivanovich, join the column, bundle under your arm, quick march!

I cannot say how far our march took us. Maybe four or five kilometres. From the transit prison to the siding behind the main railway station. I cannot remember what the surroundings looked like. But I can clearly recall walking over the snow-covered sleepers of the railway embankment in a column of a couple of hundred men, guards with their dogs in front, at the sides and behind, like one great black centipede, jointed and winding, over white snow, and I recall the rank stench which we suddenly smelt coming from ourselves and the clean wind which blew in gusts into our mouths. And one tall swarthy Rumanian next to whom I happened to be walking.

He was around thirty-five years old, a stately young fellow of the Ancient Roman type, against whom I harbour strong prejudices, not to mention downright aversion. Maybe this is based on jealousy as to imagined prowess with women, perhaps it was jealousy of their culture, which they just happen to possess, and which they trample on with indifference, maybe jealousy based on genetic experience, showing that men of such physique tend to prove to be bastards when coming in contact with a genus such as mine. But my one-hour acquaintance with this man was, at any rate, a pleasant one. He had an admirable command of

French, too admirable for my liking, and he managed cour-
ageously, for four of the five kilometres we had to walk, to recite
Baudelaire from memory. And for the sake of his Baudelaire, I
felt the distance could have been twice as long. My French was
– as those who remember my school reports will appreciate –
somewhat on the weak side, but thanks to Monsieur Ledoute
with his special method I had managed to commit to memory
six or seven Baudelaire poems: "L'Albatros", "Élévation",
"L'invitation au voyage" and so on. We muttered them – piece-
meal – in a low recitative duet:

> *Mon esprit, tu te meus avec agilité,*
> *Et, comme un bon nageur qui se pâme dans l'onde,*
> *Tu sillonnes gaiement l'immensité profonde*
> *Avec une indicible et mâle volupté.*
> *Envole-toi bien loin de ces miasmes morbides;*
> *Va te purifier dans l'air supérieur,*
> *Et bois, comme une pure et divine liqueur,*
> *Le feu clair qui remplit les espaces limpides*

We muttered – talking on this march was forbidden – under our
breath, our mouths half-closed, striding over the frozen sleepers,
stumbling along, the routine shouts of the guards, the barking
of the escort dogs and the crunch of our footsteps all seeming
somehow to stem from beyond the snowflakes and these verses.

The Rumanian was an officer, a major, and I believe that he
really held his stated rank, though soldiers in such situations often
add a couple of stripes to their sleeve with pathetic self-assurance.
The fact that he was an officer shone through in his aloof attitude
and curt correctness. And yet he was the son of an academic, a
professor of history whom I had heard of then but whose name
now escapes me, and it was clearly this cultural family heritage
that somewhat broadened and softened his strait and stiff officer's
bearing and made him seem sympathetic, at least on that march
for that one hour. But why have I begun to describe him in such
detail? Ah yes, because in conversation with that Rumanian I
learnt a French word, or to be more exact, rediscovered it. Words

and situations are sometimes interlinked in a peculiar manner. My weak knowledge of French was characterised by the fact that I frequently had to search for the word for the most mundane objects, my knowledge having been acquired in a bookish manner and not through practice. A particularly weak side of my French is the slightly more unusual words connected to those which are most common. And when we paused from reciting Baudelaire or rather when we had got through our Baudelaire, I do not quite remember if it was while he was speaking about his family – did he not mention King Michael himself in connection with his office? – he all of a sudden screwed up his dark eyes and said:

"But what have we now become? The garbage of Europe!"

I have always had difficulties in reacting to a southern temperament. The likes of us – or at least of myself – do not understand it entirely. One never knows how thick the space is between outer shell and core. Where theatricality ends and gravity begins. Is everything merely stage-setting, or does it all come straight from the heart? And for a split second I weighed up what I should reply. Whether to answer: How do you mean, garbage? Perhaps it is just grains of a specific density picked out by centrifugal force, etc., etc. . . . ? No, my language knowledge was simply not up to it and too childish to convey a cautious scepticism. Or should I simply agree – whether or not it sounded cultivated for me to do so, and say bluntly in any case: "Garbage, alas, garbage. And putrefaction our most likely prospect."

I do not quite remember, perhaps I allowed my gaze to roam in search of an answer – over the alien earth, dappled with grey snow and black soil as far as the eye could see and the low sky which was sprinkling a little fresh snow like white ash onto our dark heap. And somewhere in all this Baudelaire – And then suddenly I knew what I should reply – But it had to be translated into French! All the necessary words were there – apart from one, and that the most important of all: I had forgotten the French for "ashtray". I was obliged to explain: You know – a vessel, into which you throw fag-ends – *les mégots* – I even knew the word for "fag-ends", but the one for "ashtray" escaped me.

"*Eh bien, vous voulez dire – le cendrier?*"[5]

Exactly! I said:

"You know what we are? Fag-ends. In God's ashtray."

"In what way?"

"Those who have gone out, have gone out. Anyone who still has a spark of life in him – anyone who hasn't yet burnt out – if . . ."

He instantly grasped my meaning: "If God notices him, and breathes life into him and starts him burning again – and then passes him to someone who can draw a puff out of him? Ha-ha-ha-haa. Are you hoping He's going to do so in your case too?"

What could I answer? I didn't want to look a fool. But I did want to be honest. Or perhaps I was willing my answer to come true.

"Hm – not exactly. But something like that."

"Well, good luck!"

Since that time, the word *cendrier* has stuck in my memory. But by that time we had arrived at a siding behind the station, had walked along it and were being herded into carriages. Me into one, the Rumanian into another.

A fellow-prisoner with a bent for philosophy once said, not on that occasion but during another helter-skelter deportation, that normal life must surely be a variant of prison life distorted by the magnifying glass of time: one is forced by circumstance, one's contacts become charged with inevitability, some are moved to this end of the horizon, others to the far end, some to one city, others to another. Here, the *starshiná*, the warrant officer, bawls orders for some to enter one carriage, some a second, some one compartment, others another, for some to get out at one station, others at a different one. The chop comes, of course, to everyone in the end, only more abruptly and sharper as time goes on. More lacerating, if you like. So why keep the arse of your soul too near the blade? As that fellow-prisoner once put it.

The compartment into which I was ordered to climb was a normal "Stolypin" compartment with the yellow wood of third-class carriages, now somewhat grey with wear, and with bars

across the window and doorpanes. Such barred carriage windows
are indelibly printed on the consciousness of a great many people
of my generation – I mean to say, if not through personal experience, then by way of postcards from grandfather's time and from
an illustration by a now forgotten artist in *The Great Book of
Russian Art History*, which shows a barred window and behind it
a pair of bearded men, a woman and a child who are attempting
to throw breadcrumbs out to the pigeons busy pecking on the
platform in the foreground. Sheer sentimentalist naturalism. And,
of course, a political protest against the spirit of the age and its
soul-destroying carriages which His20Excellency Prime Minister
Stolypin had begun to bring into use in 1905 – or perhaps they
were already being used then but gained popularity at just that
time – which immortalised at least the name of the Prime Minister in common parlance right up to the epoch I am describing.
And even, to a lesser extent, afterwards as well.

As is common knowledge, such a compartment was, in civilian
use, intended for four persons. Under these special circumstances
it had been converted for use by – indeed, by how many? In order
to accommodate as many as possible, an extra platform had been
constructed between the ceiling and the upper bunks with a small
opening to enable you to wriggle your way up and down and on
which, by using a sardine technique, four or even five men could
lie or rest on their elbows. The four remaining bunks were each to
seat (how they managed to lie was their business) four men in a
row, and this could almost be done comfortably, except that those
on the upper level had to let their feet dangle, which was no problem though you had to sit hunched up, since there was no room
to sit up straight – then there was room in each compartment for
twenty-one men. And in that way, the little iron-edged window-
table would remain entirely free for the travellers to eat or play
cards on – if the guards happened to be elsewhere and the players
could manage to play silently or at most in a whisper.

I was shoved into one of these compartments – the eighteenth
man as it happened. And as no more were added, it was quite
cosy in there: one free place on each level. The other seventeen

were, as far as I could gather, all Lithuanians and all of a decent sort. Decent, that is, in the sense that none were *blatnoi*s, pickpockets, thieves, burglars or gangsters. So I did not have to worry about my reasonably respectable coat nor my medium-sized bundle. For as rumour had it, such worries were very real on such transports. But in other respects my travelling companions were a wretched lot. For they were wearing uniforms, presumably from the time of Lithuanian independence, from which all the insignia had been removed as well as the brass buttons which had been replaced by wooden toggles. These uniforms were representative of what former Estonian soldiers would have worn in the corresponding situation – the Estonians having been former Omakaitse[6] officers, while these Lithuanians were ex-members of the LAF or TDA military units from the time of the German Occupation.

In the course of two days and one-and-a-half nights, I managed to communicate with these men to the necessary extent. They spoke Russian with a heavy Lithuanian accent, although their knowledge was, on average, better than mine. I had nonetheless already had a one-year intensive course in the language, albeit with poor learning materials. So that we did have a lingua franca. Besides, they asked me little and I asked them nothing at all. For as regards my attitude to the situation in general and the question of merging with my surroundings in particular, I was, if not yet at proficiency level, then at least at that of basic orientation: I related to my surroundings like an observant tourist and merged with my environment just enough to keep trouble at bay, while *deep inside* not thawing to anything, or anybody. And so I outwardly felt quite at home in this somewhat cocksure but harmless company and was prepared to travel along with them for a day or two more, a week or two as far as I was concerned, no matter how far, no matter for what reason, as it did not depend on me anyway. The rumour spread that we were on our way to the Pechora coalfield and at this slow pace (we were constantly uncoupled at stations and recoupled to the next train, or the one following) the journey had to last another day or maybe even two. And this period at least would be a reasonably secure one.

So it came as a most unpleasant surprise when I started out of my sleep in the middle of the night to hear:

"Мирк, Пётр Иванович? Где же он?! Здесь? Ёб его мать! Быстро! С вещами!!"[7]

Thank God we were not sleeping in our pyjamas and that our things were not strewn around a hotel room. I was in the corridor in ten seconds. I do not know how they checked that I was who I was. Presumably against a photo which the guard or head of the convoy had attached to his documents. The train nonetheless stood panting in the darkness and within two minutes I was doing likewise – the train far away, now almost gone, now vanished completely, and all around me an absolute void, utter snowy darkness and the stupefyingly pure frosty air.

I called out "Hello there!" lightly into the darkness to see if perhaps someone else had been dropped like myself. But not a soul. And if there had been, it would not have been clear by which logic such games were to be played here in the middle of nowhere. At any rate, there I stood quite alone – even the stars in the sky were absent and I thought to myself: all I need to do now is locate the rails with the toe of my boot and start walking south-westwards. And in two thousand kilometres I'll be home – (And I would like to add, for the sake of young people who are not expert in these matters and who wonder why I didn't try to escape, that such an action was a lost cause right from the start. The only way of escape would be along the railway itself which was the only way of any sort in these parts. And the only buildings along the line were prison-camp huts and the guards' barracks, the kennels and exercising grounds of the guard dogs. And the private individuals, insofar as there were any out here at all, having themselves had a taste of the camps, were quite prepared to turn in any suspicious persons at the drop of a hat, be it for the fear of the penalty, or the temptation of the reward, connected with handing the culprit over.)

Someone would obviously have been sent to fetch me. But there was no one there. This was a breakdown in the system which was certainly a relatively less frequent occurrence in the army, and especially in the prison-camp service, than elsewhere in society. Nor was the breakdown allowed to last long this time either. I had been standing there for several minutes, had stretched, breathed deeply, now realising from *what* stuffy carriage air, laden with cheap tobacco smoke and bodily odours, I had emerged, when I began to make out a string of lights in the distance. And at the same time I noticed: in amongst those stationary dots of light, there was one wagging its way towards me.

A short while later a lantern approached, steaming. A leather glove pushed it out of the darkness into my face. The other glove dealt with my papers:

"Фамилия? Имя? Отчество? Год рождения? Срок??"[8]

I answered and was acknowledged as one of theirs.

"Дошлн!"[9]

We began to walk along the line. The man with the lantern walking behind, of course, and me in front and not vice-versa. I could have made an attempt to ask what the name of the settlement was and the number of the prison camp to which we were going. From experience I knew it was not unlikely that my escort would have told me, alone as we were in the darkness. But it was just as likely – presumably more likely – that he would have snorted "Молчать!"[10] And that would, however you look at it, have been too humiliating to provoke yourself. And so we walked the kilometre or so in silence, turned off the track and in a few hundred metres found ourselves at the gates to the camp.

Around an electric lamp in the control post under the watch-tower sat three men in white sheepskin warders' coats and red epaulettes. The stove was roaring. The men's faces were red with night warmth and their eyes filled with sleep.

"A newcomer –? Oh damn. Lock him up in the transfer barrack until the morning. Then we'll see where he's to go."

But I had heard enough about what happened, or could happen, in the transfer barracks for me at least to make an attempt. I said:

"Citizen Commandant – I am wearing more-or-less decent

clothing. Are you so sure it will still be on my back, come morning, if you have me overnight in the transfer barrack?"

The wall-eyed red-faced guard was patently a sensible man. He muttered something and then said, though not to me but to my warder:

"Very well. Let him spend the night in the sick bay. We'll sort the rest out in the morning." He cranked the phone and summoned the sick-bay orderly who arrived within two minutes and took me along to where he was ordered.

I trudged after this gnarled old orderly a couple of hundred yards across the camp along boarded footpaths, covered in snow, and we crossed two bridges over ditches, with their arched Rococo handrails. The deserted snowy roads were well lit despite the sparsity of lamps and the whole camp that night took on the aspect of an absurd Christmas card.

The waiting room to the sick bay which was housed in a barrack similar to the rest was almost grand: the whitewashed brick stove was hot, the floor swept and there were muslin curtains in front of the windows, in the corner narrow-footed flower boxes made from white planks and containing a row of pots with bright green asparagus plants. And against the whitewashed walls stood a few wooden settees. The orderly pointed one of them out with his chin:

"You can kip there till six. At six comes the doctor."

"Why so early?"

"Work starts at seven. Before work begins, those who have reported sick have to be examined. So get yourself off the sofa by six."

I stretched myself out and the orderly turned off the light. The settee was short and could hardly be described as soft. But, compared with that of the cell and carriage of my recent sojourns, the *air* in this spacious waiting room was miraculously pure. And what was most important: I was sleeping for the first time in goodness knows how long in a dark room. And so I – despite the uncertainty of what lay in store for me and the certainty that this could prove to be hell on earth if I was out of luck, and even if

I had good luck my stay would be no holiday – I fell into a deep and restful sleep in that sick bay.

"Get up! Get up! The doctor's on his way!"

The servile zeal of the orderly did not bode well for how the doctor would turn out to be. What was more – the doctor had not yet put in an appearance. I still had ample time to get up and wet my three-day growth of stubble in a bowl provided by the orderly and wipe myself dry on a towel. Only then did the doctor himself come in. He was of medium height and around thirty-five years of age. A prisoner too, that went without saying. But an élite prisoner. He was wearing a clean dark-blue padded jacket and a high-collared black camp tunic around whose black upright collar peeped a millimetre of snow-white vest. He had the ordinary, slightly bored but not unfriendly face of someone well2ofed, clean-shaven cheeks and, in accordance with the privileges enjoyed by men of his station, neatly cut brown hair with a parting. I spoke first:

"I was sent to the sick bay to spend the night here . . ."

"Aha, you must have arrived in the night? Where have you just come from? And where are you from?"

I explained. And at the same time I thought I detected in his brief questions that selfsame Lithuanian accent which my *Darbo apsauga*[11] men on the train had filled my ears with. And so it turned out to be:

"Aha, from Tartu? I'm from Kaunas." He now shook my hand: "Doctor Kačanauskas. Regret I've never been to Tartu. Have you ever visited Kaunas?"

"Yes. Very briefly. I've been to the Čiurlionis Museum.[12] And the Opera to hear "Birutė". But I can actually say that I've *stayed* in Klaipėda.[13] Two whole summers."

"Oh, and when was that? And in what connection? But – do take a seat." He had hung his padded jacket up on a peg and was washing his hands in a bowl brought by the orderly and placed on a tripod. And I explained. How before the war my aunt and uncle had lived in Klaipėda. And how my uncle had represented some Dutch firm which sold shipping equipment, ropes, paint, et cetera. And how I had stayed with them two summers running.

Doctor Kačanauskas washed his hands, dried them on the towel brought in by the orderly and came to sit by me:

"If you've stayed two summers in Klaipėda then you may know people there?"

I thought for a while. Aunt Juuli and Uncle August no doubt did. They had lived there for over ten years before moving back to Tallinn the year before the war broke out. But me? I had basked in the sun in the Juodkrantė Dunes from morning till night along with my cousin and we had swum in the sea, lain on the beach reading books through sunglasses so that our eyes grew dappled and our necks green. Friends? Ah yes, *one* person came to mind who visited Uncle August to dine on a couple of occasions:

"Well, there was for instance, Captain Bačenas – some pilot or other down at the port."

"Captain Bačenas?" asked the doctor. "From Klaipėda? What did he look like?

"Well, how should I describe him? Taller than average. Sturdy. Have you ever seen a portrait of Admiral Makarov?"

"I'm afraid not," the doctor had to admit.

I said: "Captain Bačenas had just the same kind of forked full beard."

Doctor Kačanauskas burst into laughter and stood up: "Captain Bačenas with his full beard was a very good friend of my father's. Listen, let's go over to my bunker for a moment."

We got up. I could see that five or six wilting individuals had already appeared in the waiting room – the first of today's batch of sick cases, presumably. The doctor addressed the orderly:

"Ivan Borisovich, come and get the thermometers and hand them out," and then, so that the aspiring patients could hear: "And keep an eye on them to make sure they don't fiddle their temperatures."

The three of us stepped into the doctor's tiny surgery. Two metres by three. A small white table. A diminutive instrument cabinet. Three white chairs. When the orderly had gone out with the thermometers the doctor asked me to sit down at his desk and himself took a seat behind it. He said smiling wryly, then growing serious:

"Well, if Saint John Nepomuk[14] has arranged things so – look, here in the camp life is almost bearable. But also quite unbearable. In an hour the prisoner-overseer will find you and then you can end up doing all manner of things: making flowerpots, felling trees, loading planks, digging ditches – they get dug even at this time of year. And doing such work in November is no joke. Especially for someone who is unaccustomed to it. And I do not imagine that Estonian jurists are. You would, in any case, not be getting sufficient food rations for the work. And yet before the first letters from here reach home and the food packages reach us here, six months can have gone by. Let me put it this way. Such work can be avoided if you grease the palms of the *naryad-chiki*.[15] With goods, money, whatever you can. But they are well-fed gents, mostly from the ranks of the criminal element. So you would hardly have anything to offer them. And even if you had, you would perhaps refuse to give it them. But what I would like to say to you is this: there is likely to be a better way for you as an Estonian to find acceptable work. You see, the central administration for a large area of prison camps is located right here in the town of Knyazhpogost. The administration runs a construction office. A dozen engineers, designers, draughtsmen, copyists. The deputy engineer, who is in actual fact the boss, is a compatriot of yours. Your *zemlyak*,[16] Yakov Pavlovich Kanter.[17] A reliable chap. If he hands the chit to the head *naryadchik* on your behalf, you will automatically be taken on there."

"But what will I do there? I'm no engineer, nor a builder, nor . . ."

"There are a hundred people working at the office. There are all sorts," said the doctor.

I said (to dampen my rising hopes and out of a certain measure of self-deprecation):

"Well, my dear *zemlyaki* don't usually make grand gestures in such matters."

And unexpectedly, Doctor Kačanauskas agreed with my dubious statement to quite an unwarranted extent:

"Forgive my saying so, but you are so right. When it comes to matters of mutual assistance, Estonians are unbelievably passive. Jews, for instance, are a hundred times keener. They'll help one another as a matter of course. I believe that even my own Lithuanians are ahead of you Estonians on that count. But allow me to add: the matter is more serious than you may have realised. For this reason: Comrade Kanter will be obliged to put you through a test. He is, let's face it – an Estonian pedant. But he does everything he considers he is able to do."

I said: "Doctor Kačanauskas, I would like to express my sincere thanks. And I promise that I will – consider . . ."

He said, almost angrily: "Listen here, Comrade Mirk, there's no time for *considering* around here. I suggest I send my orderly straight to Hut 27, right away. Kanter will be here in five minutes and then you will have made his acquaintance."

I said: "Alright, if Saint John Nepomuk has so arranged things, and will bless such nepotism . . ."

Five minutes later Jakob Kanter stepped into the doctor's room. He was a small broad-shouldered man of around fifty. Perhaps even more evidently an élite prisoner than the doctor. He had a noticeably large head, short prematurely greying hair, a rather elongated pinkish face, a tiny neatly trimmed blond moustache, a small mouth and strikingly blue eyes. One's first impression was of an amiable and cultivated man, but he was undoubtedly also what the doctor had said – a pedant.

The doctor introduced us and explained why he had called out the Chief Engineer even before work had started, and added:

"But now you must excuse me. I have to attend to my patients."

The doctor went out into the waiting room, pulling the door to his surgery shut behind him.

"So," said Comrade Kanter, "I would like to ask you – what are you actually capable of doing?"

"Well now, I could draw up the regulations for the construction office – if someone could translate them into Russian. Or –

I could write – for the office in general and the workers in par-
ticular – poems for special occasions. In unlimited numbers.
Assuming again, of course, that someone can translate them into
Russian . . ."

I observed from Kanter's almost imperceptible, sour little smile
that my banter was not at all to his liking. So I said: "I can't
really see that I can do anything which would be necessary in a
construction office. Except for – perhaps I could acquire some
necessary skill – some very basic one – quite quickly, I suppose."

"Can you read technical drawings?"

"*At present*, I would say – no. But if someone were to instruct
me, then – I suppose I'd be able to by next week."

"Hmm, yes . . ." said Kanter, his manner friendly, but a little
hesitantly, "we have two chaps from Leningrad who can read
blueprints passably enough but they've been assigned forestry
work. Because in the office you have to be able to read fast and
faultlessly."

"Well, that's clear then . . ." I wanted to say, as I felt embarrassed and the feeling was increasing by the minute.

"Can you manage a technical drawer's pen and a compass?"

I said: "Only in a very rudimentary way. As much as they
taught you at grammar school – " and at the same time I was
wondering: why did this "very highly qualified engineer" as the
doctor made him out to be, use the word "compass" instead of
"pair of compasses"? And why such a clumsy expression as a
"technical drawer's pen"? With the strangely light stress on the
word *technical*? And immediately I had it: Kanter spoke Estonian
quite flawlessly. Without an accent, you could say. And yet there
was a very slight something about his intonation which did not
quite ring true. And his use of "compass" gave me the clue, as
did his way of declining loan words: this man must be a Russian-
born Estonian.[18] Or an Estonian from Russia, at any rate. I
asked:

"You yourself – you're not a graduate of the Tallinn Technical
High School, are you?"

"No, I'm not. I first studied at the Saint Petersburg Imperial

Institute of Technology. But then I graduated in Petrograd, *sans* Emperor."

"And continued working in Russia?" I added this in the first instance to avoid his asking me more about my skills. And I have to admit: to distance myself from him. In a year such as 1947, a Russian-born Estonian was only a *zemlyak*, a compatriot of mine, to a most problematical degree. Such *trusties* with their partly, or wholly, unidiomatic phrases, their doubting and distrustful eyes who had, since the war, seeped into the university, from the dean of faculty right down to posts among the teaching staff and special departments, and in everyday life from executive committee and militia down to the local apartment block administration, had instilled in me a feeling which was as mixed as what must have been going on inside them themselves: pity and watchfulness.

At any rate, we home-grown Estonians and Russian-born Estonians had lived such different lives on our respective sides of the border that our mutual alienation had become inevitable. On both sides of the border irrational things had been said and printed about the other side. In Estonia, hungry children were supposed to go about scavenging for food in dustbins. While in Russia, claimed the Estonian daily *Päevaleht* in, for instance, 1937, the year of the great show trials, it had emerged that men who had been the vanguard of revolution only fifteen years before were now infiltrators, traitors and foreign agents who had with their bare hands mixed broken glass into the butter sold to the proletariat ... Ten years earlier, nothing but such news items were to be found about Russia in our papers. And never a whisper of protest or denial from their side of the border, something which would have been quite natural in the circumstances, had these proved to be lies. So you were bound to conclude: there must be some truth in the matter. And this then led one to ask: *which side* had gone mad over there, the courts or those who appeared before them? And to answer without hesitation: the courts. For if the courts had been normal and the accused, therefore, mad, then the mass-executions of those accused would not have been able to take place. And Russia's Estonians lived right

in the thick of this madness, in this oppressive atmosphere of
mistrust which resulted from this madness, which Russia allowed
especially to afflict the minorities on her western borders. So that
people who were used to all this seemed, according to my first
impression, and soon *a priori*, more problematical, evasive, shifty-
eyed and ill-defined than others. Especially if they tried (and as
far as I could observe, they always tried) to justify that what had
been, and was still occurring in their country was right and proper
in itself; unequivocally right and proper that is, according to the
conversations of uneducated people, but to a more problematic
degree according to those arrested – well, anyway, right and
proper, not always in that cosy petit-bourgeois sense of the
expression, but in a nobler and more general sense.

"Yes," said Comrade Kanter. "First I worked in Russia, then
in Germany and then in Italy and then in Russia once again. Up
to the year 1937. Does that mean anything to you?"

I nodded: "Understood." And the matter was indeed clear to
me. Or at least the ambiguity of the situation had become so. I
had not said: "Understood. Then you must obviously be a traitor
and were no doubt an undercover agent or a spy for Germany
or Italy or both. I merely grunted "Understood!" and left it at
that. For in such a complicated case as this it was better to keep
one's mouth shut. I made as if to rise from my seat and was about
to say: "Comrade Kanter, I thank you for your kind concern for
my welfare – but it is quite obvious that the two men working
in the forest, but who could perhaps work in your office, take
precedence over me. So be so good as to add my name to the list
after theirs. And I will try and learn something in the meantime."

But Kanter beckoned me to sit down again and asked:

"Are you acquainted with technical script?"

"What do you mean 'acquainted with'?"

"Well, can you write technical texts in ink? Using standard
script."

It was an strange moment. It was as if he simply couldn't bring
himself to let me go. And I did not dare to reply: I can. And not

simply because I could very well be proved there and then, within half-an-hour or the next day, to be a fraud."

"No, I can't."

"Hm . . ." He thought a little – I started once again to my feet.

He asked: "Oh yes, you're from Tartu aren't you?"

"Yes, I studied there, at least. And worked there too. For a short while. As long as I was allowed to. But I'm originally from Tallinn."

"I'm sorry, the doctor did introduce us but what was the name again?"

"Peeter Mirk."

"Mirk? From Tallinn?"

"That's right."

"And where in Tallinn did you live?"

Why was he asking this question? Had this man ever been to Tallinn? Most unlikely. But I had no reason not to answer. I said:

"In Kalamaja. If that means anything to you. To the north-west of the centre. Vesker's machine-tool shop was out there. My father worked for Vesker's."

Kanter looked at me with impish delight:

"So you lived – past the foundry – turn right into the small side street – in Vesker's workers' flats. You then lived in the lower flat on the left?"

I was speechless with amazement. Speechless for some time. Two lists of names intertwined in my imagination: clairvoyants and detectives – Swedenborg – Sherlock Holmes – Madame Blavatsky – the Witch of Äksi – and perhaps the weary face of Major Sidorov – if he already existed at the time to epitomise his colleagues . . . Where the hell could Kanter have known that from?

He sat there savouring my consternation – for one whole minute it seemed – with the light smile of a magician on his lips, whereupon he explained:

"You see, it was like this – in 1921, me and my wife decided – she's dead now – to move from Petrograd to Estonia. In those days, there was no question of being regarded as traitors to Russia for doing so. And from the Estonian point of view, we weren't really immigrants either, if you see what I mean. I was in fact born in Pärnu.[19] I had also been allowed to leave my previous job and my papers were in order from the point of view of both countries. That was easy to arrange in those days. And there were just the two of us – we didn't have any children. But then it transpired that the theatre – my wife was a ballet dancer at the Maria Theatre – wouldn't let my wife go. Lopukhov[20] himself asked her to dance right up to the end of the season. So we decided that I would travel first to Estonia, find a job in Tallinn, arrange a flat and move in, and she would follow along the next spring. I went to Tallinn. In the autumn of '21. I got a job at Vesker's factory. As an engineer. I worked there alongside your father. We serviced "OB" locomotives from the Russian Federation. But then it transpired in the spring of '22 that the theatre still wouldn't let my wife go. So I went back to Petrograd. But during the time I worked with your father, I was at your house several times, sometimes for reasons of work, at other times I played chess with him. I remember you. You were one-and-a-half at the time. And so high." He indicated the height with his hand – a little lower than that of Doctor Kačanauskas' desk. Then he tapped the tips of his fingers against his rough black calico camp trousers: "You have sat on my knee – and quite a few times at that."

I couldn't bring myself to say a thing. He continued: "But now I must hurry. At a quarter to seven we will be leaving with the convoy from the main gate to the zone. You will stay behind in the zone for now. I will leave a chit with your name on it with the chief *naryadchik*. I will be back at six. Look me up in Hut 27. I will have the necessary equipment for you with me. Paper. Pens. Ink. I am not supposed to have such things on camp premises. But I'll bring them along with me. You will practise. If you can't find anywhere else to do so, then here will do. I'll arrange it with the Doctor. Get acquainted with the GOST technical script as thoroughly as you are able. You have one evening, two nights and one day to do so. On Thursday morning we will leave for the office. Goodbye. And good luck. By the way, how is your father?"

"Dead."

"When?"

"Last year."

"Where?"

"In Mordva."[21]

"Oh, I see." He was silent for a moment. "Well, once again, good luck. I hope that you get the hang of the script."

He smiled, a little guilty that he had been obliged to be so demanding with me, and left.

I breathed a sigh of relief and thought: he'll get his script, all right. And I also thought – and, you might say, am still thinking: this Earth does indeed contain a level at which such coincidences occur, confirming the existence of the Lord of the Ashtray.

1983–1986

Translator's notes for "The Ashtray"

1. *Sayan Mountains* – a range of mountains in Central Siberia.
2. *Vorkuta, Kirov* – mining centres. Vorkuta is in the Pechora coalfield in the Komi Autonomous Republic, Kirov (Vyatka) in the Russian Federation. The workforce included exiled people from all over the Soviet Union.
3. *Alexander Andreyevich Arakcheyev,* (1769–1834) was Minister of Defence under Czar Alexander I. Notorious for his repression of free thought, his violent and venal régime and his general cruelty.
4. *Blatnoi* (Russian) – a common criminal.
5. "Oh, you mean an ashtray?"
6. *Omakaitse* – an Estonian military organisation created during the German Occupation 1941–44. The LAF and TDA were similar organisations in Lithuania.
7 "Mirk, Pyotr Ivanovich, Where is he? Come on, you motherfucker! With your belongings!"
8. "Surname? Forename? Patronymic? Date of birth? Sentence?"
9. "Quick march!"
10. "Silence!"
11. *Darbo apsauga* (Lithuanian) – labour convoy.
12. *Mikolajus Čiurlionis* (1875–1911) – Lithuania's most significant composer and painter. Studied in Warsaw and Leipzig.
13. *Klaipėda* – Lithuanian port (better known by the German name of Memel).
14. *Ján (John) Nepomuk* (1340–93), Martyr and Patron Saint of Bohemia. Kačanauskas comes from Catholic Lithuania, hence the keenness on saints.
15. *Naryadchik* (Russian) – a prisoner who acts as foreman and is responsible for work quotas.
16. *Zemlyak* (Russian) – compatriot.
17. *Yakov Pavlovich Kanter* – the Russified version of Jakob Kanter's name (cf. Pyotr Ivanovich Mirk).

    Jakob Kanter bears an intriguing resemblance to the real-life Estonian Aleksander Kurtna (1914–1983) – the surnames are almost anagrams! – who studied at an Orthodox seminary then with the Jesuits in Rome, became a Soviet spy at the Vatican, was recalled and became a contemporary of Kross in the Russian labour camps. Kurtna was rehabilitated and ended up as a translator of children's literature, and the A. Kurtna Translation Award is named after him.
18. *Russian-born Estonian* – Communists who fled to Russia during

Estonian independence (1920–1940) and returned to Estonia to take up leading posts after the Communist takeover there in 1944, as did First Secretaries Vaino and Käbin. Regarded with great suspicion and contempt by the average "home-grown" Estonian.

19. *Pärnu* – Estonian seaside town on the west coast popular with the Russian artistic intelligentsia, e.g. Andrei Tarkovski and David Oistrakh.

20. *Fyodor Vassilievich Lopukhov* (1886–1973) – Russian ballet dancer and impresario.

21. *Mordva* – autonomous republic. Home of a Finno-Ugrian people (like the Estonians) but also a region of Russian prison camps.

The Day Eyes
Were Opened

The Day Eyes
Were Opened

An ordinary train bound for Tartu one September morning in the late 1950s. Standing outside the new, or rather the old Baltic Station building in Tallinn which has been reconstructed out of the postwar limestone rubble.

The train is a typical six-carriage milk train. One of those that stops at every halt for a couple of minutes and every station for five or ten, all the way to Tartu, taking one-and-a-half hours more than the Pskov, Moscow or Riga expresses. So that it is incomprehensible why, apart from those passengers getting on at the halts, it should also be used by so many who are travelling all the way to Tartu. If not for the reason that the journey is a few dozen copecks cheaper this way. So that even among those who wish to arrive in Tartu by a specific hour, there are nevertheless those who are not too exact about an extra half-hour one way or the other.

The carriages are of course no longer those narrow little toytown rattletraps, booty of the hostilities, as they were immediately after the war – where you stepped straight out from either side into whatever weather you were served up, whether sunshine, rain or the biting cold. Carriages whose axles had been lengthened to suit our gauge so that the wheels stuck out like ducks' feet. No, no, these carriages are our own quite mundane prewar third-class ones. Over the linoleum floor-covering hangs the mixed smell of dirt and the cleanliness of the mop. The seats are hard wooden benches, their brown oil-paint fading, the headrests the trusty old veneer, shiny with wear. And above the backs of the seats can be seen necks and foreheads, cloth caps, trilbies, ladies' hats, headscarves, berets and a variety of bare heads.

On this occasion, the travellers are, in fact, not all that many in number. At the outer end of the double row of seats where I have seated myself by the window, there was only one boy with a freckled face who got off at Aruküla, I think, and whom I don't really remember, and in the window seat facing me, a woman.

She is around sixty, her fair hair now greying, with high cheek-bones giving her the appearance of a mixture of a blue-eyed Estonian farmer's wife and an Indian squaw. With both a childish eagerness for contact and an element of fastidiousness written on her face. Which is all making me begin to think I might have seen her somewhere before and ought to recognise her. So I can do no better than open this morning's *Rahva Hääl*[1] and bury my head in Nikita Sergeyevich's[2] umpteenth speech on wheat production, so that the paper will shield me from all social obligations.

A minute before the train is due to leave, one more passenger climbs into our carriage. A tall, thin man of around forty-five wearing a light-grey suit, too light for September, a deeply-furrowed brow beneath a thinning pate. If his nature springs from the masks of Thalia and Thespia, then there is more tragedy than comedy in him, and yet his face contains an undeniable inner arpeggio of humour. The man sits at the outer end of our group of seats, glances at the woman opposite me and gives a slight, rather hesitant, but unmistakeable, bow of recognition and greeting. In so doing, it seems as if a slight blush appears over the worn regions of his face. He then asks me in what, in the circumstances, is a half-articulated mumble whether the place next to me is free and, on my nodding, takes a seat next to me.

The train moves off. The grey corrugated-iron and chipboard houses of Lilleküla, wet with morning, slip by beyond the rain-drops on the windows. I peep out from behind my paper and make numerous attempts to work out the human and social status of my neighbours. The woman can no doubt be pigeonholed as a *housewife*. A housewife, not so much in the sense of one who comes from an urban, suburban home, more from a small town, a small house with a garden and an orchard somewhere near the community centre and the library. The woman's cheap but new and clean grey canvas shoes and her cheap, but hardly worn bluish-grey autumn coat and her blue silk headscarf from under whose edge, lifted by the draught, her greying hair peeped, all point to this. And always that troubling hint of authority, unpretentious and at ease with itself and the attitude of self-evident importance, an attitude whose public or official presence is all the more manifest in a woman than in a man.

As for the man, I can't make him out. Only as far as to say he could under no circumstances be a bureaucrat. He gives the impression of having the nervous disposition of an intellectual and takes everything in. A person who, in his jealously guarded freedom, is instinctively and naturally insecure and is, on account of this insecurity, easily alarmed. I cannot quite interpret his appearance but he must no doubt be artistic in some way or other. Perhaps artistic more in spirit than as a career. This could, of course, always be said of someone working as the bookkeeper of a second-hand shop such as *Utiil*. And all the more reason to distinguish between guise and essence in these inclement times in which our story is set. For the end of the 1950s was, as we all remember, a time where artists and poets no longer found themselves jobs in second-hand shops, and nightwatchmen or stoker poets were not yet in fashion.

My neighbour turns to look out of the window. In doing so he has to look right past the end of my nose. He has very bright grey eyes and the way he is turning his face towards the window strikes one as just a shade forced. Then the woman seated across from me takes a hand out of her sleeve where she has been keeping it on account of the cold. She is wearing a solid gold wedding ring and her hand, despite being clean and manicured reveals traces of autumn work in the garden. She extends her hand and touches my neighbour on the shoulder:

"Excuse me, young man – but haven't we met somewhere before?"

Her voice is unexpectedly clear and resonant, and also unexpectedly loud. So sonorous, in fact, that the question must be audible several seats away.

My neighbour turns politely towards the speaker with a smile and reddening once again:

"I was a student of Comrade – Mr – your husband's. At Varbola Grammar School. Mr Kaasik was my headmaster. He taught us Estonian. And you were –"

Mrs Kaasik – for it has to be her – raises her hand, palm towards my neighbour, smiles and motions to left and right, the message clearly being: please stop talking. My neighbour seems to have understood Mrs Kaasik's gesture and falls silent, still blushing. His expression is full of the question implicit in his upbringing and in the current situation: why ask me a question in a public place if you don't want me to name names and reveal connections in an audible manner . . . ?

But that very moment Mrs Kaasik anticipates his question and comes with an explanation:

"My dear young man – I'm afraid I'm hard of hearing. But let's try and remedy the situation. Just one moment, please . . ."

She opens a large and rather worn leather handbag with a metal clasp and takes out a strange device. This consists of a torch casing such as was sold twenty years ago, i.e. a blue and green striped tin casing, the end where the reflector and bulb used to sit having been replaced by a small wire-mesh-covered funnel. Out of the casing sticks about one metre of wire, ending up in an old-fashioned spectacle frame sidepiece. In the middle of the bow of the frame attached by three wires, like a spider in a web, sits a light-metal audio-crystal, a rarity obtained from Japan, no doubt.

Mrs Kaasik pushes back her grey hair under the edge of her headscarf, puts the frame to her ear so that the crystal sits in her ear, and points the mesh-covered funnel in the direction of my neighbour's mouth:

"Let's try again. Sometimes the gadget actually works. I was asking where we had met before."

My neighbour speaks in a normal voice into the funnel:

"I was a pupil at Varbola Grammar School. I left school in 1935. Mr Kaasik was our headmaster. And you, now and again, taught us Natural History and Geography."

Mrs Kaasik shakes her head. "No. It's not working again," she says, so that half the carriage can hear. She opens up the device and takes out an ordinary torch battery – "Let's have a look and see whether there's any current left. You can do so with your tongue, you know. At least, that's what they taught us in Standard II at junior school, didn't they?"

My neighbour nods patiently and Mrs Kaasik tests the two terminals:

"Well, they *are* still salty. At least in my opinion they are. You try –" She thrusts the battery under my neighbour's nose and he tests the terminals too:

"Yes. There still seems to be some current left –"

"What did you say?"

"Allow me –" says the man, takes hold of the tin casing, inserts the battery and says into the funnel, which must be the microphone:

"Yes. There seems to be some current left."

"There you are, you see," says Mrs Kaasik triumphantly, starting on hearing his voice, suddenly loud, "I told you it sometimes worked. You see my hearing deteriorated suddenly. For a long while I could more-or-less manage. But things are worse than they were a year ago. And now I've resigned myself to the fact. I'm on the waiting list for a hearing aid. But that takes time. And my nephew Ain, who's a bit of a handyman, made me this as a stopgap solution. Well: where have we met before?"

The man repeats his answer for the third time.

"And what was your name again?"

"Suursepp," says the man, "Edgar Suursepp."

"Goodness me –" yells Mrs Kaasik, "that's most vexing –"

"I beg your pardon?" says the man, nonplussed.

"Quite typical! This gadget" – Mrs Kaasik flourishes her device – "has gone on strike again! What was the name again?"

"Suu . . ."

"No, no. Don't speak now. I can't hear you anyway. Do you know what we'll do? We'll use the old well-tried method. Just a moment . . ." She again opens her large handbag and produces a medium-sized notepad and a pencil. "Please write your name down here!" She looks at Suursepp, and it would seem that he is hesitating. Perhaps he is, at that. Mrs Kaasik says: "It's quite safe to write your name down here. There's nothing suspicious about my notepad. All the names here are jumbled up with others. Important ones and insignificant ones. Mostly insignificant ones. Are you afraid? Whatever for? One conversation in a carriage doesn't mean a thing, you know. And talking with you is so very interesting. Your face sits in my memory as if it were somewhere deep down at the bottom of a well. But I can't remember the name . . ."

The man writes his name on Mrs Kaasik's notepad.

"Of course!" yells Mrs Kaasik, once again for the benefit of half the carriage, "I remember now: you were that boy with the long curly hair – you were in the ninth form if I remember rightly – who we thought they ought to call Tomtit. You were in the same class as Taaveri and the others."

The man nods smiling and Mrs Kaasik reminisces:

"Taaveri, who has now become an academic, and Maripuu who was a minister for a while, and then there was – Randmäe who the Germans gave a – what did he get from them?"

"I don't rightly remember –" murmurs the man but remembers nonetheless. "The Iron Cross, with Oak Leaves, I think –?" (And I can see clearly from behind my *Rahva Hääl* that he is embarrassed at the name Randmäe –) "But he died recently, didn't he?"

Mrs Kaasik continues to reminisce: "Yes, his legs were blown off and then he died. Poor lad. What could he do? His legs blown away from under him then that medal around his neck. – But listen now – you yourself – tell me who and what you are now. But speak quickly. My thingummygig is working again."

My neighbour shrugs his bony but broad shoulders a little to the right and left as if searching for a way out of the question:

"Me – I have begun to learn gardening. My father was a gardener, after all. I'm not trained to do anything else. I happened to have trained in Denmark. My father had trained over there and he had friends there. When the Germans invaded Denmark – in the spring of '40 – I only just managed to get out in time. And since then I have been rooting about here in the soil. And taught how to root around in the earth. And have tried to write a bit. For twenty years now. Very quietly, very inconspicuously . . ."

"Why so inconspicuously?" asks Mrs Kaasik. I get the feeling that it does not please her that one of her husband's and, indeed, her own former pupils has remained so inconspicuous.

My neighbour answers in a half-whisper, smiling bitterly:

"You know, somebody who was here during the German Occupation. A person who's studied abroad. A person who's not always satisfied. It's better in such circumstances to keep as low a profile as possible."

"Oh dearie me – I didn't get the last bit –" yells Mrs Kaasik, "it's gone dead again!"

"There must be a loose connection," says the man, "but now that everything's shaking with the train in motion, there's nothing can be done about it."

"What d'you say?" asks Mrs Kaasik and hands the man her notepad.

The man writes a few lines. I cannot manage to read them as I don't want to make it obvious that I am eavesdropping.

Mrs Kaasik glances at what he has written, nods, looks out of the window for a moment and then turns again to face my neighbour:

"Are you married?" She hands him the notepad.

He nods and that is clear at least.

"And what does your wife do?"

The man takes the pad from Mrs Kaasik and writes on his knee so that I can read it:

Also roots around – i.e. a landscape gardener.

"Oh how delightful," says Mrs Kaasik with a sigh, "do you know, in my opinion it's so good for a man and wife to work in the same field. Don't you agree?"

Mrs Kaasik's enthusiasm can once again be heard throughout several bays of seats. The loud conversation and its semi-telephonic nature has by now attracted the attention of several of the travellers. Two girl students in the bay opposite to ours have now been so involved in following the conversation that they can hardly be more than pretending to read their books. Their exchange of glances and the corners of their mouths reveal the true nature of their focus of attention. A middle-aged woman who is sitting behind Mrs Kaasik, only the nape of whose neck is visible to me, plus her freshly permed brown curls, has risen for the third time and adjusted her suitcase on the luggage rack where no adjustment is required, simply to be able to peer over at Mrs Kaasik, her eyes as beady as blackcurrants. Beyond the young girl students by the other window, two men are playing cards at the window table. The younger one with badly cropped fair hair and a fresh face of the *Mechaniser of broad swathes of meadow* type, the older one who is thinner, darker, more the smug, drinking card-sharp and is, shall we say, some sort of state-enterprise supplier. Redface says in passing, through his blond eyelashes:

"Listen how the old dear's plumbing the depths of marital bliss . . ."

"And why ever not?" says the Supplier "Look what curves she's still got. You can bet she still goes, where her old man's concerned. If she's got an old man, that is – "

Mrs Kaasik notices from Suursepp's and my glances over at the girls who are blushing that something is being said about her by the card-players. She turns in their direction with a smile – I notice that her dark blue eyes are still pretty – and looks at the two smiling faces, one red and one a muddy grey:

"Have you got anything interesting to add to our conversation? Here you are – " She hands the men the notepad and I detect for an instant the ugly dissonance in their kinds of smile. Then, judging by experience, she realises what the men's expressions denote. Before the Mechaniser manages to take hold of the notepad while shouting "I sodding-well said 'pass'!" at the Supplier, Mrs Kaasik has already turned back to Suursepp, seemingly a trifle saddened for a moment, then asking him, unperturbed:

"So, don't you agree with what I said about husband and wife being in the same field?"

Suursepp says: "Just a moment, please – ", takes Mrs Kaasik's device and removes the battery. He wiggles the terminals, jerks the lead, strokes the earpiece a little, puts back the battery and talks into the funnel microphone. Meanwhile, the train stops at Raasiku station. Then it moves off again and the clickety-click of the wheels reduces the audibility of the speakers to a wider audience. Suursepp hands the earpiece part of the apparatus back to Mrs Kaasik and she puts it to her ear.

"Well, is it working now?" asks Suursepp into the microphone.

"Well, I'll be . . . – it's working!" yells Mrs Kaasik.

"That's fine," says Suursepp with a smile, "my answer is rather too long to write down on that pad. So – " He changes from his louder and more confident tone of voice to that of someone dictating instructions, which clearly embarrasses his fellow-listeners slightly, and in so doing manages to speak quite quietly. But Mrs Kaasik's emergency hearing aid seems to be working pretty well by now:

"Well anyway. The husband and wife being in the same field is fine. Not only in theory. In practice, too. Mutual understanding, responsibility, demands and assistance. But in a marriage they are not all that important. In my experience. There are *so many* things which have to be compatible. And so many things which are not which in a marriage become compatible nonetheless. My marriage is not a so-called happy one. No, no. Tiiu herself would be the first to admit it. So I have nothing to be ashamed of. And yet we do the same job of work together. That has gone on for fifteen years now. Fifteen years. But we have been on the point of getting a divorce a number of times. And are so right now. There is a need for happiness – I just don't know of which kind. But happiness, nonetheless. In such circumstances having the same job doesn't work miracles."

"Who said anything about *miracles*?" says Mrs Kaasik somewhat placatingly, "But, indeed, why not!" she adds suddenly growing lively. I would almost have added "coquettishly" but that would not have quite been true. "What do you consider a miracle to consist of? In my opinion it all depends on the person performing it. *Whether he sees it or not –*" Then she suddenly asks: "Do you have children?"

"We've got one son," replies my neighbour with slight weariness.

"Oh dear, my gadget has gone dead on me again! Please write it down –" And she hands him the notepad. He writes and Mrs Kaasik yells, with complete candour:

"An only son? Why only one child? What do you think you'll achieve with only one?"

My neighbour reddens visibly: "Well, you see – it just turned out that way . . . And you?" he asks in a sly attempt to change the course of the conversation, "You have several children if I remember rightly."

"My gadget isn't working! I didn't catch what you said. Please write it down!" says Mrs Kaasik handing over the notepad.

My neighbour writes and the lady replies instantly:

"Yes we do. Or rather, we did have. If we'd only have had one boy we wouldn't have any left. We had five. Four boys and a girl. In order of age and fate: Vello was killed at Velikiye Luki. On the right side. Meelis fell in the Sinimäed hills. On the wrong side."

Suursepp's face is half a metre away. I can see in great detail his upper lip drawn up in acrimony, his lower lip protruding in self-defence, his barely noticeable evasive shake of the head, his half-closed eyelids and the flicker of his eyelashes. Yes, I can see quite clearly how Mrs Kaasik's words spoken too loudly and with childish clarity, pain him. Clearly only the breeding he obtained from the Kaasiks themselves obliges him to remain in his seat and continue the conversation. Mrs Kaasik explains:

"Aksel was on neither side. He left for Finland in '43, moved to Sweden and is now in Australia. He wanted to become an archaeologist. He had already been on digs on Saaremaa with those Vassars and the Schmiedehelms and who have you, back in '39. But once abroad, there was no longer any question of archaeology. In Sweden he worked in a gramophone factory. And now in Brisbane he makes ties." – Mrs Kaasik gives a faint sad smile – "a manufacturer, so to speak. He himself and nine workers. Three of them are Estonians. But his wife is an Australian and so are their children. Then there's our Jaanus. He wasn't accepted to study physics at Tartu in '51. His father was out there at the time. Jaanus went to Moscow and there he was good enough for the university. And there he has remained. Last year he got his Master's and is hoping to go on to do his Doctorate. But now he's married to a Russian woman and they've got Russian children . . ."

"Well, so what?" says Suursepp, "As long as she's nice and the kids are too – " I am not incidentally sure of the weight of conviction behind these words. The desire to comfort is certainly present, but has he really forgotten that Mrs Kaasik's device is not working again? And is he really not aware of the fact that his words will reach the ears of all and sundry, so to speak – and that in saying what he has, he will at least have been making an attempt to counter Mrs Kaasik's rampant nationalism . . .

Mrs Kaasik hands him the notepad: "Write it down. I didn't understand you."

Suursepp writes and Mrs Kaasik says presently:

"Yes, his wife is nice. And so are the children. Nothing concrete to complain about. Love is something you don't enquire about. Only the thought crosses my mind: if there's too much of that kind of love, our nation will disappear off the face of the earth, won't it?" She continues to look Suursepp in the face a little demonstratively: "Listen Suursepp – Suursepp is your name or have I mixed you up with someone else? No? I can see your expression and can't help asking: have I said something untoward? Is it still forbidden to mention such matters? That can't be the case! I simply can't believe it! Tell me, how has *your* life run its course so that you have become – such an easily startled Tomtit! In our time we used to think this too, but we didn't dare say so in public. But times have changed! Or have they remained the same in your imagination?" Mrs Kaasik hands Suursepp the notepad. She even goes as far as to thrust it into his hand and watches him with a challenging expression. He takes it and I can read what he is writing along with Mrs Kaasik. He writes:

I just don't know ! And underlines his words. Then he writes in order to return from doubtful side issues back to the main topic of conversation:

What about your daughter?

And Mrs Kaasik begins to explain, now that the train with its clickety-click must be the other side of Tapa:

"Then there's still our Helvi. Our youngest. Twenty-one she is now. She's fine. Studying Estonian language at teacher training college, following in her father's footsteps. She'll get into university without any problems. Now that her father is back . . ."

"Oh really? So your husband has returned!" says Suursepp with obvious surprise, and hardly at the fact that the story has now moved on from daughter to father. "I had heard, incidentally, that . . ."

He clearly wants to continue – "heard that Mr Kaasik had died *out there*." But in his joy at hearing to the contrary he stops short of saying so right out. Mrs Kaasik hands him the notepad and he writes:

And how is Mr Kaasik?

This results in at least our half of the carriage receiving a detailed account of the life and times of Mr Kaasik, Suursepp getting to know more personal details than he should perhaps have liked.

Mr Kaasik's story began a good while back. In the summer of 1940 during the Vares[3] government, a provincial newspaper had conducted an interview with the headmaster. Why did it have to be him in particular they interviewed? Perhaps because he was well known at the time for his left-wing views on education. And most definitely because he had, shortly before, been involved in a clash of principles with the generals of Päts'[4] Ministry of Education. So that in the eyes of sympathisers he became something of a hero of the day. And the ambitious new editor of the paper had printed the following sentence – which, as it happened, came right at the end of the interview: *But what flag is more beautiful than the red flag – under our blue skies, over our black earth and in the pureness of our hearts?*

"Suursepp, you remember, don't you –" says Mrs Kaasik smiling indulgently, "he *was*, after all, a bit of a romantic . . ."

Suursepp nods and writes on the pad, so that I too can see: *Like many teachers of Estonian of his generation.*

And Mrs Kaasik nods gratefully.

"Anyway. During the German Occupation, the school authorities threw Mr Kaasik out of his headmaster's post and even banned him from continuing as a teacher on account of his *Weltanschauung*. First he was found a job as a librarian with the local evening school. But then orders came from above to purge the library, along with a list of those works which had to be destroyed. Mr Kaasik had travelled to Tallinn to protest – and a week later he had been dismissed from his post. And by that time his words in praise of the Red Flag had been brought to the attention of the authorities. And in March '42, they came to arrest him . . .

"Why do I bother telling all this? Those who have experienced it for themselves already know. And those who haven't will never know. Anyhow, I contacted all the old school officials. At least those with whom we had had reasonably good relations. Suursepp, you are old enough to appreciate: such visits brought more grief than joy. But sometimes joy sprang up in the most unexpected places . . ."

Mrs Kaasik had managed to find a lawyer who had written a grand petition. "And a statement," she says with emphasis, "which was certainly not beneath my August's dignity. That was of great importance, you understand . . ." And the lawyer had offered his services for free: "Look," he said quite frankly: "There's nothing you've got that I want! Give me a couple of packets of cigarettes, *Maret* or *Ahto* brands will do, or *Karavan* . . ."

Five or six courageous men among Mr Kaasik's colleagues signed the petition nevertheless. And his wife took it wherever she felt necessary.

"At the time the children and I were living with August's sister and brother-in-law in the country. In town there was nothing to feed the children with. And Linda and Martin were very kind and tolerated us at least. And about a year after that, August was set free. There was no longer any question of school work, either for him or myself. I tended Martin's pigs and August dug ditches. And by that time the Germans had left too. Then our new masters, the likes of Andresen and his buddies, re-installed August in his old post of headmaster at Varbola. And I became a full-time natural history teacher. Anyway, life took its course. You yourself remember what I am talking about now. We had lost three boys. But the four of us were still there. So far, so good. But you remember Suursepp, don't you, that August *was* a bit too quick-tongued. And a little vain. As men tend to be. So that he shot off his mouth on a number of occasions. As spirited people have the habit of doing. And so he on one occasion explained to his pupils – God's truth, I heard it with my own ears – the kind of utterance he had been arrested for by the Germans. But in those times, this was the '50s you have to remember, the whole matter was blown up out of all proportion. So that Mr Kaasik, head-master under the bourgeois régime, was openly promoting the blue-black-and-white colours of the illegal bourgeois flag! For had he not mentioned the blue of the sky and the black of the soil? And what other colour but white could be implied by the purity of our hearts? And what added to the dubiousness of the vile utterance led to the question: what else could the story of the beautiful Red Flag and the pure heart imply? Nothing other than that children should wave red flags in public, but that in their hearts they should remain white! So once again August was drummed out of his post and – sent to prison. Things had simply gone too fast for August for him to have been able to adjust to his re-education . . ."

And I have to admit: I have not been able to judge whether this last sentence of Mrs Kaasik's was uttered ironically or not. And if so, what proportion was irony as to the political situation and what proportion can be attributed to human stupidity and a surfeit of self-assurance. Or perhaps the utterance was a totally neutral one . . . It is indeed this last way that Suursepp seems to have taken what was being said. During the whole of Mrs Kaasik's long story, he has been tinkering with the hearing aid and now says into the microphone:

"An Estonian is, of course, slow in matters of re-education . . ."

The device has clearly starting working again, since Mrs Kaasik now says:

"Not always. But in the case of August – yes, very. I remember back to the 1940s. *How* difficult all those bouts of re-education were for him. Imagine: going one morning to school and suddenly having to address the Deputy Head as *Comrade* Kopp. When he'd always been just plain *Mr* Kopp before. And when he's always been your colleague, but never your friend. August just was like that. But that selfsame Comrade Kopp – You remember him? Of course you do! The Deputy Head was –"

"No, he hadn't yet been appointed when I was at school . . ." said Suursepp.

"Such a fussy type, always flitting about arranging things, a quiff hanging over his forehead and always a bit sweaty," Mrs Kaasik continued. "I remember him as clear as day: two weeks before the June coup d'état – I was standing in for the history teacher and was in assembly at the time – Mr Kopp made a speech, under Päts' portrait, you remember, and, pointing to the portrait talked of *our dear President* with tears streaming down his cheeks. I saw it with my own eyes. I was only three paces away. But in the autumn, he made a speech to the assembled

school also in that same hall. Except for the fact that instead of
Päts' portrait there was now a portrait of Stalin. Once again, I
was three paces away. And Kopp talked about *the Great Leader
of the workers of the world*. Once again the tears. Buckets of them.
August wasn't like that. In his whole life he was so stingy with
his tears that . . ."

"Why talk of tears if Mr Kaasik is back safe and sound?"

Suursepp says this a little hastily and a little cheaply. So that
I have to hide my smile behind my newspaper. A bitter smile at
my neighbour's attempts, made in the face of all logic, at steering
the conversation around every potential reef. But Mrs Kaasik's
device has cut out right in mid-sentence:

"What did you say? Why shouldn't I speak about tears any
more?"

She hands Suursepp the notepad, but Suursepp is jiggling the
lead on the side of her device, and I can't help thinking: is he
doing this to avoid her tearproof reply – for such it is likely to
be – from reaching the ears of whoever may be listening . . . ?

"Well, can you hear me now?" asks Suursepp.

"Yes I can!" yells Mrs Kaasik joyfully, "why shouldn't I mention tears any more?"

"For the reason," says Suursepp into the microphone, and it
seems to me he really is using a louder voice than necessary,
". . . for the reason that Mr Kaasik has come back safe and sound,
as I hear . . ."

"Yes –" says Mrs Kaasik dully, "he's back alright – these last
three years –" And I notice that she heaves a sigh – "But I wasn't
talking about *those kinds of* tears! *They* have been shed long ago.
Hardly by him though. Oh no, not by him. But by me. I won't
deny it . . ."

And now Suursepp gets his just deserts. For the reason that
just now he tried to suppress any mention of tears, for such
attempts are punishable. Especially if you are not yourself the
cause of such tears. For in the latter instance, you can forgive
such attempts. But Suursepp gets his just deserts because by trying
to wriggle out of shedding tears of worry he succeeds in shedding

a mixture of those of stupidity and sham. Mrs Kaasik continues:

"I clearly remember *one* crying attack . . . You know when I was standing in the corridor to the tribunal – in February, I think, February 1951 – on Roosikrantsi Street, or one of those buildings where rich people used to live – and was waiting and knew that in one of those rooms there August was being sentenced . . . And none of the relatives of the accused were allowed to attend the hearing. But they didn't manage to remove me. And when I had waited a couple of hours and paced over the parquet, sprinkled with sawdust – then August was brought out between two soldiers into the lobby right past my nose – I hadn't seen him for a year. I wanted to get a look at him so I could remember him. He had grown old and grey and kind of transparent – but I only really noticed his mouth. His mouth looked especially red and youthful. And I was all ears and hoped to hear what that mouth had to say. For it *had* to utter the length of his sentence. And I couldn't bring myself to say anything. And he said as he passed by me, quietly but clearly: 'Ten years. We'll try and survive, won't we?' And I nodded vigorously and smiled with all my might . . . But then he was past and beyond the glass doors and was gone. And I just stood there – and burst into tears. It's embarrassing to say so, but I just couldn't stop. For I had got it into my stupid head that he might be set free nevertheless. But those ten years – which I had also considered as possible – now that they were suddenly reality, seemed like being buried alive – I stood there, my shoulders against the wall and gave myself over to crying. Then a young soldier passed close by. I don't think he was from that building. God only knows. But on passing me he said in a half-whisper and kindly, you understand – *kindly*: 'Ну мамаша! Ну эачем ты плауешь Детский срок же старику дали'[5] And was gone. And in the first instant I did not understand whether what he said was said in sympathy or mockery. I closed my eyes and thought: which could it be? And then my glance fell on the acne'd childish face of the soldier and I felt terribly ashamed that I had doubted the sincerity of his words. So that I wanted to run after him and say: 'Dear boy – you don't really know what you're

saying, but – thank you nonetheless! For what you said, you said
with a good heart!' And I now understand that ten years is but
a children's portion – when they're doling out twenty-five years
with five of exile right, left and centre . . . But the boy's thread-
bare greatcoat and rubberised kersey boots were already too far
away, and it would have been embarrassing to run after him . . .
So I dried my tears and travelled back home to Varbola. Jaanus
and Helvi were waiting and wanted to know what tone I was
going to adopt. And I didn't want to look too much as if I had
been crying for their sakes. And, believe it or not, when it came
to telling the children I cried relatively little. For I was thinking:
who could comfort them if their mother also turns on the
waterworks . . . ?"

"Of course, of course," agreed Suursepp, "what's the use of
crying . . ."

"Oh, I don't know," said Mrs Kaasik, "perhaps crying in mod-
eration has its merits. It is unlikely that God gave us human
beings the ability to cry for no reason at all. It does, after all,
flush something out of you. But I had no time for blubbering.
There was no longer anything left for me to do in Varbola. I had
been dismissed from my teacher's job and they were beginning to
put pressure on me to leave the flat. As a new teacher was already
coming down from Tallinn to replace August and myself. So I
got to swap flats with him. One-and-a-half rooms in Tallinn as
against four in Varbola, but anyway. And I even managed to find
work in Tallinn: as a shop-assistant in a bookshop. True, they
didn't keep me long as senior saleswoman. I was, after all, the
wife of someone who was inside. And perhaps I didn't keep my
mouth shut to a satisfactory extent. So instead of senior saleswoman of new books they made me junior saleswoman of old
books. In the second-hand department. At fifteen roubles a
month, the minimum salary possible. But if I had been a Christian, I'd have said: as God himself had willed it. For from that
salary I couldn't really afford food. Jaanus was already a strapping
young man by then and Helvi a big girl too. And I had to send
August his parcel once a month and a few copecks of money

as well when possible. So I had to sell something. And they'd confiscated everything we had to sell. Apart from three beds and chairs and the kitchen table. There were only, by some miracle, books left. They'd been transported to Martin's place in the country. Still a couple of thousand of them. And well-chosen works, too. When August had been sentenced and the bailiffs came to confiscate what they could, I might, according to a certain ethic, have told them about the books. But I chose to follow another moral code. I said nothing. And then I began bringing them in small numbers from Martin's place into town and selling them in the second-hand book section. And do you know, when I went to work in the second-hand book section, Comrade Soekõrv[6] – that was our boss, an understanding fellow – I don't know if you know him – he gave me five or ten roubles more for each book than he would have paid to strangers for them. So I made ends meet and Jaanus could even go off to university with a new winter coat on his back. And then those who'd been sent away began to trickle back and this soon became a flood. August never was one of the first in anything, nor was he one of the first to come back this time either. But in the spring of 1956 he finally returned home . . ."

Mrs Kaasik looks Suursepp and then me in the eye with such joy of life as if she had just announced that her August had won the silver medal in the decathlon during the 1956 Olympics in Melbourne rather than having come back after six years of a ten-year sentence . . .

Suursepp's lower lip creases from its worried pouting into a smile: "But *then* you must have had a real weeping session?" he says – a little to show he has indeed noticed the harmless tears of joy.

"*Then* – oh yes indeed!" says Mrs Kaasik victoriously. "But those were tears of a third, completely different kind. Of those I will not speak."

"You 'eard 'er, Juss!" The Supplier who has, in the meantime managed to keep completely silent, sniggers over his cards at the Mechaniser and then winks over in the direction of Mrs Kaasik:

"Yon tears will have come with all that merriment and the creaking bedsprings when the old man came home after six fallow years! But I wonder if old Pig's Ear or Droop-Ear Soekõrv got the droops when dad returned, know what I mean? Hi-hi-hi-hii — "

This is said far away from Mrs Kaasik's microphone and it could be assumed that she hasn't heard. But there is also something of "I don't have to listen to everything" in her expression. For she is silent for a moment, then says as if in passing, quietly but quite audibly and, of course, in Suursepp's direction:

"Do you know, my deafness and my hearing-aid they're both an evil and a burden. But they do have one advantage: I don't have to listen to everything. To the imbecilities of those badly brought up. Even when I hear them, I don't, so to speak. It is an art I have managed to learn."

"A useful art, of course," says Suursepp hastily. He no doubt fears that the Supplier will feel hurt and will begin whingeing – so that he asks in the same breath: "But everything must be alright with you now? The last years, I mean. What does Mr Kaasik do now?"

"Yes, I suppose everything is basically alright now," says Mrs Kaasik straightforwardly and looks Suursepp in the eye, her eyebrows raised in joy. "We moved from Tallinn back to Varbola. August said that he had always felt a stranger in the big city, and especially now. He had spent over thirty years of his life in Varbola. We've found a tiny house there. We get a pension. Eight hundred roubles for the two of us. So we don't starve. And we still have plenty of books. Both to read and to sell. We'd be doing pretty nicely really – as well as we can do without the boys, that is – if it wasn't for our misfortune . . ."

"What misfortune?" asks Suursepp – carefully and partly out of curiosity, but partly because the question simply cannot remain unasked.

"The misfortune with his eyes," says Mrs Kaasik.

"What's wrong with Mr Kaasik's eyes?" asks Suursepp with what I feel is a certain measure of relief – with eyes there can only be medical, not legal, problems, can there not? And so is indeed the case here. For Mrs Kaasik now says:

"Cataracts."

But she says this in a most strange manner. Not only without tragedy but even triumphantly, you could say. Almost in such a way as if it is hard to suppress the smile forming at the corners of her mouth.

"Erm . . . you mean cataracts? Or glaucoma?" asks Suursepp.

"Cataracts," says Mrs Kaasik fighting with the same smile as previously, which puzzles me.

"And so how much of his sight has Mr Kaasik lost?" asks Suursepp.

"He's completely blind," says Mrs Kaasik. No, no. Not really joyfully, not really triumphantly, that would be too much to claim; but nevertheless with a twinkle in her eye. "Yes, he went completely blind, and the doctors said he had to go completely blind before they would operate . . ."

"But anyhow, cataracts are easier to cure than glaucoma," says Suursepp, "though I'm not sure. Perhaps it was the other way round . . . But how did he go blind? Didn't he wear glasses all the time?"

"Who knows," says Mrs Kaasik smiling apologetically. "It had begun before he had become aware of it. One eye-doctor whom we consulted said: 'it comes as a result of harrowing experiences.' You know what he was referring to. But I don't believe it. Now some say one thing, others another. Some say half the cases of gangrene are caused by the camps. Owing to undernourishment and cold affecting their legs. Others say that the eradication of TB is thanks to the camps: the diet of sauerkraut and the crystal clear air of Siberia. And let's face it, August didn't have such a hard time out there. He only worked for a short time in the forests. He was then sent to a ceramics workshop. He says, that even without my food parcels – 'I hope you'll forgive me for saying so,' he says, 'but even without your food parcels I wouldn't have gone really hungry out there.' He says it isn't that which is hard. What is depressing is that it's all taken for granted. He says

that *one year* would have done to see all he got to see in six.
But nevertheless, everything was so terribly *interesting*. All those
different species of animal and the myriad of ways of self-
preservation, in what was a furnace and a cold-store at one and
the same time. August says that it's a pity he's no writer..."

"You know," cries Suursepp, "in that case it would be a good
thing..." But he leaves unsaid *what* it is that would be a good
thing. So that you can only presume that what he meant was: in
that case it would be a good thing if Mr Kaasik stayed blind and
didn't start, God preserve us, writing it all down...

No, no, Suursepp does not say anything of the kind. Suursepp
merely asks quite eagerly, or, God knows, perhaps from the shelter of my newspaper I have been doing him injustice after injustice
right from the start, interpreting everything as having a far too
cheap, superficial, and all too platitudinous undertone! Perhaps
I have simply transplanted myself, Peeter Mirk, into a chance
passenger on a chance train on a chance autumn morning? At
any rate, Suursepp asks, eagerly in my opinion:

"But how is it now – are they going to operate on Mr Kaasik?"

"They've already done so," says Mrs Kaasik with the same
secretive, joyful, take-it-or-leave-it mien as before.

"When was that? And where?" enquires Suursepp, now with
undisguised interest.

"A fortnight ago. In Tartu. In the eye clinic there."

"And how did it go?" I get the feeling that both Suursepp and
I are asking this question.

"We don't know yet..." says Mrs Kaasik, almost in a whisper
and then explains, returning to her former volume: "The Professor said that August's case was a complicated one. The chances
were fifty-fifty. We'll know how it went today. Today they'll be
taking the dressings off his eyes."

"Oh... So is that why you're travelling down to Tartu?" I
now do not know whether it is Suursepp or myself who is asking.

"That's right," says Mrs Kaasik, "I would have travelled anyway, of course. But the Professor phoned. We haven't got a
phone ourselves in Varbola, but I gave him the number of the

school. They don't mind. So he rang and asked me to travel down. Since he said he'd asked August, *what* he, August, would like to see first when they take off the bandages, assuming, that is, that he can see anything at all."

"And what did August say?" We interrupt one another, Suursepp and I, and apologise for doing so for we do not want to prevent Mrs Kaasik from having the chance to tell us what August did say.

"And August said . . ." says Mrs Kaasik, looking in the direction of Suursepp, then at me and the student girls in the seats across the aisle with bright eyes, "August said that he would be grateful – if what he saw first was his wife!"

Mrs Kaasik looks us straight in the eye, her silent smile implying: You all understand what I mean . . .

But then she feels there is a risk that her happy eyes could fill with tears right in front of us and that would be overdoing it, despite all this open-heartedness. So she snaps open her large handbag and hides her face behind the large flap (which has a mirror on the inside, no doubt) and begins to push strands of her grey hair under the edge of her headscarf and over the frame of her hearing device. Still wrestling with the constant smile of triumph on her lips. Just as, ten minutes before arrival in Tartu, the milk train crosses the ringing iron bridge over the river swollen by the September rains.

1982

Translator's notes for "The Day Eyes Were Opened"

1. *Rahva Hääl* – an Estonian national daily newspaper, then the mouthpiece of the Communist Party.
2. *Nikita Sergeyevich* – i.e. N. S. Khrushchev (1894–1971), First Secretary of the Communist Party of the Soviet Union from 1953 to 1964.
3. *Johannes Vares* (1890–1946) was Prime Minister in the puppet Estonian government after the Soviet takeover in 1940. Vares, who died under mysterious circumstances, most likely suicide, during his second period in office after the Soviets pushed out the Germans in 1946, was a well-respected Modernist poet (pseudonym – "Barbarus") during Estonian Independence. His Foreign Minister in 1940 was Nikolai Andresen (1899–1985), a literary critic, and his Minister of Education, Johannes Semper (1892–1970), erstwhile poet and translator of Gide, Whitman, Verhaeren, etc. A classic case of "la trahison des clercs" and the naïveté of literary figures who enter politics.
4. *Konstantin Päts* (1874–1956) – President of Estonia during Independence. His autocratic government from 1934–1940 was unpopular but he did manage to prevent the growth of Fascism as such in Estonia. Päts was persuaded to stay on after the Communist coup in June 1940, so the "generals" with whom Kaasik clashed will be people under the governor Andrei Zhdanov, who dictated policy. Konstantin Päts died in Siberia in 1956, and was reburied in Estonia, 1991.
5. "Hey, Missus. What are you crying for? It was only a kids' sentence what they gave the old man . . ."
6. *Soekõrv* – the surname means: "wolf's ear" or "warm ear" and causes the Supplier to pun later in the story, creating "pig's ear" and "droop-ear".

Harvill Paperbacks are published by
The Harvill Press

1. Giuseppe Tomasi di Lampedusa *The Leopard*
2. Boris Pasternak *Doctor Zhivago*
3. Alexander Solzhenitsyn *The Gulag Archipelago*
4. Jonathan Raban *Soft City*
5. Alan Ross *Blindfold Games*
6. Joy Adamson *Queen of Shaba*
7. Vasily Grossman *Forever Flowing*
8. Peter Levi *The Frontiers of Paradise*
9. Ernst Pawel *The Nightmare of Reason*
10. Patrick O'Brian *Joseph Banks*
11. Mikhail Bulgakov *The Master and Margarita*
12. Leonid Borodin *Partings*
13. Salvatore Satta *The Day of Judgment*
14. Peter Matthiessen *At Play in the Fields of the Lord*
15. Alexander Solzhenitsyn *The First Circle*
16. Homer, translated by Robert Fitzgerald *The Odyssey*
17. George MacDonald Fraser *The Steel Bonnets*
18. Peter Matthiessen *The Cloud Forest*
19. Theodore Zeldin *The French*
20. Georges Perec *Life A User's Manual*
21. Nicholas Gage *Eleni*
22. Eugenia Ginzburg *Into the Whirlwind*
23. Eugenia Ginzburg *Within the Whirlwind*
24. Mikhail Bulgakov *The Heart of a Dog*
25. Vincent Cronin *Louis and Antoinette*
26. Alan Ross *The Bandit on the Billiard Table*
27. Fyodor Dostoyevsky *The Double*
28. Alan Ross *Time was Away*
29. Peter Matthiessen *Under the Mountain Wall*
30. Peter Matthiessen *The Snow Leopard*
31. Peter Matthiessen *Far Tortuga*
32. Jorge Amado *Shepherds of the Night*
33. Jorge Amado *The Violent Land*
34. Jorge Amado *Tent of Miracles*
35. Torgny Lindgren *Bathsheba*
36. Antaeus *Journals, Notebooks & Diaries*
37. Edmonde Charles-Roux *Chanel*
38. Nadezhda Mandelstam *Hope Against Hope*
39. Nadezhda Mandelstam *Hope Abandoned*
40. Raymond Carver *Elephant and Other Stories*
41. Vincent Cronin *Catherine, Empress of All the Russias*
42. Federico de Roberto *The Viceroys*
43. Yashar Kemal *The Wind from the Plain*
44. Yashar Kemal *Iron Earth, Copper Sky*
45. Yashar Kemal *The Undying Grass*
46. Georges Perec *W or the Memory of Childhood*
47. Antaeus *On Nature*
48. Roy Fuller *The Strange and the Good*

For the full list of titles please write to:

The Harvill Press,
84 Thornhill Road, London N1 1RD

enclosing a stamped self-addressed envelope.